I0665533

Game of Lies

Amanda K. Byrne

LYRICAL PRESS
Kensington Publishing Corp.
www.kensingtonbooks.com

Lyrical Press books are published by
Kensington Publishing Corp. 119 West 40th Street New York, NY 10018

All Kensington titles, imprints, and distributed lines are available at special quantity discounts for bulk purchases for sales promotion, premiums, fund-raising, and educational or institutional use.

To the extent that the image or images on the cover of this book depict a person or persons, such person or persons are merely models, and are not intended to portray any character or characters featured in the book.

Special book excerpts or customized printings can also be created to fit specific needs. For details, write or phone the office of the Kensington Special Sales Manager:
Kensington Publishing Corp.
119 West 40th Street
New York, NY 10018
Attn. Special Sales Department. Phone: 1-800-221-2647.

Kensington and the K logo Reg. U.S. Pat. & TM Off.
LYRICAL PRESS Reg. U.S. Pat. & TM Off.
Lyrical Press and the L logo are trademarks of Kensington Publishing Corp.

First Electronic Edition: January 2017
eISBN-13: 978-1-60183-650-2
eISBN-10: 1-60183-650-31

First Print Edition: January 2017
ISBN-13: 978-1-60183-653-3
ISBN-10: 1-60183-653-8

Printed in the United States of America

The ties that bind, the vengeance that severs...

Cass Turner, promising UCLA student, is gone. All that remains now is Cass the rogue assassin. Her target: all those who've sworn their loyalty to Isaiah, a man so ruthless Cass won't find peace until he's destroyed. Yet Cass's brazen killing spree has driven a wedge between her and the man she loves. As a lieutenant in LA's largest crime family, Nick Kosta has his own reasons for wanting Isaiah dead. But if Cass continues to play by her own rules, she'll have to choose between Nick and getting even.

When her one chance at the ultimate revenge is snatched away, Cass's world begins to fall apart. Now they're going to play by Nick's rules—even if it means betraying her trust. Because the danger to their lives, and their future, is far from over. But with the body count rising, and a target on Nick's back, Cass will have to find a way to unearth the lies that surround the Kostas and find the killer in their midst...before it's too late.

Books by Amanda K. Byrne

Game of Shadows
Game of Vengeance
Game of Lies

Published by Kensington Publishing Corporation

To my parents. Because I don't say I love you often enough.

Acknowledgements

A huge thank you to my editor, Corinne DeMaagd. This whole trilogy wouldn't be as amazing as it is without your guidance.

I'm convinced my critique partner, Liv Rancourt, has an unending store of patience. Liv, you always listen to me, and give me a well-timed smack upside the head when necessary. Thank you so much for everything.

And as always, the BF, Aaron, for putting up with me when I was a giant ball of stress. I love you!

Chapter 1

This place is a prison.

I drop my keys on the kitchen counter and don't bother with any of the lights. It would only illuminate the chaos. Cleaning the apartment after the mess Josef and I made is pointless. Once I've finished what I've set out to do, I'll be leaving it.

For now, it's my prison. One of my own making. I don't *have* to be here. I could have stuck with the plan. A single day, multiple hits, crippling Isaiah's little uprising where it would hurt the most.

Then he decided to balance the scales by killing my father right in front of me. So. Here I am. Carving away little pieces of his infrastructure every day, and every night I come back here because it's familiar. I know every creak, every whisper of sound. If I have to be constantly on guard, I want to do it in a place where there are no surprises.

I pull open the fridge for the pitcher of water and see my dinner sitting on the middle shelf. Nothing fancy, just a sandwich and a salad from the deli a few blocks over. Last night it was Chinese. There were leftovers when I went to bed last night, so Nick must have eaten them when he brought the sandwich by.

I snag the food and bump the door shut with my hip, then set everything on the counter before pulling out my phone. It powers on in silent mode, vibrating once in my hand as the screen flashes to life. One new text and several voicemails. I ignore them and call my mother.

The answering machine picks up, same as it has for the last thirteen calls. "Hi, Mom. It's Cass. Can you pick up today? Please?" I asked the same thing on my previous calls; she never does. I stifle a sigh and give her another few seconds of silence. "I'll be by tomorrow. You can tell me if you need anything when I see you." I swallow hard. "I love you," I whisper. "I miss you."

I hang up before I break and bite into the sandwich. Turkey with avocado. The man's a quick study. Tell him once that turkey sandwiches are always better with avocado, and he makes sure it's on every one I eat.

I dial in for my voicemails and listen to them on speaker while I work my way through the salad.

"Cass, it's Denise. Um. I hope everything's okay. Nick called me the other day and said you were, but I still want to hear it from you. I wish there was something I could do. Just…call me, okay?"

Maybe someday when I feel more like a person than a machine, I can talk to her again. But I have to use this numbness while I can. I'm not ready to let it go yet. I delete her message and fork up more lettuce. I'll text her in the morning. *That* I can do, and I owe her that much.

There's a message from Lia, her voice timid in a way I've never heard from her, asking if there was anything she can do. Another from Con, telling me to come back, the guest room isn't the same without me.

But nothing from Nick.

In a life full of ghosts, he's become the newest one. The food is one way I know he's been in my apartment. Sandwiches, soup, a new box of cereal, a small carton of milk. Have to keep my strength up.

I wonder if I'll see him before I fall asleep.

I ball up my trash and toss it into the garbage can, then wander to the couch and switch on the lamp. Another sign Nick's been here—the box holding my cleaning materials is closed up and moved to a corner of the coffee table. I used the whetstone this morning and forgot to put it away. I won't need them tonight. Today's marks were pretty clean, both dosed with potassium chloride. No blood to wash off.

I pull up my pant legs, unstrap the knife sheaths from around my ankles, and set them on the table in front of me. Slumping into the cushions, I tip my head back and shut my eyes, letting the exhaustion drag me down.

Revenge is tiring. It's this physically, emotionally, mentally demanding monstrosity that swears it's only looking out for me and wants me to be happy. It's a fucking liar. Sometimes I picture it standing in a corner, snickering at me. Because as demanding as it is, it responds with a kick of adrenaline every time I get a step closer. Can't give up now, Cass. Can't give up after you've taken out two men in one day.

Only five more to go.

Rubbing my temples, I sit up and glance over at the door. Locked, of course. He won't come to me while I'm still awake. Lucky for him, I'm about ready to keel over.

I make my way to the bathroom and strip, turn on the water as hot as I can stand, then let it stream over me as the steamy heat fills the small space. Nine men down. Five left at the top of Isaiah's hierarchy, not counting him. Tris, his shadow, will be the most difficult. I've spent most of my spare time trying to find a way to get him alone, but he's either at Isaiah's side or surrounded by his fellow SWAT team members.

I blink away the water dripping into my eyes. Maybe that's the solution. Maybe I should be focusing on the time Isaiah's alone rather than trying to take out Tris. He usually leaves Isaiah with another guy when he has to go into work, but Isaiah doesn't seem to have much confidence in the other guy; he won't leave his latest base of operations without his shadow.

My brain ramps back up, pushing aside the dregs of fatigue as it tries to find a solution to this problem. I get out of the shower and dry off, annoyed with myself. Now I'll never get to sleep. I *have* to get to sleep.

Sleep is when I see him.

It's the one time of day I let my guard down because he's there, surrounding me, making it possible to catch a few hours of rest. Those scant hours, four, five at a time, give me the strength I need to keep going.

We don't talk. Or I don't, anyway. Occasionally he'll whisper to me in the dark. Tells me he loves me. Asks if I'm all right, even knowing I won't respond. Not with words. Because the truth is I'm *not* all right. I haven't been for a while, and Turner's death only made it worse.

I ignore the goose bumps prickling my skin and braid my wet hair back. If I'm lucky, it won't come loose during the night. Those are the nights he holds me tight enough I can't move, the faint cinnamon scent of his soap lulling me to sleep.

I force myself to pick up my clothes and take them with me to the bedroom. I dump them into the hamper before I crawl into bed. The light's still on in the living room, but he'll turn it off when he comes in. I pull the covers up over my shoulders, shut my eyes, and settle in to wait.

The nightmares come first. They always do. Fragments of the moment I discovered Turner, bound to a chair with a gun to his head. Those horrifying seconds when I stare at my mother's battered face. Scott's pale skin as he realizes he's been shot. Nick's terror that I'm trapped in his house as fire eats away at the walls.

"Cassidy."

With a shudder, I strain toward his voice. He repeats my name, my full name, not the quick and easy "Cass." I roll over and grope blindly, swallowing a sob when my hands connect with warm skin. I scoot toward him, not stopping until my face is buried in his neck, his heartbeat sure under my palm.

Nick.

He wants me to stop. Wants me to come home despite the fact we don't have one. It's there in the way he holds me, in those murmured words I can't always understand. I won't go with him, and he knows it. So this is the compromise he's reached. Every night, wrapped together in my old bed, and then he sneaks out in the pre-dawn light to leave me alone.

I need more tonight. I need him everywhere, anchoring me, letting me fly. I need to forget. I want to lose myself in him. We sleep naked. It's never been a conscious taunt on my part, but the skin-to-skin contact is soothing. Tonight, I did it on purpose.

He murmurs a soft protest as I trail my mouth up the side of his throat, the stubble on his jaw rough against my lips. But he kisses me willingly, eagerly, as needy as I am for this connection.

It's like a circuit coming online. The instant our mouths connect, my body lights up and my brain says *yes*. Legs tangling together, hips rocking, his tongue strokes mine, and I dig my nails into his shoulders, ready for more.

He loosens his hold and I whimper, afraid he's pulling away. "Let me touch you, love," he whispers.

Touch. We're practically glued together, but our hands can't slip between our bodies, explore all those places we found before. I ease back, my skin cooling instantly with the distance, but heat flares once again when he tweaks a nipple.

I lose track of time. My world consists of Nick's hands and mouth on my skin, his low groans and shudders, warm darkness, and a strange, sweet tenderness I hoard for later. He props my leg on his hip and plunges into me, then rolls me onto my back and pins me to the mattress.

I can't move. I don't *want* to move. I wrap my limbs around him and hold on tight, his weight a comfort. Stroke after slow, shallow stroke, I climb with him, my mouth on any part of him I can reach. And when I finally break apart, he's not far behind, leaving a rush of heat and love.

I moan quietly and reach for him as he shifts away, not comforted at all by the kiss he places on my palm. He leaves me huddled in the bed, slick between my thighs and listening to his movements, hoping he won't leave but unable to tell him not to go.

The mattress dips behind me, and I turn over to see him sitting by my hip, washcloth in hand. Oh. Right. Sex is a messy business, and the smart thing would have been to get out of bed and clean up. Instead, he brings the cleanup to me.

After, he slides in beside me, skin to skin, my body warm and loose. "I miss you," I mumble, lips moving over his collarbone.

He glides his hand up my spine and cups the back of my head. "It's time to come home, Cass." His chest rumbles with the words. "Time to stop. Come home with me."

I hold him tighter because I know in the morning he'll be gone.

Chapter 2

He's still here.

Don't ask me how I know this. We haven't been together long enough for me to have developed that mythical sixth sense of knowing when my boyfriend is in the same space as me, but he's *here*. A giddy bubble of happiness rises, then pops when I remember my task for the day: eliminate crony number five.

The walls come back up, the shields slam down, and I get out of bed and pull on a pair of jeans and a long-sleeved shirt. I tug the band from the bottom of my braid as I walk out of my bedroom.

Nick's on the couch, dressed in jeans and a dark blue button-up with the sleeves rolled halfway up his forearms. "You look like shit," I say, working my fingers through the remains of my braid.

He does. Despite the tidiness of his appearance, there are lines digging in around his mouth and between his brows. His hair has progressed beyond the casually messy stage and into the unkempt stage. But it's his eyes that threaten to break me. They're as weary-looking as I feel. If the hours of solid sleep I manage are few, his must be fewer, given he wakes before I do and steals out of my apartment.

"You don't look much better." He stands and gestures to the kitchen. "Coffee?"

I nod. "This is a change. You're usually gone when I wake up." Braid finally undone, I duck into the bathroom, retrieve my hairbrush, and run it through my hair, wincing as it snags on a few tangles. I pull it into a ponytail and step back into the living room, murmuring my thanks when Nick hands me a mug of coffee.

"Circumstances necessitated the change. We can do this two ways— the easy way or the hard way." He swallows coffee and takes his seat on the couch. "You have to stop, Cass."

I arch a brow as I sip my coffee. "I assume this must be the hard way you're referring to? Talking me out of it? Isaiah's still alive, Nick. I'm not stopping now."

"You've done plenty of damage on your own in the last two weeks," he agrees. "But some of the families are asking questions, and while we've gotten to most of the bodies in time, there were a couple discovered before we could take care of them."

"And the police can't bury the cases?" Clean up isn't in my wheelhouse, and while I did my best to take out my targets in concealed spaces, it wasn't always possible. Leaving Nick to deal with my fallout is a selfish move on my part.

It's eating at me from the inside out.

"Our pull with LAPD only goes so far. You go after Tris, and we'll have none."

"Actually, I think I have a way around that." Worried by the sudden weakness in my legs, I make my way to the opposite end of the couch. Guess I didn't sleep as well as I thought I did. I gulp more coffee. "Whenever Tris has to report for work, he leaves another guy with Isaiah, but I get the feeling Isaiah doesn't trust him. He won't leave his safe house until Tris returns." I lean forward and set my mug on the table. My hands are starting to shake, and I'd rather not burn myself. "If I can get inside the safe house, or get Isaiah out *without* Tris dogging him, I can end this." I dig my nails into the side of my thigh. The pain is a weak, brief flash that does nothing to overtake the encroaching fatigue.

"It doesn't matter, Cass. You've lost the family's backing. Any more bodies turn up, they won't help you hide them." He sighs and places his mug on the table.

I scrub my hands over my face. "So I refocus on Isaiah. That's fine. Another week, it'll all be over." My head is heavy. I turn sideways and rest it on the back of the couch.

He shifts around to face me, the weariness in his gaze absolute. "That's just it. I can't run damage control for you any longer. You don't get another week. My father, Con's father, they're not disagreeing something needs to be done, or even the way it's being done. You changed the plan, and no one knows where you're going to hit next. *That's* what they object to."

Goddamn patriarchy. "I'd rather hit first, apologize later." I'll come up with a different plan. Tris doesn't strike me as a leader. It'll take the remaining five men some time to figure out how—or if—they're going to continue with this little revolution.

Why am I so fucking tired?

He shakes his head. "You don't have a choice in this matter anymore." My eyelids droop as he stands, jostling the cushions. I can't even lift my head as he bends over me, lips brushing a kiss across my temple. "I'm sorry, Cass," he whispers.

Sorry? What's he sorry for? I try to ask him, but all I manage is an unintelligible mumble. Every part of me feels like it's encased in cement, the battle to stay awake a losing one.

Sorry.

The coffee.

He slides one arm under my knees, the other behind my back, and I want to hit him.

The bastard drugged my coffee.

* * * *

This bed is not mine. It's not one of Nick's, and it's not the bed in Constantine's guest room. I push my nose into the pillow.

It's too *clean*.

I slit open an eye. There's a table beside the bed with a small lamp and a bottle of water. I reach out to grab the water and stop.

Coffee.

Drugs.

My boyfriend *drugged* me.

I shoot up in bed fast enough to trigger a dull, aching throb behind my eyes, and I squeeze them shut. Whatever Nick doped me with has given me a headache and a mouth desperately in need of water. After several deep breaths, the throbbing fades to a manageable level, and I open my eyes again.

The room is dim. Light's coming in from somewhere, and I twist around to find the source. High windows line the wall behind the bed. The room itself is long and kind of narrow, the walls white. Other than the bed and the table, the only other furniture is a tall cabinet in the corner.

I push aside the blankets—how considerate of Nick to make sure I was comfortable while I was unconscious—and plant my feet on the floor. At some point, he took off my pants, and the air in the room is cool enough to make me shiver. My legs hold me up, so I walk to the cabinet and pull open the doors.

Why are my clothes hanging in here? I tug on a sleeve and frown. I left most of my clothing at Constantine's. Flipping through the hangers, it looks like all my clothes have been moved here. What's not hanging up is in the shallow drawers below. I snag a pair of fleece pants I haven't seen before and pull them on, then head for the door.

Nick earns back a point when the knob turns easily in my hand. I half expected him to have me locked in the room. I step onto what appears to be a catwalk and peer over the railing to the floor below.

It's a warehouse.

Nick's got me in a *warehouse*.

Granted, it's a small-ish warehouse. The floor below is mostly covered in mats, though one quarter of the space holds free weights, a couple of cardio machines, and other random exercise equipment.

I study the length of the catwalk. The room I'm in is on one end. I open the door next to my room, a groan of relief escaping when I see it's a bathroom. Even if the bottle on the nightstand is sealed, I don't trust it. I wash my hands, turn the hot water to cold, and cup them under the stream.

I drink.

And drink.

And drink.

Water dribbles down my chin, trailing along my neck, but I don't care. Whatever the hell Nick put in my coffee dried my mouth out worse than the Mojave.

When I've finally drunk my fill, I fumble a towel free of the rack and wipe the water from my face. Then I go back to the room, find a pair of shoes, and head for the stairs at the other end of the catwalk.

If he's around, he must be in one of the other two rooms because the main level is empty. There's a wide set of double sliding doors on the far side of the warehouse and a sturdy-looking metal bar secured with a heavy lock across them.

Beside me is a single door with a bright green sign overhead that reads EXIT. I glance up at the catwalk and step toward the door.

This one *is* locked. I study the deadbolt for a moment. It must lock from the outside. Which means either anyone outside can unlock it or Nick had a double-sided deadbolt put in. Dangerous in the event of an emergency. Perfect if you want to keep someone prisoner.

"You can have your own key when I'm confident you won't try to escape."

"Your trust in me is overwhelming," I say flatly, glaring at the door. I turn around and scan the lower level. I missed the kitchen area spread out under the catwalk. He's lounging against a counter, bottle of water next to his elbow.

"Preemptive strike." His voice is just as flat. "You and I both know you wouldn't have come willingly. It was either drug you or wrestle you to the ground and handcuff you, and there was still a risk you'd get away." He flashes a sharp smile. "You're wily like that."

I give the door a hard thump with the side of my fist and stalk to the middle of the mats. I kick off my shoes and drop to the floor. "Your diplomatic skills need work. You have no way of knowing I wouldn't have agreed with you."

He pushes off the counter and strides across the room. My breath hitches as he drops to his knees in front of me. "If you expect me to apologize for what I've done, you'll be waiting a fucking long time." Lightning fast, his mouth is on mine, hot and firm and gone in the next blink. "You're not doing this alone," he says softly. "You were never supposed to."

I will not scoot back. I will not be the first to retreat. I absolutely *will not* hit him, no matter how much he deserves it. "I was always supposed to do this alone. I just never told you."

Nick settles on the mat. "Isaiah's done more than murder your father, Cass. His actions have split the organization. He has to answer for that. That's the reason why my father and my uncle agreed to this plan."

I arch a brow. "You failed to mention the part where we were supposed to report to them what was happening."

"Had you stuck with the original plan, there would have been no need. One day, hit 'em all, and it'd be over. Not easy to cover up, but doable with advance notice. We'll come up with a new plan, and I highly recommend you cooperate." He points behind me to the exercise area. "In the meantime, feel free to use whatever you want. If you want to go to the shooting range, let me know, and I'll arrange it."

Arrange it. I feel like I'm trapped in that old song—I can check out any time I like, but I can't leave. "Why are you doing this?"

He gets to his feet, and for the first time, I see the anger behind his bland expression. "You abused my trust. You pushed too far, too hard, too fast. Right now, I'm the only one standing between you and the rest of the family. I'll help you, but it will be done my way."

I'd do it again, too, and *that* brings on a wave of guilt. Not that I've used him, but that I'd do it again. "How long are we staying here? Where *is* here?"

"When you stop acting like a selfish, immature girl, I'll tell you." He stands and heads for the door.

Shame burns through my veins long after he's gone. Nick's right. I've been selfish and immature, too focused on that hideous beast called revenge to care what my choices did to others.

The burn flares hotter as I realize I don't care, and I wouldn't change a thing. Flopping over onto my back, I stare at the ceiling high above. Does it make it better, knowing I'm ashamed of my actions, even though I wouldn't change them?

No. Because the fact remains I wouldn't do anything differently. Each kill has been a brick in a wall, separating the old Cass from the new. What Nick wants will tear that wall down, and if he succeeds, I will become a babbling, incoherent mass of grief and pain.

I roll onto my side and prop myself up on an elbow. Somehow, I'll have to get out of here. The easy way is to allow Nick to help me take out Isaiah. The idea has its appeal. The only thing holding back the aching loneliness is that half-built wall, and if we do this together, I won't be alone.

Physically, anyway.

The hard way involves finding the damn key he's promised me, not getting caught, and most likely destroying whatever's left of my relationship with Nick.

I wish revenge wasn't such a greedy fucker.

Chapter 3

Most of my life with Nick is crammed into this cabinet. When I left Constantine's for my old apartment, all I took with me were some clothes, my phone, and the weapons Nick bought me. The gun's locked in a box on the top shelf, next to the one holding the whetstone and oil I use to clean the knives. The knives themselves are stored in their original box, next to the supplies.

Three little boxes and a bunch of nearly new jeans and shirts. It's so far from a complete picture it's laughable. It doesn't show the quiet evenings full of getting-to-know-you conversations, or his casual acceptance of my ability to take care of myself. There's nothing of the meals I've made for us or the hells we've gone through.

Then with one move, one choice, he screwed it up.

I grab a sweatshirt and shut the cabinet doors. Maybe I'm overreacting. Maybe Nick did when he doped my coffee. Whatever the answer is, it's not one I have time to search for. Isaiah's still alive. I pull the sweatshirt over my head and go back downstairs.

The refrigerator is full, as are the cupboards. Everything I could possibly need to feed myself a healthy, nutritious meal is in this kitchen. I take out a glass and fill it with water from the tap while I debate my dinner choices. Part of me wants to be annoying and contrary and make Nick pick up take-out. He deserves it for locking me inside.

"Dammit!" Water slops over the sides of the glass as I slam it onto the counter. I promised Mom I'd stop by to see her today. She might be a member of the walking dead, but I promised. On the off chance she notices I haven't been around, I don't want to cause her any more worry.

Any other time, I might have waited until Nick gave me my key, shown him I'm not the *selfish, immature girl* he says I am, but this is my mother. The only family I have left. She trumps proving anything to my boyfriend. He's got to have it squirreled away in one of the rooms upstairs.

The door swings open with a loud squeak as I'm hurrying toward the stairs. Nick shuts it behind him and twists the key in the lock.

"I told my mother I'd stop by and see her today. You said there was a key I could have?" I ask.

"I dropped by your parents' house and told her you would be out of touch for a few days," he responds. "She said she was going to visit your aunt for a while and would call you when she got there." He starts up the stairs. "Come on."

So Mom will talk to Nick, but not to me? The hits won't stop coming. I follow him to the second level while trying to wrestle the hurt into place.

He opens one of the two closed doors and waves me inside. The long, narrow room reminds me of his study and the second bedroom at the condo. A U-shaped desk sits in the near corner, three monitors cluttering its surface. When he reaches under the desk and boots up the computer, the monitors flare to life.

I wander farther into the room. There's not much else. A couch is pushed against the far wall, a neatly folded blanket topped with a pillow on one end. A duffle bag is tossed in the corner, the top of it zipped tight.

Something about the blanket and the pillow throws me. I stare at them, trying to understand what they mean. He fucked up, yes, and he hurt me, but I assumed we'd still be sharing a bed, like we have all the other nights.

I don't want him in here. I want him next to me. I want everything to go back to the way it was. Before Turner was killed.

The only way I'll get that is to kill Isaiah.

I relax my shoulders and turn around. "You're still willing to work with me?"

He regards me steadily, his face giving nothing away. "Have a seat." He points to a chair beside the desk. "Yes, I'm still willing to work with you. That was what should have happened in the first place."

I pick up the stack of papers on the chair and sit, searching for the words to tell him why I'd done what I had. "Before," I say quietly, slowly, "it was personal, but not...overly so, I guess. Like there was still some distance. Isaiah already admitted he underestimated me, and up until he shot Turner, I thought he'd keep doing that. After? It wasn't enough for his men to die. I needed him to be afraid. I *need* him to fear me. I want him to realize that I don't play by his rules and he made a huge mistake thinking he could get me to do things his way. If you and Constantine helped, it became too much like a business transaction."

I look down at the papers in my hands. "You didn't even try, Nick. You said there was an easy way and a hard way, and the hard way was talking me out of it. If you really meant to try, you wouldn't have gone straight for the drugs. How do you know I wouldn't have listened?"

He sighs. "Because you wouldn't have, Cass. You plowed through those nine men with a singular focus. The Cass I know, the Cass I love, would have hesitated. That lack of hesitation proved I wasn't dealing with her anymore."

He's right. There was no hesitation. My timid, remorseful self is there, though, and she likes to poke her head up at the most inopportune times. "How do I know you're not offering to help me now so you can kill Isaiah yourself?"

"You don't," he says bluntly. "And I'm not going to tell you I won't. Because if getting to Isaiah means putting yourself in danger, you won't get anywhere near him. I'd rather have you alive and hating me than both of you in the ground. His life is not worth yours."

He takes the stack of papers from me and shuffles through them. He finds the one he's looking for about halfway through the bunch. "Map of the surrounding houses." He passes the paper to me. "Haven't had a lot of time to run surveillance on the street, so we'll need to do that for a few days."

I put my anger and hurt on ice and study the paper. A few days of inactivity could have the benefit of keeping Isaiah on edge. Given how quickly I eliminated the other men, he might be expecting me to rush at him. Sneaking up from the side has some benefits.

The downside is this won't be over quickly.

"You said my mom's leaving town?" Aunt Carol lives in Montana. Her house is near Flathead Lake, surrounded by trees. It's quiet, peaceful, and this time of year, covered in snow. It's also in the middle of nowhere. They could be in danger, and there'd be no one around to hear them scream.

"Isaiah's stretched too thin, thanks to you. Going after your mother wouldn't be a smart move on his part. I can bring her here if you'd rather." He slides the keyboard toward him and types in a command. I scoot the chair around and lean in.

It's a schedule, complete with approximate times and destinations. I reach for the mouse, brushing Nick's hand in the process. The brief touch sparks a wave of longing, and I hold my breath, willing it to pass.

I could touch him. Kiss him. Let him break me down and put me back together. And if I did, I'd spend more time wondering about his motives than accepting his gestures at face value, and it would destroy whatever we have left.

It was easy to ignore his concern and affection in the first few days after Turner's death. When I left Constantine's for my apartment, when he started coming to me at night, little chinks began appearing in my armor. Never large enough to cause much damage, but I felt him. It didn't take long for my brain to re-wire and accept that with Nick there I could relax, snatch those precious hours of sleep.

"I don't get it." I tuck my hands in my lap. "If what I've done isn't sanctioned by the organization, why didn't you stop me sooner?"

Nick's gaze remains on the monitors, two new programs springing up on the remaining screens. "Partly because my father and Uncle Anton agreed something should be done about Isaiah's men. And because if it had been one of my sisters, my mother, or you, I would have done the same thing."

The muscles of his jaw twitch and relax as I wait for him to continue. "There's this rage," he says quietly. "It'll burn you from the inside out if you let it fester. You should have come to me first with your new plan, Cass. Not gone ahead without me and assume I'd be there to clean up your mess."

It doesn't burn. It freezes. It's this thick, heavy layer of ice that threatens to kill all the good, leaving only the bad. How does Nick know about the rage? From everything he's told me, he's never been in the situation I'm in. "You talk like you've experienced it."

He shakes his head. "I've got an imagination. And I've seen this before. It happens every once in a while in the family." The look he sends me is one of quiet resignation. "Everyone has the capacity to kill. Some will never need to use it. Others will channel it in different ways, becoming soldiers, terrorists, hunters. Still more will access it in a moment of fear or anger."

A capacity to kill. We've exercised ours more than most. "There's another category," I say. "The hardened. The ones who kill without compunction."

His eyes turn to stone, and his mouth firms into a thin line. "I'm not going to let you become one of them. I'm not letting you walk away, either. We finish this together." His gaze flits over my face, and then his eyes meet mine. He taps the monitor with the schedule like the interlude never happened. "Isaiah's schedule, such as it is. It's more a schedule for the house than for him personally."

The switch in topic almost gives me whiplash. All right. We're done with the soft, tender portion of our talk for now. I turn my attention to the monitor. "Do we know when the LAPD schedules will change? Will Tris be on this shift for a while?"

"We don't know, which is why we'll be doing surveillance for a couple of days to confirm this schedule."

I reach for the mouse again and scroll through the schedule. "I've seen the house wake earlier than seven. Don't know how often it happens, but there were at least two instances where someone left before six."

"Do you remember what days?" Nick rummages through the drawers and comes up with a pad of paper and a pen.

"One was last Friday. The other might have been this past Monday, or possibly Tuesday. Guy leaving the house was the same one both times. I couldn't get close enough to see who it was. Dark hair, on the skinny side. Wore a dark blue windbreaker." There aren't enough hiding spots for me to stick around for any length of time.

"Might have been Michael." Nick hits a few keys, and a picture appears on the middle monitor. "This him?"

"Maybe. Like I said, I wasn't very close."

A satellite map of the neighborhood pops up on the third monitor. He taps it with his finger. "Show me where you were."

"Zoom in."

Slowly, the houses and cars become clearer. I trace the line of the street with my finger, pausing in front of a house three houses up on the left, on the opposite side of the street. "Here. The owners have been out of town for the past week, so I've been able to use their yard to watch the traffic. Not ideal, but I've been able to track some of the comings and goings." I point to the house directly across from Isaiah's. "They were out one night. There's a large shrub next to the front porch that provided some cover, though there wasn't a lot of activity that night. Isaiah's men seem to be in the house by eight in the evening." I haven't had a chance to pull an all-nighter, mostly because there isn't any place on the street for me to hide. Smart choice on Isaiah's part. The residential neighborhood limited what I could gather without being seen.

"We'll go back tomorrow night. I'll see if there's any traffic cameras nearby."

Over the next few hours, we fall into the rhythm we developed over the last few months, and it's as though the problems of the past twelve hours never happened.

The false sense of peace continues when we break for food. "How long should we wait?" I ask, dumping the ground turkey into the skillet. "I've already got him on edge. I know we need more information, but I don't think we can risk more than a few days."

"At least three." The look of fierce concentration on his face is pretty funny, like the pepper he's slicing is going to jump off the cutting board and run away. "Given that Tris's schedule could change at the last minute, we'll need to be prepared. Constantine's working on getting us into one of the houses across the street. Couple of vacant ones with people on vacation for the holidays."

The mention of vacation stops me cold. I set my wooden spoon aside and turn to Nick. "I would feel a lot better if my mother were here. Aunt Carol's closest neighbor is about a half mile away, and on the off chance Isaiah decides to go after her, they're too vulnerable."

He doesn't speak, just places the knife next to the cutting board, wipes his hands, and pulls out his phone. I take it from him and find my mother's contact information.

It rings once, twice, three times. If it gets to five, it will automatically switch over to voicemail. The ice creeps back in as it starts on the fourth ring. She's an adult. More, she's the one who lived with Turner all these years. I have to trust she'll be able to take care of herself.

But I don't think the broken shell she's become is capable of doing that.

"Hello?"

The ice doesn't recede completely, though it retreats enough I feel relief at the sound of her voice. "Mom?"

"Cassidy. I'm glad you called. I'm assuming Nick told you I'll be staying with your Aunt Carol for a while?"

She sounds almost...normal. "He did. I'd like you to stay with us. It's safer."

She's quiet for a long moment. "I can't," she says at last. "I'm sorry, sweetheart. I love you, but I need some time."

Time? Time for what? What is she sorry for? "I don't understand."

Another stretch of silence, and her meaning penetrates. She needs time away from *me*. Her daughter.

The ice surges and spreads, swallowing me whole. "You'll call when you get to Aunt Carol's?"

"I will. I'll call you every day at four too. It's only for a couple of weeks, Cass. When I get back, we'll have a long talk about what to do." After a slight hesitation, she tells me she loves me and hangs up.

I give Nick his phone and pick up the spoon to poke at the meat.

"Everything all right?"

"Fine. She's going to check in daily until she comes back. Are the peppers ready?" Everything is not fine.

Unfortunately, this is one thing Isaiah's death won't fix.

Chapter 4

I've lost track of the minutes and hours I've sat here staring at the house across the street. The binoculars remain clutched in my hands, though they're mostly useless at this point. No one's moving. If it weren't for the lights in the upstairs and downstairs windows, I'd assume everyone is asleep. They very well could be.

There's a smug sort of comfort in thinking I've scared Isaiah into sleeping with the lights on.

The quiet is broken up by the clicking of Nick's keyboard and his occasional muttered responses to Constantine's questions, something about the app launch that isn't ready. After the virus breach a few weeks ago, they had to push back the launch. From the snatches of conversation I've heard, it'll take a miracle to make the new date. He should be at work, or at least not here, but he refused to leave me alone. So he's glued to his laptop, Bluetooth fastened to his ear, as he tries to be two places at once.

"You don't have to be here. I'm not going to do anything tonight." The empty house, courtesy of Constantine, is a blessing. I have a clear view of the street and the front door of Isaiah's current hidey-hole. A few nights of surveillance, and I'll hopefully have the information I need to finish the job.

"You'll understand if I don't trust you to stay put." Nick continues typing.

I stand and stretch my arms over my head, my gaze never leaving the street. I'd forgotten how quiet suburbia could be at night. I glance at my phone. Barely eleven o'clock, and no one is stirring. It's strangely bright outside, though. It's the sort of neighborhood where people leave their porch lights on at night, and there are streetlights every hundred feet or so.

The last person to enter the house was Tris. He's easily identifiable, even in the dark. It's his walk. He's got this way of walking that demands you watch him. Coupled with his height and muscular build, there's no mistaking the big, burly SWAT officer.

Nick joins me at the window. "Go take a break for a few minutes. I'll tell you if anything changes."

I'd argue, but my legs are stiff from sitting still. I pick up my water bottle and wind my way through the darkened living room to the kitchen in the back. Something makes a soft *click*, followed by a shuffle, and I stop and press myself to the short wall dividing the kitchen from the living room.

More shuffling like muffled footsteps.

Someone else is in the house.

My first thought is the owners. Supposedly they're on vacation and will be for a couple more days. Constantine could have been wrong, or he could have lied, though the house *was* empty when we arrived. We went through the rooms one by one before setting up in the living room.

I bend over and set my water bottle on the floor, then withdraw the knife from the sheath strapped to my ankle. Squinting into the shadows, I inch toward the corner, grip loose, hand steady, mind blank.

Those are definitely footsteps. And they're getting closer.

A set of cabinets at the entrance to the kitchen blocks my view into the main part of the room, which means I have two choices: I can round the corner and confront the intruder, or I can wait for him to come to me and surprise him.

The first option isn't really an option at all. Who would willingly want to confront a potentially violent intruder?

I soften my knees and exhale quietly as the footsteps pause near the edge of the cabinets. The intruder steps forward, and I slip behind him. I whip my hand toward his neck, blade poised to sink into his throat.

He shoots out a hand and catches my wrist before I can make contact. "Careful there. Can't get blood on the floor." Constantine keeps his fingers locked around my wrist, gently pushing it down. "Dom around?"

"Living room, watching the street." He still hasn't let go. I flex my hand around the knife handle. "Wasn't aware you'd be joining us."

"Last-minute decision." He drops my hand and steps around me. "Anything happening?"

The hairs on the back of my neck prickle in awareness. I squint at him, trying to make out his face in the shadows. "Street's been dead for at least an hour. All the lights are on, and no one's come or gone in a while, unless they're sneaking in through the back." The timing's off. Nick *just* hung up with Constantine. Their office is over a half hour away, and Constantine's condo is even farther. "How'd you get here so quickly?"

"Multitasking," he murmurs. "Put the knife away, Cass. You won't need it tonight." He walks into the dark, leaving me frowning after him.

For Constantine to get here as fast as he did, he would have had to be in his car, on his way here, while he was talking through the latest bugs with Nick. Unless he's got some sort of encyclopedic brain, he couldn't have had all that information at his fingertips.

The puzzle threatens to distract me from the task at hand. Pushing my doubts into a box to examine later, I replace my knife, pick up my water, and continue into the kitchen.

I skirt the dim pool of light spilling onto the floor from the light over the stove and lean on the countertop. Something scuttles across the backyard, dashing toward a small tree in the far corner. Probably a neighborhood cat or a raccoon.

The low murmurs of Nick and Constantine's conversation drift toward me, bringing Constantine's odd appearance to the forefront. I tiptoe across the kitchen and edge around the cabinets, straining to hear.

A trickle of guilt that I'm eavesdropping on my boyfriend and a man I've come to consider a friend tries to worm its way through. I ignore it. Constantine's behavior in the last five minutes triggered my instincts, and the only way to soothe them is to find out what they're talking about.

"I get it, Dom. I do—"

"Do you? Because it sure as fuck doesn't sound like it."

An argument. Awesome. This is just what tonight needs. I let out a shallow breath.

"Cass isn't present. Not completely. I don't want to stop her because she's taking care of our problem. But I'm going to be there to keep her from derailing completely." The quiet determination in Nick's voice has a thick thread of steel. I curve my lips in a smile. This is why I love him. He might not like my methods, might not agree or approve, but he knows I need this, and he'll give it to me.

How many people can say that about their partner?

"It's not just her vendetta, though I have to say it's been an education to see her in action. Only other time I've seen kills that clean is her father's work." The reluctant admiration weaving through Constantine's words hurts. It's the sort of compliment that would cause Turner to praise me in his faint, damning way, and I want to cling to it even as I push it away.

"She's a distraction, man. Guys at the office have been wondering what the hell you're up to. We've got a launch in two weeks on a product that's not ready, and you're playing babysitter. She's costing us money, and if she's as out of it as you say she is, she could get you killed."

Each word is a paper cut. String them together as an argument, and it's like someone's poured lemon juice over them. On their own, they sting. Coming from Constantine? Someone I like? The sting becomes a burn.

I ease away into the kitchen, then over to the back door. The knob's loose under my hand, and I turn it slowly to minimize the rattle. Cool air washes over me as I edge through the door onto the porch, and the door shuts with a soft *click*.

It's a little too cool to be outside without a jacket. I rub my arms through my long-sleeved shirt and wander down the back steps to the damp grass. When this is over, I'm going to take another look at Nick's cousin. My initial reaction to him may not have been wrong.

I may have just interpreted it incorrectly.

My phone buzzes against my hip, and I glance around the yard before pulling it out and answering. "Hello?"

"Cassidy? Why are you mumbling?"

Mom's response is so normal, so *her*, I lose my cool remoteness for a minute, sudden tears burning my eyes. "Sorry, Mom. Nick's trying to work, and I don't want to disturb him." The lie flows easily, and I scan the yard again, straining to hear beyond the tiny night noises.

"I won't keep you long, then. I'm at Carol's now. There's two feet of snow, and we're expecting more by morning."

It's amazing what a change of location and a few hours will do. Last night when she told me she was leaving, she sounded better, but still fragile. Twenty-four hours later, her voice is stronger. Some of my anger fades. The distance she's put between us is a slap in the face, but if it's what helps her heal, I'd be a selfish little bitch to begrudge her that. "Are you sure you'll be safe there?"

Her smile is evident, even through the phone. "The only person who could ever out-shoot your father is Carol. We'll be all right. I'll call you tomorrow at four. I love you."

A lump forms in my throat. "I love you too, Mom." We hang up, and I slide the phone back into my pocket.

"How touching."

How the *hell* did he get here? I turn toward my right. Isaiah remains near the fence in the deepest part of the dark.

I wonder if he's alone.

"Did you sneak away from your bodyguard? And isn't it past your curfew?" The knives are strapped to my ankles. There's no way to retrieve them without giving away what I'm doing. I stay where I am and cross my fingers that Isaiah's alone and not armed.

Of course he's armed, and if someone isn't behind me, he's slipping. Confronting me without a weapon is stupid, and if there's one thing we've learned over the past month, it's that Isaiah's not stupid.

"I underestimated you. Again. I assumed because you'd become part of my world, you'd play by my rules." Using the dark to hide, he's a fuzzy, vague Isaiah-shaped outline. Coward.

But I can't taunt him into coming at me. I do the next best thing.

I say nothing.

"You've done a good job. Kept me on my toes, and made it damn near impossible for me to go anywhere. Did me a favor too. I needed to make some cuts, keep everything lean. Easier to control that way."

If I remain where I am, silent and still, will he continue his movie villain act and keep talking? The longer he talks, the more time I have to figure out a plan. This is too good an opportunity to pass up. Isaiah came to *me*. I need his cockiness to be his undoing.

"You've decided against taking out Tris, I'm guessing."

"The risk is a big one," I agree. "Though I haven't ruled out eliminating him as well. In your absence, he's the only one that seems to have the balls to do what you're doing. I imagine Andreas and Anton would be happy to see him gone."

A hand closes around my throat. "My balls are none of your concern."

Tris's voice is nothing like I imagined it would be. The soft, sibilant hiss is strangely calming. "Isaiah thinks you're a smart girl," he murmurs. "So let's see how smart you are. A smart girl would walk away and let the damage she's caused stand instead of creating more." Cool metal presses into my temple, and it takes all my willpower not to tense up.

A gunshot will attract attention we don't need. He has to know that. I can *use* that.

Two against one, and I have to assume both are armed. Both men are taller and stronger than I am. I can't see either of them, and of the two, I only know for certain where one of them is. Getting out of this situation unscathed is unlikely. Getting out alive is possible—it'll just take some ingenuity on my part. Tris won't let down his guard, so expecting him to lower the gun is out.

"Why are you here, Isaiah? You know Nick and Constantine are in the house, and you know Nick's going to come looking for me any minute." I shift my feet, bumping my head against the barrel of the gun.

"You're right." The frown's evident in his voice. I peer into the shadows, frustration growing the longer I stare at his indistinguishable face. I need to see him. Isaiah continues. "Dom's been distracted tonight, though, hasn't he? The launch is coming up. Has he managed to fix the app?"

Nick *has* been distracted, now that I think of it. If he wasn't, he would have forced me to change places with him more often.

"How did you find me, anyway?" I slouch a little, my back brushing against Tris's chest. His grip on my throat tightens in response.

"That's none of your concern."

Huh. Cryptic. I switch to a more immediate problem. "So are you going to make a lot of noise and take me out here, or do you have a plan to smuggle me out of the backyard and over to your house?"

"The gun's a precaution," he says. "An insurance policy of sorts. Tris won't have to use it as long as you cooperate."

Yippee.

"You still didn't answer my question. Why are you here? And are we going inside sometime soon because I'm getting cold."

The night quiet settles around us while I wait for Isaiah's answer, Tris's hold never wavering, the gun steady. My best shot is to drop down, away from the gun, rather than grabbing his hand and trying to pull it away.

"I'm here to get you, Cass. So we can discuss this like adults." Isaiah finally moves from the shadows. "We can talk here or across the street, though if we have the conversation here, it will likely be cut short when Dom comes looking for you."

From one heartbeat to the next, several things happen at once. The back door opens and Nick steps onto the deck. Two more men enter the yard, heading for Isaiah. Constantine comes up behind Nick, talking like they were in the middle of a conversation. I jerk in Tris's hold, dropping to my knees to get away from the gun, Tris falling with me as he tightens his grip.

This is not going to end well.

Chapter 5

Someone shouts. A dark blur races from the porch to the yard, and one of the two new men goes down hard as he's tackled from the side. It takes a second for the other guy to realize what's going on. He yanks the tackler to his feet, and from the hoot of laughter, I can tell it's Constantine.

I can't believe he's *laughing* about this. The man sure has a bizarre idea of a good time. A shot rings out, Constantine's attacker stumbling and falling to the ground, leaving Constantine to face off with Isaiah and the guy he tackled.

Nick takes a step toward us, blocking my view of the fight behind him. He hasn't said anything. Why hasn't he said anything? I push the rising panic down and scrabble for calm. Nick's thinking. That's all this is. Tris hasn't let go of my throat. His hand squeezes hard, choking the air right back out, and my heart's pounding in my ears. He shoves the gun into the side of my head. "Nice try," he says. Before I can recover, he lets go of my throat, grabs first one wrist, then the other, yanking them behind my back and cutting off my only route to a weapon.

Memories of Isaiah binding my arms and legs, his knife slicing into my skin, threaten to overwhelm me. I shut my eyes, the sounds of Constantine's fight echoing in my ears. He can handle himself. He's not my concern. I need a plan. An escape route. Isaiah rendered me helpless. As long as the safety stays on, I'm not this time.

Tris is behind me, and while he's holding my wrists, I can move my hands. His legs are spread, knees on either side of my calves, evening out the height difference a bit. I hope it's enough.

"Drop the gun."

My eyes snap open. The first lick of fear dances up my spine as Nick stands in front of me, gun pointed at Tris. I shake my head, heedless of the oily metal pressed to my temple. Bad plan. Horrible plan. He's got more to lose than I do. I won't have him shot because he got in the middle of my problem.

A *click*, and Nick's flicked the safety off. The fear races higher. Tris is a highly trained law enforcement officer. If I do anything now, the risk he'll squeeze the trigger is much, much higher than it was twenty seconds ago.

Another *click*. The safety on Tris's gun. There's nothing standing between me and a bullet in the brain now. I bite my tongue. This isn't happening. I'm not on my knees with Nick in front of me, gun trained on a *police officer*. He said so himself; he won't be able to bury Tris's death. Someone will have to pay.

Tris laughs. *Laughs.* "You want to test your reflexes against mine?"

"I want you to let Cass go. Isaiah's the one who wants her. You don't think he'll be angry if you get to her before he does?"

"I think he's a bit busy at the moment." But Tris moves the barrel away from my head, and I don't bother hiding my sigh of relief.

Then I go for his balls.

I sag into him, hands spread as wide as I can make them, and take advantage of his surprise and grab him, squeezing hard. As he releases my wrists, his gun goes off and I roll away from him, going for the knife strapped to my ankle.

Nick staggers, drawing my attention, and I watch in horror as he collapses in slow motion, his legs folding under him like a newborn deer's. "Nick!" The fear takes over completely, and I forget the knife, crawling over to him. He's propped himself up on one elbow, his dazed expression barely visible in the dark. I run my hands over his chest and arms, searching for the wound and not finding it. "Where is it?" I mutter.

"Leg," he rasps. I grope down his right leg, snatching my hands away when they come into contact with wetness. I'm dimly aware of the sounds of Constantine's continued fight, the sounds of flesh slapping flesh broken only by their grunts of exertion.

Hands like titanium close around my upper arms, and I'm pulled to my feet. A violent, sudden fury crashes into me. Tris and his *fucking* gun. It's always about the guns. Their absolute immediacy, the lack of accuracy that causes damage nonetheless. *That gun* needs to go.

He releases one arm to shift his hold, and I jump, his chin connecting with the top of my head. Ignoring the pain radiating through my skull, I free a knife from its sheath and dive to the ground as another shot rings out. I roll onto my back as Tris lunges for me. I plunge the knife into his thigh, yanking it free when he stumbles. Five seconds to rise to my knees, and I strike again, this time at his groin.

His gun drops to the ground, and I scramble for it as he does his own slo-mo collapse, staggering sideways. He lands on top of the gun. I shove my hand under him. He's a dead weight, pressing down on my hand as I try to wrap it around the butt of the gun. I barely jostle him as I slide it free.

I flick on the safety and get to my feet. I back away slowly until I'm at Nick's side. Tris hasn't moved, just stares up at the sky, one hand at his groin, his chest lifting in short, sharp pants. I drop to the ground beside Nick and lay the gun next to me.

He's taken off his shirt and pressed it to the wound. I cover his hands with mine, applying even more pressure. "Hey," I say softly. "Tell me what to do."

"Get something to tie this off with. Con will call a crew to clean this up."

As I head for the house, the lack of noise and movement from Isaiah's section of the yard hits me, and I glance over.

The world stops.

The two unidentified men are lumps on the ground, neither of them moving. Isaiah lies a few feet away. Constantine's kneeling at his side. My feet move of their own volition, leading me to Isaiah. Constantine looks up, his expression blurred in the shadows. "I'm sorry, Cass."

I sink down and bend over Isaiah's prone form. He's still breathing. He has to be. His chest *has* to be moving. I place a hand on it, willing it to move.

It doesn't.

* * * *

Isaiah is dead.

Killed by a stray bullet. Shot from his own bodyguard's gun, according to Constantine.

I stare out the window at the passing streetlights, Nick's hand clasped in mine. We had to leave the bodies where they fell, the scream of approaching sirens ticking down the seconds to discovery.

This is why I don't use guns.

The car hits a bump in the road, and Nick hisses, his hand tightening on mine reflexively. "You should have left the knife," he says.

I pull my attention from the street. "Huh?"

"The knife. You should have left it with the body."

It's still clutched in my other hand. I need to clean it. My fingers are sticky with drying blood. Nick's. Tris's. Isaiah's.

So much blood.

"No." I hear myself as though I'm at the end of a tunnel. "I might need it again." I wipe the blade on my jeans and release his hand to slip it into the sheath.

Isaiah is dead. The monster should be sated. Instead, it's confused. There's no adrenaline rush. No crushing need to push forward.

All these weeks since Turner's murder, I've been betting on this one last death to set everything right. To take my crooked, turned-around world and reorder it into some semblance of structure I can understand. This was supposed to end with my knife slicing a brilliant, gruesome smile across Isaiah's throat.

It didn't account for the possibility he might die some other way.

The car hits another bump, causing Nick to swear under his breath. Nick. He hasn't left me. Not after everything I've done or how carelessly I've treated him. He was shot because of me. It's my turn to be there for him, to hold his hand and tell him everything will be all right.

The words won't leave my mouth. I can't get them out. Maybe my tongue has finally developed a mind of its own and knows any reassurances I could offer would just be a lie.

I can't lie to Nick.

I lean over his leg to inspect the makeshift bandage. His bloody shirt is held in place by a length of twine I found in the kitchen. It's not very sturdy, and the cloth is dark and damp to the touch. While I'm pretty sure the bullet missed the femoral artery, I don't like that he's still bleeding. "How much farther?" I ask Constantine.

"Twenty minutes if we're lucky," he says grimly. He meets my eyes in the rearview for a brief moment before checking his blind spot and changing lanes, speeding up to pass the car in front of us.

We've already passed Huntington Hospital, the closest trauma center. "Hermosa Beach is too far." Hospitals mean questions, but there's discretion and then there's life-threatening. Simon's too far away, and Nick could need blood. The longer it takes to get him the care he needs, the worse he'll get—and the longer his recovery will take. With Isaiah gone, though, he'll be able to focus on getting healthy without constantly looking over his shoulder.

His life will go back to normal.

"Not Simon's house." Nick's voice is quiet and tired. "He's on staff at General. He's meeting us there."

Angels General Hospital is crowded. Crowded, busy, underfunded, and understaffed. In other words, perfect for people who can't risk questions.

With effort, I push thoughts of Isaiah and his death from my mind. "How will this work?"

"Bypass the ER. Surgery's on the fifth floor. Tish will meet us at the south employee entrance." Constantine swerves around another car.

"Hopefully she'll have a wheelchair," I mutter. Nick shouldn't even *try* to walk on his leg. It'll only make everything worse.

"With a wheelchair," Constantine agrees. "She gets us up to surgery, Simon goes in and stitches Nick up, we get him home."

"*Cass* takes me home."

Constantine risks a glance over his shoulder. "She's not strong enough to—"

"I'm strong enough, thank you," I interrupt. "I can get us home." I have no idea how he'll get up the stairs, and he needs to spend at least the first night in an actual bed. "You won't be staying overnight in the hospital?"

"We can commandeer an operating room for a couple of hours, and it won't cause too much of a hassle. Can't do the same with a hospital bed." Nick tips his head onto the seat back and shuts his eyes. His skin looks sickly in the passing flashes from the streetlights, and I bend over to check the wound again. I can't tell if it's bleeding as much as it was or if it's slowed.

He taps my hand. "I'm okay," he murmurs.

I lift my head and stare at him. "No. You're not."

"Listen to your girlfriend, Dom." Constantine takes a corner too fast, and I fall into Nick's side, my blood-covered hand smacking into the center of his bare chest.

"You're not okay. And no offense, Cass, but Dom will need help getting around immediately after the surgery. Let me take you guys back to wherever you're staying."

So Nick's cousin doesn't know where we are? Interesting. I lean in and place my lips next to his ear. "Why can't he drive us home?" I whisper.

Nick's hand comes up to cover mine, and too late, I try to jerk it away. All that blood, that symbol of my failure, tainting Nick. "He agrees with my dad and his," he whispers back. "I don't trust him not to rat us out, and the last thing I need is someone taking you from me." He manages a smile. "Besides, he's a motherfucking asshole at launch time."

"I heard that." Constantine scowls at Nick in the rearview. "You want your privacy, I'll give it to you."

"You said that the last time. Then you woke me three times in the middle of the night, every night, for a solid week before the last launch. I'm not out of touch, Con. Just need to ensure some space."

Constantine grumbles and turns another corner.

She's costing us money.

She could get you killed.

I figured Nick's trust in his cousin was absolute. The chink is unexpected, and I'm not sure what to do about it.

I pull my hand away from his chest as the hospital looms into view, the sprawling complex lit with spotlights. We bypass the emergency room, and Constantine screeches to a halt outside an unmarked door. Tish, the blonde from Simon's house, is waiting beside a wheelchair. She jerks the car door open, and Nick struggles to push himself out and into the chair.

I get out of the car and hurry around to the other side. I slip under one of his arms to support his weight. We manage to get him into the chair. Tish starts for the hospital door, and I check the back seat to make sure we have everything. We barely managed to grab Nick's laptop, the surveillance equipment, and my water bottle before the first cop car showed up. I'm paranoid we forgot something.

Before I can shut the door, Constantine says my name. "I need to call his father. Fair warning. Andreas *will* come."

Great.

Constantine drives off, and I run to the door, catching it before it can close completely. I follow Tish to a bank of elevators and get my first good look at Nick since he was shot.

I was right. His skin is sickly, practically gray, his mouth tight with pain, a frown line digging deep between his brows. My rusty handprint is dead center of his chest, a grotesque reminder of the night. More blood spatter dots his abdomen and forearms, and the right leg of his jeans is stained dark with blood from hip to knee. The shirt is soaked through where it's pressed to the wound, the edges still the faded blue the fabric was before it became a tourniquet.

The elevator arrives, and it's thankfully empty. Tish pushes Nick in first, hits the button for the fifth floor.

"Constantine was going to call your father. He seemed certain Andreas would come."

Nick laughs weakly. "He will. He'll sit in the waiting area, not saying a word, and when Simon comes out, he'll tell him that in no uncertain terms am I to die." He takes my hand, and I stare down at his large one dwarfing mine.

When Simon stitched me up, Nick stayed by my side the entire time. "Will Simon let me in the operating room?" I ask Tish.

She shakes her head and pushes the chair through the doors. "There are some rules he's willing to bend in this hospital. That's not one of them. No unauthorized personnel in the operating suite."

I don't want to let go of his hand. It's awkward, walking alongside the wheelchair and trying not to trip, but dread creeps in with every step toward Simon. He's clad in blue scrubs and waiting at a set of swinging double doors.

He acknowledges me with a dip of his head and points to the right. "Restroom three doors down. Cafeteria's on the second floor." He turns to push through the doors.

"Wait." What if I never see Nick again? What if he doesn't wake up? Panic whips through me, clearing away the numbness. I've lost too many people. I can't lose him.

Nick's hand flexes in mine. "There's an observation room, isn't there? She can watch there."

"That room is for medical students, here to learn," Simon argues. "Friends and family stay in the waiting area. No exceptions."

Incredibly, Nick straightens, power rolling off him even as he sits bleeding from the leg and in obvious pain. "Make one."

Simon's expression freezes into stone. "Dominic—"

"Make. One."

They glare at one another, each beat of Nick's heart pumping more blood out through his wound. I'm about to let go of his hand and back off when Simon jerks around and pushes through the doors, waving his hand for me to follow.

"Bathroom." He points to a door as he passes. "Wash your hands. I'll have a nurse bring you a set of scrubs to change into. She'll show you to the observation room."

Tish pauses long enough for me to kiss Nick good-bye, and then he's rolling down the hall. Away from me.

Half an hour later, hands washed, clad in clean scrubs, I stand at the window of the observation room watching as they bring Nick in for surgery.

Chapter 6

Operating rooms are nothing like they appear on television. They made me think the room would be a table in the middle of a dim space, with blinding lights hanging overhead to amp up the drama. There would be far too many heads bent over the table, and sooner or later the conversation would devolve into a discussion of who was fucking who in the supply closet.

There's hardly anyone in the room, and it's bright and sparkling clean. Everyone is calm. Nick's even grinning. It's a loopy expression, and it gets loopier when he turns his head toward the observation room. He raises his fist and gives me an agonizingly slow thumbs-up.

The scrub-clad people crowd around the table with Tish next to Nick's head, blocking my view of his face. All I get are peeks when she shifts to check a line as Simon works to repair the damage to Nick's leg. Alone in the observation room without any way of knowing how badly the bullet ripped him up, I'm left to pace.

And think.

We weren't prepared. Right to the end, Isaiah caught us with our pants down. He knew we were in the house. Maybe it was blind luck he got me in the backyard alone, but he was prepared.

I frown. Constantine was the one to find out the owners were on vacation, allowing us to break in and set up surveillance in the living room. His help wasn't anything out of the ordinary. So why can't I brush aside his sudden appearance moments after hanging up with Nick?

I stop in the middle of the room and watch the surgical team for a moment. Nick has utter confidence and trust in his cousin. Hell, *I* trust him. I had some doubts in the beginning, but he's proven himself over and over. There's no solid reason for my suspicions.

If it *is* all an act, Nick will be devastated.

I start pacing again, brain latching on to the mystery of Constantine's behavior like it's a life raft. If this is some kind of ruse, I'll need evidence. The list I gave Nick months ago won't be sufficient. I have to have indisputable proof that Constantine was in on this from the beginning.

I have never wanted so badly for my instincts to be wrong.

Isaiah's endgame was never in doubt, at least when it came to me. I killed Marc. I needed to die. His jealousy and anger toward Nick were understandable because everyone discounted his smarts and savvy and, well, he had us running around in circles. But it didn't quite feel like enough then. It doesn't feel like enough now. Isaiah held his position for two years. There was always the possibility that as time went on, his strengths and intelligence would be recognized and he'd be given his due.

I pause at the window. I need to see Nick's face, and Tish is still blocking my view. Since I can't see anything, there's no real reason for me to stay. Getting out of the hospital before Andreas shows up would be prudent, and I'm sure Nick would understand.

But I promised. I'm not leaving.

Rubbing my arms to warm them, I count my steps to the wall, turn, count my steps to the opposite wall. It's paranoia. Desperation. Part of me knows that Isaiah is dead and my task is complete, and the rest of me is still trying to catch up. He could have found out about the house the old-fashioned way—we weren't careful enough and someone spotted us. I could be spinning something out of nothing because I don't know what's supposed to happen next.

I press my hand to the glass. Dead, and Isaiah's *still* fucking with me. It was so clear before: remove the threat, Nick and I go on with our lives.

The threat's gone. Nick has a life to go back to. I'm not sure I do anymore.

My thoughts circle and twist as I put one foot in front of the other, stopping every so often to try and catch a glimpse of Nick on the table. Finally Tish steps back, and Simon glances up, meeting my gaze. He dips his head in that way he has and walks away from the table.

It's over.

I run from the room. Simon intercepts me before I can dash down the hall to look for Nick. "He'll be awake shortly, and you can see him then. I'll have someone come get you when he's ready to leave."

"Was the surgery successful? What happened?"

He sighs. "I won't give you that information, Cass." I open my mouth to protest, and he cuts me off with a sharp look. "Dom might trust you. Constantine might. You are not family to me. If he asks for you to take him home, I will discharge him into your care."

This is normal behavior. I shouldn't expect Simon to give me the information I want just because I ask. "You're going to talk to his father, right? If I'm there while you're talking to him, would that be a problem?"

Simon gives me a critical, considering once-over. "Andreas would be the one to make that decision." He gestures to the double doors leading to the unrestricted area of the surgical floor. "Come with me."

I'm surprised to see Andreas is sitting alone on one end of a fake leather couch and calmly leafing through a magazine. He must have an amazing amount of faith in Simon's skill. He sets the magazine aside as we approach, his gaze flitting to me before settling on Simon. A month ago, the casual dismissal might have hurt.

Tonight, I couldn't care less. All I want to know is how severe the injury is and when I can take Nick home.

Simon takes a seat on a nearby chair, so I sit in the middle of the couch, close enough to hear. He raises his brows in question, and Andreas waves it off. "Dominic?"

"In recovery. The surgery went well. The bullet tore through the muscle and glanced off the bone. Had to clean out a couple of fragments. Lucky the bone didn't break, or he'd need a cast. He'll have to stay off the leg for a while as it is. Usual instructions for cleaning the wound."

"Wait," I interrupt. "What are the instructions? He'll need drugs and crutches, right?" He shouldn't try to walk on that leg.

Andreas turns to me. "I'll take care of it, Cassidy."

I. Not including me. He's so much like Turner. So cold, so absolute. I shake my head. "Nick specifically said he wanted me to drive him home. I'm staying with him. If he's going to be a difficult patient, I need to be prepared."

"We're already equipped to deal with a wide range of injuries." Andreas switches his attention back to Simon. "When will he be ready to leave?"

"Soon. Once the anesthesia's worn off, he'll have to go."

Which gives me an indeterminate amount of time to figure out how to get Nick out of the hospital and away from his family.

Andreas's phone rings. He stands and walks to the elevators before answering. Simon stands as well. "I need to check on Dominic."

I grab his hand to stop him from leaving. "Simon. Please. I'm not lying. Constantine spent a good part of the car ride here trying to convince Nick to allow him to take us home. Nick's got his reasons for hiding from the rest of his family. I don't know what they are, but shouldn't your patient's wishes come first?"

His mouth firms into a thin line. "I will ask him once he wakes up." He tugs his hand free and stalks off, the double doors opening with an angry slam. I'm left alone with a man who reminds me entirely too much of my deceased father and no allies of my own.

Except Liana.

I slip my phone from my pocket and call Nick's sister, holding my breath while I wait for her to pick up.

"Cass? What's up?"

Her tentative, cautious tone reminds me I haven't spoken with her in a while, but I don't have time to tiptoe through this. "I need a favor. A big one. Nick's been shot, and everyone seems determined to keep me away from him. Can you—"

"Nicky's been *shot*? What? Where? Where are you?" I hear her rustling around, muttering curses.

"In the thigh. He'll be fine, didn't break any bones, just the usual risk of infection and such. Simon just finished working on him, and he's in recovery. Your dad's here, and he wants to take him home as soon as he's awake. Constantine tried to convince Nick to tell him where we were staying, and Nick refused. He wants me to take him home, and no one believes me."

"Ha, well, lucky you because I do. Dad's a worse mama bear than Mom is, and if Nick doesn't want Con to know where you are, it's probably because they're in the middle of a project, right?"

"Launch is a couple of weeks away," I confirm. "I can call a cab to pick us up, but I need to get Nick out of the hospital before Andreas kicks me out."

"Hospital? So you're at General then. Nicky will probably sleep off the anesthesia for another fifteen, twenty minutes. I need about a half hour unless traffic's with me. Can you distract everyone until then?"

Dragging Lia into the middle of this mess wasn't my intent. "I thought maybe you could call your dad or something in a couple of minutes, keep him on the phone while I try to get Nick out."

"Cass. You're my friend. I love my brother. I want to help."

She's the only one. "How do you know he'll be asleep that long?"

Something slams shut on the other end of the line. "I know Simon. He's a stickler for procedure and patient safety. Not even Dad can get him to budge, and since having Simon on staff at a major hospital is a good thing, he doesn't try too hard." She sounds a little out of breath.

"Half hour," she repeats. The call disconnects, and I shove my phone back into my pocket.

Somehow I have to keep both Simon *and* Andreas occupied until Lia arrives.

Nick's father is still on the phone, and Simon hasn't returned, so I take my first good look at the waiting area. The elevator bank is to my left. The hallway runs through the waiting area and off to the right. The double doors to the surgical suites are in front of me. Using the elevators to the left is out. Nick won't be able to walk down stairs. A place as large as Angels General will have multiple elevator banks. The question is finding the next one and figuring out where it ends up.

A quick glance shows Andreas hasn't moved. I walk to the hallway entrance to my right, searching for a *You Are Here* map. What I get is a diagram directing me to the nearest emergency exits. I hurry down the hall, ready to stop the first hospital employee I find to ask for directions.

Up ahead, a slim blond woman turns out of a doorway, and I rush to catch up with her. "Excuse me." She half turns, and I stop short. It's Tish, and the last person I expect to help me. "Never mind," I mutter.

"It's Cassidy, right? Are you looking for Simon? He's back the way you came."

I inch closer as a couple of people pass us, discussing some hospital policy. "Actually, I was looking for the elevator. I know where the one we came up in is," I add hastily. "Is there a different one I could take?"

She makes a sympathetic noise. "Andreas is a pain in the ass. If you want to avoid running into him, just continue down this hall and turn right. There are two elevators there."

I flash a smile. "Thanks." Next order of business: get to Nick. If I can get him in the wheelchair and to those elevators, we can figure out where the exit is once we're on the ground floor. "Restroom's behind me?"

"There's another one near the elevators I told you about, but yes, the one behind you is closer."

I thank her again and turn around. The restroom is about halfway between where I ran into Tish and the hallway entrance. I duck inside, count to a hundred, then do it again. I poke my head into the hallway. No Tish. I make my way to the waiting area. Maybe I can talk Andreas out of taking Nick home, and I won't need Lia's help after all.

But he's nowhere to be seen.

Heart thudding, I push through the double doors to the surgical suites and scan the hallway. Two men in green scrubs are standing far enough away I can't hear what they're saying, but no sign of Andreas or Simon. I tug at the hem of my scrub top as I weigh my options.

I glance down slowly as an idea forms. Simon did me a favor when he gave me these scrubs to wear. As long as no one looks too closely, I should be able to get Nick in a wheelchair and push him right through the front doors.

Straightening my spine, I start down the hall, straight past the two men. I sneak a quick look at the doors as I pass. All I see are operating rooms, and my heart rate kicks up the farther I get from the waiting area. Recovery *should* be on the same floor, and with the layout, it makes sense it would be nearby.

I round a corner, still scanning doorways. Another set of double doors is ahead, which will be convenient only if it connects with the rest of the floor and doesn't dead end in a more restricted section.

I'm starting to lose hope I'll find Nick in time when I look through an open door and spot him. He's still unconscious, blankets halfway up his chest, his face pale. A wheelchair's conveniently sitting in a corner. I step inside and shut the door. My shoes squeak lightly as I cross the room.

He stirs, eyelids fluttering, then opening completely.

"Hey," I say softly. I ease a hip up onto the bed and take his hand. Relief slides through me as he curves his fingers around mine. "Your dad's here."

"Where?" he mumbles.

"Not sure. I figured either he or Simon would be in here waiting for you to wake up." He shuts his eyes and mutters something. I ease in. "Sorry. What did you say?"

"Get me out of here."

"Lia's on her way to run interference. I thought I could get you out with her help, but I need your crutches and pills first, and I don't think Simon will hand those over voluntarily."

Nick lets go and strokes his hand roughly up my arm, coming around to cup the back of my neck. "Dad wants to take me with him, right?"

"He mentioned it."

"He won't allow you to come along. Get me in the chair. We'll worry about the rest of it later." He releases me and pushes at the blankets, his movements feeble and weak. He's not ready to move. Not yet.

I place a hand on his shoulder. "Stay in the bed for a little bit longer. You can barely move."

"No time. Help me into the chair."

Sweat breaks out on his forehead, his mouth pinched tight as we maneuver him off the bed and into the chair. I rip one of the blankets free of the bed and cover his legs. My phone buzzes as I'm attempting to open the door and push Nick through at the same time. Thinking it might be Lia, I pull the chair back into the room and answer. "Where are you?"

"A few blocks away," Lia replies. "Where do you need me? Is my father around?"

"I don't know. I'm trying to get Nick out of recovery, but we need his medications and his crutches." I don't tell her my growing fear of leaving the room; I don't want to get us lost, but I think that's exactly what will happen.

"If Dad's not around, it might be simpler to just get to the front. If Nicky gives the okay, I can drive you home."

I tip the phone away from my mouth. "Lia's offering to drive us."

"Fine," he grits out. "We need to go, Cass."

When we get back to the warehouse and Nick's had a couple of pain pills, I'm going to ask him why he's so insistent on avoiding his family. I tell Lia we'll meet her outside the front entrance, hang up, and stick the phone into my pocket.

As soon as I open the door, I hear voices. Familiar ones.

Andreas is coming toward us.

Chapter 7

"What are you doing?" Nick reaches out to grab the door as I roll him back into the room. "We're leaving."

"Your father is in the hallway. I'm really not in the mood to find out what happens if he confronts me. Get in the bed." A bead of sweat slips down the back of his neck. He shouldn't be up yet. "Let me text Lia. She should be here by now. She can come up and distract him."

It's a mark of how poorly he's feeling when he doesn't argue. I shut everything out, my rising panic, the growing pile of questions, worry over Nick's recovery, and get him in the bed and snap the blanket out. I'm smoothing it over his legs when the door opens.

"Good. You're awake." Andreas strides into the room. His eyes narrow a fraction as he takes in Nick's face. "Anesthesia not quite worn off? Simon assured me it should have by now."

Nick grunts. "I'm awake enough to know I feel like shit. I need pain pills, but I don't see anything. Could you go find him?"

"Cass can go."

"You know Simon won't hand them over to her. Besides, I want to speak with her alone. Give us a minute?"

Andreas flits his gaze between his son and me and back again. "Rest for a few minutes. I'll get the pills and arrange to have the crutches delivered to the house." His mouth curves into a faint smile. "Your mother is looking forward to having you home, if only for a few days." He spins on his heel and stalks out the door, off to look for Simon.

Nick sits up so fast a hiss of pain escapes, and he swallows audibly.

"You okay?" I ask, moving to his shoulder. I slip an arm around his back, and he pushes the covers aside.

He swallows again and shuts his eyes. "Little nauseous. Need a moment."

I stare at the door, willing it to stay closed while Nick fights to get his stomach under control. He squeezes my fingers, and I help him into the chair a second time. I tuck the blanket around his legs, unlock my phone, and hand it to him. "Text Lia. I'd feel better with her up here getting in your dad's face than having her waiting out front to drive us." We'll have to get the pills some other way. I'm most concerned with the antibiotics. I've heard too many horror stories about the bugs people pick up in hospitals, and the thought of Nick getting sick on top of all this makes me ill.

He taps at my phone as I ease open the door and stick my head into the hallway. Someone wearing scrubs and studying a chart is at the corner, and there's a man walking away, but other than that, it's empty. I push the chair out of the room and move toward the double doors. "Any idea where these lead to?"

Nick shakes his head and puts my phone down. "The building's set up like a series of interlocking rings. Eventually this hallway will dead end in either a T or an upside-down L. If we hurry, we might be able to make it to the elevators in the west hallway before they come looking."

Running through the halls pushing a wheelchair is a great way to attract attention, scrubs or no scrubs, but we're low on time. I jog as fast as I can, occasionally checking over my shoulder to ensure no one's seen us. I slow to a walk as we pass an admin desk of some kind.

The hallway ends in the upside-down L Nick mentioned, leaving me with no choice but to go right. Tish mentioned the next bank of elevators was in this hallway, but I don't see them. It's busier, too, forcing me to slow down.

My phone buzzes in Nick's lap, and he picks it up. "Password?"

"I can't exactly enter my password right now. Unless you've magically developed the skills to steer this chair yourself." I glance down the adjoining corridor as we pass, searching for Andreas or Simon. At the far end is a tall man with dark hair stalking toward us. He's too far away for me to make out his face, but his stride is purposeful, almost angry.

I abandon all pretense of belonging and pick up the pace to a jog, mind clicking along as I think through the next steps. Into the elevator, down to the ground floor, out through the front. I'll check my phone in the elevator.

And once Nick is able, I'll ask him why the hell we're doing all this sneaking around.

I skid to a halt in front of the elevators and jab at the down button. "Did you happen to look down the hall we just passed? I think I saw your dad, but I'm not sure."

"Might have been him." The elevator doors open, and I push him inside, hit the button for the ground floor, and stab the door close button repeatedly. They slide closed seconds later, and I take my first deep breath since we left recovery.

Five floors aren't a great distance. Nick hands me my phone, and I barely have enough time to unlock it before the doors open again and we're forced into the corridor. I toss my phone onto his lap. "What did she say?"

The hallway is busy, fluorescent lights flickering and buzzing. An intercom squawks overhead, and a group of people with stethoscopes hanging out of their pockets walk by. A sign hanging on the wall in front of us points to the ER on our left.

I go right.

"She's heading to the fifth floor to intercept our father. Says she'll try and get the meds from him while she's at it." He hands the phone to me, and I shove it into my pocket.

Someone steps into our path, and I run into the back of the chair, jostling Nick in the process. He swears, and I straighten, going ramrod stiff when I see who it is. "Mr. Kosta."

Andreas ignores me and frowns at his son. "Dominic. I asked you to wait."

Nick barks out a bitter laugh. "If I waited, you would have squirreled me out some side entrance and Cass would have been wondering where the hell I was."

"Someone would have ensured she arrived home safely."

Oh, well that's nice. A man in pink scrubs gives us the side-eye as he edges around us. "Mr. Kosta, I'm sure you have your reasons for not wanting me around your son at the moment, but it might be better if we discussed them somewhere else. People are starting to notice, and Nick does need to get out of the hospital before we get Simon in trouble."

He says nothing, only arches a brow and dips his head once before heading toward the front entrance. My phone buzzes in my pocket, and I pull it out to answer. "Lia?"

"Where are you?" She's out of breath. "Where's my dad? No one's up here."

"Andreas caught us on the way to the exit. Here, talk to your brother." I pass him my phone and resume pushing his wheelchair. Andreas waits at the edge of the main atrium, gesturing for us to proceed through the front doors.

I roll Nick's chair off to the side, out of the flow of traffic. He's still talking to his sister, though his side of the conversation is one-word answers and the occasional affirmative noise. "Mr. Kosta, may I speak with you for a moment?"

"You can call me Andreas, Cassidy. I don't mind." But he stays where he is, some distance from Nick, allowing us a bit of privacy.

A gust of wind blows through the circular drive, and goose bumps spring up on my bare arms. "Is there a problem?"

"A problem?"

"A problem with me," I clarify. "Nick has turned down two offers of help from family members tonight. Constantine offered to drive us home after the surgery, and he refused. It doesn't seem like he wants to go with you tonight, yet you were going to send me home alone. To me, those are indications of a problem. If I'm in the middle of it, I need to know what it is."

Andreas studies me in the dim light, his careful, detached scrutiny annoying. I fight the urge to cross my arms over my chest and wait.

"You have proven reckless and selfish. This is a danger to the family. More, you have abused my son's trust and dragged him into a personal vendetta."

"There was no dragging," I say mildly. "I left Nick. He chose to help. I realize I took advantage of his resources, and for that, I apologize. But your son has been a great help to me, in more ways than one."

What would have happened to me if he hadn't been there, night after night? If he hadn't fought to keep me tied to him in some small way?

"Besides," I add, "Isaiah is dead. My 'vendetta,' as you put it, is over."

"Dad."

In concert, Andreas and I look over at Nick sitting in his wheelchair. Nick's face is cool and blank. "Stop. You're wasting your time."

Andreas's footsteps echo off the pavement as he makes his way to Nick's side. "You would endanger the family for her?"

"She's not endangering anyone."

Andreas points to Nick's leg. "A lie."

"An accident," Nick counters, and I want to slink back inside, find another exit and a way back to my apartment. I know there's an ongoing disagreement between Nick and his father about how large the family's gotten and what should be done about it. From the weariness in Nick's voice, it sounds like that tension's increased drastically. I don't want to be the breaking point.

I straighten my shoulders and walk to Nick's other side. I'm not about to let his father scare me off, either. "I can call us a cab."

"Let it go, Dad." Nick cuts his father off before he can speak. "You really want to talk about this, we can do it later."

Andreas looks me up and down, and I stiffen. "Don't," I say quietly. "I'm not leaving him, and don't force him to do anything."

"Cass!"

I crane my neck around and spot Lia exiting the main doors, her cheeks flushed. "You couldn't have stayed in one place?" She hurries over and gives me a quick hug. "Everything all right?" she murmurs.

"He's okay," I whisper back. "Just needs to get home."

"Sure thing." She wraps her fingers around the handles and pushes Nick toward the curb. "Coming?" she calls back.

I smother a grin. Hard to believe anyone could bully this mafia princess. I offer a stiff nod to Andreas and follow Lia to her car.

The two of us manage to get Nick into the back seat, and I climb into the front passenger seat over his protests. "You need the space for your leg. Uh-uh, no arguing," I say when he opens his mouth. "Where are we going? Back to my apartment?"

"East Temple. Near the railroad tracks." He tips his head back and shuts his eyes, and I tug my seat belt into place.

Lia waits until the hospital is in her rearview to start on the questions. "The truth, Cass. Are you really okay?"

Fatigue swamps me, and all of a sudden I'm barely holding it together. "No. Isaiah's dead. Tris killed him. Tris is dead, too, and your dad's going to have a hell of a mess on his hands." I give her a rundown of the night's events with the sensation that it all happened ages ago. I glance at the dashboard clock. Almost three AM. Well, that explains the exhaustion.

"I don't know how Nick's going to get the pills he needs." I scrape my teeth over my bottom lip. "Simon's too much of a rule abider to hand them over, and Andreas isn't about to."

"You mean the pills that Simon happily passed over to me? They're in my purse. Go on and get them out. You can get crutches at any drug store." She flicks on her turn signal and smoothly changes lanes, roaring through a yellow light.

"I'm not bleeding anymore, Liana. You can slow down."

Lia flips off her brother and grips the wheel once more. "Shut up. You need to rest. The sooner you get home, the sooner you can do that."

Nick grumbles and goes quiet, and when I peer into the backseat, he's in the same position he was when we left the hospital. Lia's bag is at my feet. I pick it up and set it on my lap. I find the pill bottles and squint at the labels, trying to read the directions in the passing flashes of the streetlights.

"Give him one of each when you get him into bed," Lia says quietly. "The first twenty-four to forty-eight hours are the critical ones. If he spikes a fever, call Simon, even if Nick tells you not to. I'll e-mail you some instructions on how to change the dressing and keep the wound clean, though Nick'll probably tell you what to do."

I stare at the bottles. "How do you know all this? I thought you and your sisters mostly stayed out of the business." At least, that was the impression Nick gave me.

Her mouth twists in a mocking grin. "You spend any length of time in my family, you'll understand why. There's no escaping it."

No escape. The comment had been reiterated in one fashion or another by several people. This is my life now. This blood and violence, this never-ending cycle, is my life.

I settle deeper into my seat and clutch the bottles tighter.

"You can relax, Cass. No one's going to steal them from you." Lia slows for a red light.

"How do you know? You can make some real money peddling pharmaceuticals." But I loosen my grip. "Are we being followed?"

The light changes. "Don't think so. Why?"

"Because I wouldn't put it past your father to follow us so he can get to Nick." With the most immediate danger over, a new one pushes to the forefront. Someone could easily take him from me.

She's quiet for a few blocks. "He might," she says at last. "Dad's a hardass, no doubt. And like I said, he shifts into overdrive when it comes to protecting one of his kids. But he's not unreasonable."

I wonder if unreasonable would be Andreas removing Nick from my presence against Nick's will. He has to understand that doing so would only increase the friction between them.

I hope. Nick's stood by me even through his anger. "I can't lose him," I say softly.

Lia reaches over and squeezes my hand. "You won't."

Chapter 8

It's early. Or late, I guess. Early because it's almost seven AM, and the sun's rising. Late because I'm awake, and I haven't slept.

Nick's sound asleep in the bed I woke in a few days ago. Fearful of injuring him further, I opted for the couch over sharing the bed with him. He didn't protest too much, either. So I'm lying on the couch, staring at the high, narrow windows, watching the sky lighten outside. My eyes are dry and gritty, and I've spent the last few hours willing my body toward sleep. It's not working.

I roll onto my side and shut my eyes. If I can sleep, I don't have to remember what happened last night. If I can sleep, I can forget my life's a total mess. I pull the blanket higher up over my head to block out the light.

The dreams are fragments at first. Blips and snapshots of the face-off with Isaiah. Tris's gun goes off, Nick falls to the ground, and that's when it gets really weird. Nick's flat on his back, not propped up like he's supposed to be. There's blood everywhere, not just on his leg. Searching for the wounds, I run my hands over his chest. His skin is riddled with them. Blood flows thick and almost black.

He grabs my wrist, smearing blood on my skin. Bubbles of it slip out between his lips. "It's time," he rasps. "You need to stop." The light goes out of his eyes as red slicks over his face, and it morphs into Isaiah's. He laughs. It's a frightening sound, scraping over already raw nerves and fraying them even more.

"Poor little assassin," he says with a chuckle. His face is coated in slippery dark red, dripping into his mouth as he laughs. "You'll lose everything." The hand holding my wrist turns skeletal, bones rotting and turning gray, then black, spreading through the rest of his body. "Everything."

I shoot out of sleep with a scream lodged in my throat, panic clawing at my chest. A dream. Only a dream. Something straight out of a cheesy horror movie.

I fall off the couch, blanket tangled around my legs. I yank it away and run out of the room. Nick. Nick is alive. He was alive when we came home. I helped him up the stairs myself. I gave him pills from the bottles that Simon provided. I have to go to the drug store later and get Nick some crutches.

A vise closes over my throat. I throw open the bedroom door. The sheets are rumpled, Nick a lump in the center of the bed. The sight of him doesn't magically allow me to breathe. Gasping and panting, I dart across the floor and climb up on the bed.

He makes a snuffling noise and shoves weakly at the comforter around his head. "Cass?" he mumbles.

Relief doesn't come. I still can't breathe. He's alive and awake, but it's not enough. I grope under the covers for his hand, sit up, and focus on a point on the wall. *Air goes in. Air goes out. Nick is fine. I am fine.* Nick's hand is warm and solid in mine, his fingers curling around my palm. *Air goes in. Air goes out.* The vise opens a few inches, and I draw in a breath, the tightness in my lungs dissipating.

I resettle myself on the bed as Nick pushes back the covers with his free hand, exposing his broad shoulders. "Nightmare?" he asks. I nod, and he squeezes my hand once, then releases it. The loss burns. I make a fist to keep from reaching for him again. The last twenty-four hours haven't erased the pain we've caused each other. It only put it on hold. I'm still the girl who assumed he'd be there to clean up my mess. He's still the guy who thought drugging me was the best way to get me to cooperate.

"You want to tell me about it?"

I meet his eyes; the spark I saw flicker out is bright and steady. "You died. We were in the backyard, and the bullet didn't hit you in the leg. You were full of holes. There was blood everywhere. You...told me to stop. Then your face changed, and you were Isaiah. He laughed and said I'd lose everything. The whole getup was something straight out of a zombie film. One of those super gory ones." I rub a hand over my face. "He didn't have to do anything, and he still won."

Nick shifts around and pushes himself into a sitting position, the blankets falling to his waist. My bloody handprint is gone, leaving unblemished skin behind. "He didn't win. He's dead."

I shake my head and crawl off the other side of the bed. "No. He did win. He might be dead, but I didn't get a chance to do what I'd set out to do." I push my hair out of my face. "Do you want some help downstairs? I'll make breakfast before I get your crutches."

"Cass."

I hate that tone. That calm, commanding, brook-no-arguments tone. It's so damn *reasonable*. There is nothing reasonable about this.

"You're letting him win."

He's right. "Only because I don't know what else to do. I can only tell myself so many times Isaiah's not worth kicking myself over before it starts sounding false. And it *is* false." I lift my hands, let them fall to my sides. "How am I supposed to grieve for a man I thought I'd lost years ago? No, don't answer that." I don't want to know. Isaiah's death at my hands was supposed to bring me closure; all the deaths before his were steps in the grieving process. Break off a little more of the old, still-sweet, naive Cass and replace it with something harder to kill.

I round the end of the bed and walk to the cabinet, pull out a sweatshirt, and slip it on. "Breakfast?"

He sighs. "Yeah. Help me to the bathroom first?"

I leave him in the bathroom and run downstairs to start the coffee and find a skillet for scrambled eggs. While I wait for him to finish, I check my e-mail. I click on the one at the top of my inbox, a notice from UCLA. "Shit." Classes start in a few days. I picked my classes when I stopped at the registrar's office a couple of weeks ago, but I haven't paid my tuition bill or bought any of my books.

"Shit what?"

I glance up. Nick's hanging over the railing. "Classes start in a few days. I completely forgot about it." He turns away, and I dart to the foot of the stairs. "Stop moving. I'll be right there."

"I'm not completely helpless, Cass." Bracing himself with the railing, he hops to the head of the stairs, then turns down. Each hop tightens his mouth more. By the time he's at the bottom, his lips have folded so far in they've practically disappeared.

"Maybe this place isn't the best for you." I duck under his arm and take his weight, the pair of us slowly limping into the kitchen. Once he's in a chair, I drag an empty one close so he can prop up his foot. "The lease on my old apartment is up at the end of January, but I can talk to the landlord about going month to month." Nick could stay there while his leg heals. "If you don't want to move back in with Constantine, that's a better option than staying here."

He hisses as he adjusts his foot on the chair. "Not yet. I managed to keep this space off the family radar so far. They know about your apartment, and I wouldn't put it past them to smuggle me out while you're in class one day. Once we find a new apartment, we'll move."

We. Before everything went sideways, Nick and I were going to move in together. We even looked at a few apartments. Now we're sleeping in separate rooms, dancing around like we're waiting for the other to explode. Our mutual trust is in shreds, and he's still talking like there's no reason to change our original plan.

My fear of losing him is still there, but it's muted, tempered by his presence. I identify the crawling sensation as discomfort and push it aside. There are more urgent matters to discuss. This is the third or fourth time avoiding his family has come up in conversation. I busy myself with the coffee, going over everything in the last few days, searching for clues. I find none. All I have is this feeling his excuses are nothing more than that—excuses. I carry a mug to the table and set it in front of him, then retrieve his bottles of pills from the counter and hand them over.

Quiet settles over the kitchen area as I prepare breakfast, my curiosity growing the longer it stretches, yet unable to find the words to ask Nick what the hell is going on. And I need to. I've spent too long on high alert, triple-checking every dark corner, and there's no way I can come down without Nick telling me the truth.

Finally the normality of the scene does me in, and I slide a plate of eggs and toast in front of Nick with a little more force than necessary. He takes the fork I hand him with a wary look. "Got something to say?"

I thump down in the chair opposite him. "What's going on? And please don't try to placate me or pass it off as no big deal. You're avoiding your family, and I'd like to know why."

"I've already explained myself, but sure, we can go over it again." He scoops up a bite of egg and sticks it into his mouth.

"Nick." I sigh. "That's exactly what I'm talking about. Something's… Well, if it's not wrong, it's definitely not right. I can sort of buy wanting to get away from your cousin. And Lia said your dad's worse than your mom when it comes to hovering. But it's more than that. I wish you'd tell me what it is."

He chews egg, picks up a piece of toast, and crunches off the corner. "There's been some discontent within the family." When he doesn't continue, I arch a brow and pick up my own piece of toast. He stabs his fork at the pile of eggs. "You know my father and uncle are unhappy with your choice to move on Isaiah's circle without help."

I nod. "Your father said I was"—I tap my chin—"'reckless and selfish.' I got the distinct impression he was trying to shut me out and keep me from seeing you." I fork up egg as I debate telling him what I overheard of his conversation with Constantine. "Constantine said I was costing you money. Funny thing, Isaiah said the same a few weeks ago." I pop the egg into my mouth. Nick holds my gaze, dark and steady, while I chew. I set my fork down. "Am I costing you money, Nick? Is your father intent on splitting us apart?" I must have inadvertently stepped into a remake of *Romeo and Juliet*. "Is someone going to come along and curse both our houses?"

He draws his brows together. "What?"

"Sorry. I must not have said that part out loud. The whole splitting us apart thing reminded me of *Romeo and Juliet* for some reason."

He laughs, and a tight knot of anxiety unravels in my chest. "Nice analogy." He reaches for his coffee. "Yes. My father believes that it would be best for the family and organization as a whole if I stopped seeing you. From a business standpoint, Constantine agrees with him."

The lighthearted feeling his laughter brought on sluices away. "So, what, I'm just an all-around bad choice?"

He sobers. "If I have to answer that, we're in a worse place than I thought."

I turn my attention to my breakfast. The sooner I finish, the sooner I can escape. I make a mental list of errands as I scoop up the last of my eggs. Plate empty, I scoot my chair back and stand. I carry both plates to the sink and rinse them off before setting them on the counter to wash later.

I know I'm not a bad choice to him. Sometimes his words lash out like a whip, but he's shown me every day and every night since Turner's funeral that he chose me.

I don't want to be the reason he splits from his family.

For the first time in weeks, I'm the one who initiates the contact. I need to touch him, ground myself, feel the heat of him against some small part of me. I reach out and cradle his face in my hands. "I have to ask," I say quietly. "Not because I'm doubting you, but because I don't want you hurt any more than you already are. Are you absolutely certain I'm worth it? What's the worst case scenario?"

He turns his head, presses a kiss to my palm. "Worst case scenario, they cut me out. I give up my place within the family and go straight. I won't lie. It would be a major adjustment to me. One I'm not sure I can make." I hate the bleakness and resignation in his eyes. "This is the life I was born into, love. I've never had to imagine what it might be like without it."

Whereas I've spent too much time imagining my life beyond killing. I step into him, and he rests his head on my stomach. "Tell me. All of it. What would you be giving up?"

"It won't be like it is for my sisters, if that's what you're asking." His voice is muffled by my shirt. "They'll withdraw protection from my businesses. I'll lose some assets. My personal net worth would take a hit. I'll recover it eventually." He nuzzles my stomach through the soft cotton. "It'll be like losing my family. They'll constantly be on guard about what they can say and what they can't around me, and eventually communication would die. And that's just with those who don't cut it off immediately."

He might as well have punched me in the stomach. I don't want him to lose his family over me. "Then let me go." He tips his head back and glares at me.

"Losing family is like being sliced open," I whisper. "I can't be the reason that happens to you."

His glare deepens. "Do you love me?"

More than I thought possible, and it frightens me. "Yes."

"Then don't get any ideas about doing the noble thing and leaving me." His expression softens. "We've got some shit between us to take care of. But I love you, and it's going to take a hell of a lot more for me to end this."

I wish I could say I suddenly forgive him and that all is right between us. I don't. I can't. I can give him this, though. I bend and kiss him, savoring the feel of his mouth on mine. "I love you too."

He lets out a shuddering breath. "I needed to hear that. You have no idea how much I needed to hear that."

I did, because I needed to say it.

Chapter 9

"Cass, I'm trying to understand. And thanks for calling me. I'd much rather hear from you than Nick. But it's been almost three weeks. I just want to make sure you're okay."

I shut my eyes in a feeble attempt to block out Denise's voice. I haven't seen her since the funeral, haven't heard from her other than the voicemails she's left. We haven't spent any real time together since the day she and Charlie packed for Colorado.

I don't want to be around her. I don't have it in me to pretend I'm grieving for my father when I don't know *what* I'm doing. She's been my anchor for years, and it's like I've cut the rope and I'm drifting off while she remains behind.

All the destruction I've caused is etched on my skin. I'm afraid she'll see it.

I shift my phone to my other ear and settle back in my seat. "We need to go by our apartment and clear out the rest of our things. Tomorrow?"

"That's not what I meant, Cass. We'll be too busy boxing up books and plates to actually talk. I'm sorry I'm being—you know what? I'm not sorry. I'm not sorry I'm being so pushy. You're my best friend, I love you, I'm worried about you, and I don't fucking care if it's selfish of me to want to see you and reassure myself that you really *are* okay."

Despite her anger, Denise's words make me smile. She rarely swears. That she's swearing now is an indication of just how concerned—and pissed—she is.

"We *do* need to clean tomorrow, though," I point out. "Our lease is up in a few weeks, neither of us are using the place, and once classes start, we won't have much free time to do it. Might as well get a head start on everything now. Nick won't be there, either." The man in question pulls his attention from his tablet to frown at me. "So it'll be the two of us. Or three if Charlie's coming." I hold Nick's gaze. "We can grab some food after if you want."

"Nick won't be there? Why?"

"Work." Not a lie; he should be and likely will be doing as much as he can remotely. "He's got a project due in a few weeks." He grunts and goes back to the tablet in his hands.

"That works, I guess." I smother another grin at her annoyed tone. She asks, "Do you have boxes? I have a few. Have you found a new place to live yet? We'll need to move all the furniture out."

We discuss moving logistics and set a time to meet, then hang up. I toss the phone onto the kitchen table. "Neese has a point. There's a bunch of furniture in that apartment that I need to do something with."

"Storage unit." He flicks his fingers over the surface of the screen. "I don't want it brought here. We'll store it until we've found an apartment, unless we find one before your lease is up." I tense at his assumption we'll be living together; I still haven't decided what to do about that. He waves me over. "Found a couple of places. Thought we could check them out."

I drag a chair next to him, and he taps the screen. "This was one of the ones we set an appointment to see a few weeks ago and never got around to it." I lean forward, ignoring the haze creeping into my vision. We never got around to it because we were too busy tracking down my mother and Turner. A stone lodges in my chest, forcing the air from my lungs.

Blood dripping down his face.

I love you.

The three most powerful words in the English language. They can invigorate. Destroy. They're their very own shock and awe campaign.

"Cass?"

I flinch away from the hand on my cheek.

"Cassidy." He drops his hand to mine and works open my closed fingers with soothing strokes. "You all right?"

"Fine." I'm fast approaching the point where I won't be able to take another *are you okay* question. I don't know why I bother with Nick, anyway. He knows I'm anything but fine. "Not that one."

He doesn't question me, just withdraws his hand, closes the browser window, and moves on to the next one. "I know you were looking at one bedrooms, but realistically, a two bedroom would be better." He taps on a picture, enlarging the floor plan. "It's about what you and Denise are paying now."

It won't hurt anything to look at a two bedroom. I don't have to make up my mind today. "Are any of these others two bedrooms, or just this one?"

He nods, his gaze on the tablet. "I picked out a couple, though most are one bedrooms."

"Balconies?"

"No balconies. No ground floors. Here." He swipes his finger across the screen. "This one met most of your requirements and mine. We'll know more once we see it. Small building, in-unit washer-dryer combos, on the fourth floor. It's about seven blocks from campus."

I skim the listing, looking for the catch, because there has to be one. I find it at the bottom. "I can't afford this."

"I can."

"I'm not letting you pay my rent, Nick. We've been over this."

He slides the tablet away and reaches for his phone. "You have a budget. I'm paying for the portion over your budget." He types in the number and raises the phone to his ear.

"Nick—"

"Hello. I was calling to see if the apartment you listed is still available?"

Annoyed, I scoot my chair back and get up for a glass of water. I won't have Nick paying for something he may not be using. Allowing him to pay half or more on a place when I can't decide if I want him living with me isn't fair to him *or* me.

"We leave now, the property manager can show it to us first thing. She's got a long list of showings. Says it'll be first come, first serve." His phone hits the table with a clatter. There's a grating shriek as he scrapes his chair back, followed by a soft *thunk* as he positions his crutches. "Need to check something, then we can leave."

I open my mouth to protest. *We're just looking.* I'll make my mind up in my own time. I drain the water and set the glass on the table. "Fine."

* * * *

The apartment is practically perfect.

Fourth floor, exactly as promised. There's thirty units in the entire building, an elevator on one end, stairs on the other. Both the stairwell entrance and the elevator are easily seen from every doorway on the floor. The front door to the building requires a separate key. Street parking only, which will be a pain in the ass once I buy a new car. I'm tired of borrowing one of Nick's whenever I need to go somewhere. The unit itself faces the street, giving us a clear view of anyone walking up to the front door. As advertised, a stacked washer-dryer combo is tucked away in a utility closet near the kitchen, and the kitchen itself boasts plenty of counter space. There's a coffee shop at the end of the block, and the south end of campus is, indeed, only seven blocks away. I'll have to add in extra time to get to class, since most of my classes are on the north end of campus, but it's doable.

It's also five hundred dollars more than my last place.

Half listening to Nick's conversation with the property manager, I stand in the middle of one of the bedrooms. My skin's too tight. Weeks ago, I never would have heard of this apartment, wouldn't have *needed* to. Neese would have been in the next room, and I wouldn't have been calculating the time it would take to get from here to my first class.

Rubbing my arms in an effort to ease some of the tightness, I wander to the window and check the street. In deference to Nick's injury, we didn't attempt to park several blocks away, opting for the shortest route from the car to the front door. It made him antsy and brusque, barking out short commands until I wanted to slap some tape over his mouth to get him to shut up.

Then I remembered Andreas and his determination to get me away from his son, and my frustration fell away.

The street below is busy in that way a lot of the residential streets around campus are—a cluster or two of people on the sidewalks, usually students, the occasional car cruising by, searching for a parking spot. The angle of the sun prevents me from seeing into any of the cars.

It's all so fucking normal. *Normal.*

Maybe this would have been the semester Denise and I parted ways. Maybe I would have been looking for a new place. Maybe it even would have been with Nick. But *normal* would have meant I'd call my mother and ask about dinner plans, and she'd answer in that slightly harried, distracted voice that said she was in the middle of a case. *Normal* would have meant Turner and his silent disapproval. *Normal* would have been a quiet Christmas and a rowdy birthday, and I'd have all my textbooks already and I wouldn't be wondering how the hell I was going to get through the next four months without thinking one of my classmates was going to sneak up on me.

A warm, strong hand closes over mine and gently pries my fingers from the windowsill. "Hey." Nick's at my back, his strength jerking me back to reality. There's no Turner. No Mom. I didn't even celebrate Christmas this year. "Cassidy."

The soft and confident way he says my name rolls over me, easing me back from the edge. I am going to break. It will be soon. And Nick will be the one to pick up the pieces. Whether they'll fit back together, I don't know. I don't know if there's any glue in the world strong enough.

"He should be here," I whisper. My legs start shaking, and I lock my knees. "*Here*. Not a pile of ash in a metal container, waiting to be scattered."

Nick wraps an arm around my waist and pulls me close. "I know."

A shudder works its way through my body as I struggle to pack it all away. This is my normal now. A heart of cold, twisted metal and a man determined to stay with me anyway. One day, if I let him, he'll melt it down and replace it with the living, beating organ it once was.

Not today.

I stroke a finger over the back of his hand. "You shouldn't be on your feet so much."

He presses a kiss to the top of my head, the sweetness of it tearing through me like a whip. "I'll be okay for a little bit longer. I've given the property manager the check. You just need to sign the lease."

I blame Nick's attentive tenderness for the fog around my brain. He hasn't shown me much of it the last few days, so it's settled in thick. I ease out of his arms. "You did what?"

"We're taking this apartment. We keep looking, we may not find another one that works as well as this one."

There is actually a one bedroom on the list that might work, at least on paper. But I arrow in on his first statement. "*We* are taking this apartment?" I cross my arms over my chest. "Am I the other person in this *we*? Because I don't remember agreeing we'd live here. Or live together, for that matter."

His face morphs into that cold, implacable expression he has whenever he's made his decision and nothing and no one will change his mind. Well, tough shit, because he's not winning this round. I edge around him, shut the door, and let the fury out.

"We are not moving in together." I ignore Nick's shock—and my own—and push on. "You doped my coffee and then you try to pull this shit? You expect me to live with someone I'm not sure I trust anymore? And what about you? You honestly, seriously, want to sleep next to someone who has proven reckless and dangerous in the past? We can't do this, Nick. I *won't*." I suck in a breath and shut my eyes, reeling in the anger. It won't do me any good now. "I need time," I say quietly. "You hurt me. I hurt you. I need time, and space, and I want to start over."

Love is painful. Love is hell. I can't *live* with Nick, not after what he did and what he's just done.

"You're right."

Those two words mean more to me than anything he could say, including *I love you*. He's saying them *because* he loves me. I open my eyes, and the shock has been replaced by resignation. "We need time to fix this, and we don't have it. Not yet." He hops over to the windowsill and leans against it, taking some of the weight off his injured leg. "I'll give you the time you need, love. But take this apartment, and let me pay for it. I can secure this place so you're safe, and I need that for me."

It's too big for one person. "Nick, I can't stay here. I don't need this much space."

He waves an impatient hand. "With everything that's going on, I need a place to work away from the office. Unless you have any objections, I'll use the other room as my workspace. I'm not moving in, Cassidy," he adds when I shake my head. "We can't start over. We've come too far for that. But we can take a few steps back, slow it down."

The relief racing through my veins is icy cold, and I stiffen my spine to keep from trembling. "Thank you." My voice is calm and steady. I walk to the door and open it before I can change my mind.

After signing the lease agreement and handing over the deposit, we're back on the sidewalk. "What next?" I unlock the car and take Nick's crutches so he can fold himself into the passenger seat.

"I need to get some work done. Do you want to grab lunch on the way to the warehouse?"

Interesting that he doesn't say *home*. I wait until I'm behind the wheel and buckling my seatbelt before answering. "I could eat." I curl my fingers around the steering wheel. "Take out or do you want to stop some place?"

The engine roars to life, and I pull away from the curb. "El Dorado?" he asks. "I swear this time I'll get the mole sauce."

I laugh. "You better. I'm not sharing."

True to his word, he orders the mole sauce. Our meal is interrupted several times by his buzzing phone, and each subsequent text spins the dial on his mood into glower territory.

I push my plate away. "What is it?"

He shakes his head. "Nothing important."

She's costing us money.

A month ago, he would have told me. The thought we've drifted this far apart sends another pang of hurt rippling through me. We'll never get back to where we were if we don't start talking. I slide out of my side of the booth and into his. "Not gonna fly. Talk to me." When he levels a blank stare at me, I reach up and cup his jaw. "Nick. You've spent the last couple of weeks propping me up. Let me help you."

Surprise flashes across his face, and he looks away, focusing on my half-eaten dinner. "We need some to-go boxes."

Chapter 10

The texts turned out to be an app emergency. Constantine ran a last-minute test, downloading it to his personal tablet, and it failed to install properly.

Curled into a corner of the black leather couch, I watch Nick and Constantine argue over how far back to go to search for the problem. "It's not in the code," Nick insists. "The section damaged by the virus has been checked four times by four different people. If there were something wrong, it would have been caught by now."

"Those four different people weren't either of us, and the section was originally re-written by Caleb Turner, who had no knowledge of what the app was supposed to do. It needs to be checked. It's the only reason it's not installing correctly." Constantine pushes a hand through his hair, the short, dark strands standing on end.

"In order for him to restore the code, he would have needed basic knowledge of how the app functions," Nick points out. "Have you looked at the code yet to know that's the problem?"

"Hey." Both men turn toward me. "Have you checked the server it's stored on?" I arch a brow as Constantine scowls at me. "I'm not saying my father was a perfect coder and there's no way he would have made a mistake. But what if there's a server error that's not allowing the executable file to download correctly, and you're just not getting an error message?"

Nick holds up a hand to silence Constantine before he can speak. "We'll do both. The server check is quick enough. Move it to a different server and try downloading again."

Constantine straightens. "Not as fast as you'd like. It was on that server because it's the only one that has any room. The others are too full." He picks up his tablet and heads for the door. "I'll see if we have anything that can be moved or dumped. Half hour, minimum." The door shuts behind him with a decisive *click*, and Nick slouches in his chair, letting out a hiss of pain in the process.

"Maybe sitting behind your desk isn't the best idea right now." I point to the unopened laptop sitting on his desk. "Can you do everything you need on that?"

"Most of it."

I get up from the couch. "Come over here and use the couch then."

He shakes his head. "I'll be all right. You mind reheating my leftovers for me?"

I take both our half-finished dinners into the break room, dump them onto paper plates, and stick them into the microwave. Bracing my elbows on the counter, I drop my head into my hands and shut my eyes, willing the lingering tightness to dissipate.

"Has he been working? Or is he too busy playing house with you?"

I snap my head up and around. My gaze lands on Constantine. "You know, if you want to blame me for something bad that's happened to Nick or your family, you're going to need to get in line." The skin between my shoulder blades is itchy. "But to answer your question, yes, he's been working. He also just got shot in the leg. No, I don't need you to remind me it happened because of me. That point's been hammered home." The microwave dings. "Now, is there anything else you'd like to say, or can I take Nick his dinner?"

Constantine's mouth twitches, his lips finally shifting into a small grin. "Sorry, Cass. Just need this to go well, and I tend to take out my frustrations on everyone around me. Thank you," he adds, "for answering my question. How's his leg been?"

"Bothering him, though he won't say much about it." I open drawers, searching for silverware. "Do you have forks somewhere?"

"Second drawer from the left. Should be some plastic stuff in there. Going to check the server." He leaves, and I carry the plates to Nick's office. The door rattles in the frame when I bump it shut with my hip.

"Thanks," he mutters absently, eyes glued to his monitor. I peer over his shoulder. Lines of code crawl across the screen, his cursor moving along at a rapid clip. Rather than interrupt him, I retreat with my plate to the couch to finish my meal.

Half an hour later, my empty plate's on the floor and I've about drained my phone's battery. Nick's mumbling to himself. Contrary to his previous statement, Constantine hasn't returned. Nerves flash and die under my skin, and I can't stop my hands from trembling. I need to get up, move around, find something else to occupy my brain.

I get to my feet, pick up my plate, and step over to the desk to retrieve Nick's. A quick stop in the break room to dispose of the trash, and I'll take out some of my anxiety on the stairwell. Hiking up and down it a couple of times should dispel the nervous energy.

Nick looks up. "Can we test the app on your phone? There's enough room on the second server, so once we move the file, we can try the download again."

"Do you have a charger? My phone's going to die in a second." On cue, it emits the beep signifying shut down. "Make that dead."

He drags a hand down his face. "I've got an iPhone. You're android, right?" I nod, and he slouches in his chair. "I don't have one that'll work. Check with Con. He might. Bring him back with you while you're at it. It doesn't take that long to move the file."

Constantine's office is next door to Nick's. He's not in it. I take a quick tour of the rest of the floor before descending the stairs to the eighth. To the best of my knowledge, he wouldn't need to access the server room to move files, but it's the only other logical place he'd be.

I hear voices the moment I open the door to the eighth floor, and I freeze, straining to make out the words. One of the voices sounds like Constantine's. I edge through the door and ease it closed. The carpet does a decent job of muffling my footsteps as I approach the voices.

Or *voice*. Whoever he's talking to isn't responding, but the tone and cadence says it's definitely a conversation.

"Find out."

A pause, and I take in a shallow breath.

"No more excuses. Find. Out." Another pause. "No, eliminating her isn't an option. It'll only tip him off. If it happens at all, it should be the two of them at once. Don't underestimate her."

Cold washes over me, and I pull it inside, use it to sooth the jitters, wipe away the little worm of guilt over eavesdropping. Constantine could just as easily be talking about an employee issue. Paranoia's got a tight grip on me, though, and I'm not willing to give him the benefit of the doubt.

He gives one last terse order and hangs up. I dart back to the stairwell door and make more noise as I walk down the hall to the server room. I knock on the half-closed door for good measure before pushing it open. "Constantine?"

"Cass." He rounds one of the blinking black towers. "Need another minute. Got an alert that one of the servers might be overheating."

"That's fine. Nick wanted me to tell you he found room on server two. He's ready to try the download again, but he wants to do it on my phone. Do you have a charger for an android device?" I pull my dead phone from my pocket. "Kind of hard to download anything if it doesn't have any juice."

His smile is warm and genuine, rattling my shaky convictions. Maybe I misheard him. It must have been an employee matter.

"There's one in my desk. Top right drawer." He dips his hand into his pocket and comes out with a key. He tosses it to me. "I'll be there in a minute. Just need to check the temperature and adjust the sensor."

I slowly climb the stairs to the ninth floor, replaying the snippet of conversation and adding it to everything else I've observed from Constantine. Everything he's done, from helping Nick with the initial search for his would-be killer, staying with me while I was stuck in the hospital, to putting us up after Nick's house burned down, are all such kind, selfless gestures that it causes me physical pain to think it may all be a long con.

Rubbing a fist absently across my chest, I head for Constantine's office. It's tempting to snoop through his desk. He *did* give me a key. But said key means it's highly unlikely I'd find anything of interest in his desk, so I locate the charger and shut and lock the drawer.

Nick's still hunched over his keyboard, poking at the occasional button. I find an outlet near the couch and plug in the charger, then my phone. It powers on with a melodic *ping*. "We're in business. How do I connect to your server?"

"Huh?" He tears his attention from his monitor. "Con had a charger? Good." He locates his crutches and struggles to his feet.

"For fuck's sake. *Sit*." I reach down to unplug the charger from the wall.

"Don't. I'm fine." He manages to get his crutches under his arms and swings out and around the desk. Rolling my eyes, I drop back down onto the couch. *Fine*. That word is going to lose all meaning in the very near future.

I take his crutches for him as he lowers himself to the couch. Right leg stretched out in front of him, mouth pinched shut, he motions for me to hand him my phone. The cord pulls tight. "Wait. Switch places with me."

Getting to my feet, I can actually *hear* his teeth clack together as he scoots into my spot on the couch. I remain on my feet. "Did you bring your pain pills with you?"

"No," he grits out. "We weren't going to be out that long."

True. "Try the download, and then I'll go get them."

He shakes his head and points to the seat beside him. "I'll be fine. There's some over-the-counter pills in the first aid kit. Those'll be enough."

"Nick." The pain isn't worth it. "Let me get your pain pills." I take his hand. His skin is cool and slightly clammy against mine. "Tell the truth. How bad is it?"

He slips his hand free and ignores the question. My phone screen flashes on. "Five minutes," he murmurs.

Five minutes, my ass. He's injured and in pain. I can easily steal his keys. If the download doesn't work, that's exactly what I'll do.

"Is it working?" Constantine walks into the room, tablet in hand and hair more mussed than ever. He flashes me a weary smile as he leans against the desk, and my doubts grow larger. He's under a lot of stress. Both of them are. What I overheard was business related. It had to be.

But how much longer can I justify those odd little out-of-character blips?

Nick drops my phone onto the arm of the couch and slumps back. "Still won't install. Doesn't even give an error message. Could still be a server error, and if it is, that's an even bigger problem."

"Do you have anything else you can download?" I ask.

Nick frowns. "A couple. Have you called the rest of the team?"

"On their way," Constantine confirms. "Hope you're rested. Gonna be a long night."

Nick absolutely needs his pain pills. He boosts himself up, and I hand him his crutches. The two of us leave Constantine in Nick's office, and I dart a look over his shoulder to ensure we're far enough away that we won't be overheard. "Give me your keys," I whisper.

He shakes his head and veers off into the break room, the rubber tips of his crutches squeaking on the floor. The room is bright with florescent lights, two refrigerators humming quietly. He swings around the tables, pausing to push a chair out of his way. "I don't want to risk someone following you back to the warehouse." A long counter with double sinks runs along one wall, and he props his crutches against it, then opens the cupboard over his head. He pulls out a white plastic box with the words *First Aid* emblazoned across it.

Mixing his prescription painkillers with over-the-counter ones doesn't strike me as the smartest idea, but that may not matter if he won't hand over his keys. "I'll be extra vigilant. I'll park twenty blocks away and walk in. The drugs in the first aid kit are not going to cut it, Nick, and you know that. You've got too much work to do to be distracted by this."

He turns around and leans against the counter. Faint lines of pain are already sinking in around his mouth and eyes. I fist my hands and shove them into my pockets to keep from touching him. "Let me take care of you. You've done everything for me."

He shakes his head. "There's no balance sheet here. You needed me more."

I still do. But I need him whole and *un*-hurting. "If you tell me the pain doesn't affect your concentration, I'll call you a liar and set your pants on fire."

He snorts out a laugh. "If you set my pants on fire, I really *will* be in pain." A line appears between his brows. "You'll be careful? Safe? If they catch up to you, don't go to the warehouse. It's the last place I have that no one knows about, and I won't have it compromised."

"Lia knows about it." I hold out my hand for his keys. I don't know why I gave them back to him in the first place. The man isn't able to drive.

"But no one within the organization does. Lia knows how to keep her mouth shut." He dips into his left pocket and pulls out his keys, metal jangling against metal.

I fold them into my hand, welcoming the subtle bite into my palm. "This time of day, it'll probably be close to two hours before I get back. Will you be okay for that long?" Lucky me, I get to drive just as all the worker bees are leaving for home. If traffic cooperates, I *might* be able to make the drive in a half hour, but with Nick's paranoia about being found, I'll need to add time to account for a possible tail.

The grimace twisting his mouth would be comical if it weren't for what's causing it. "I'll manage." He jerks his head to the door. "I'll walk you to the car."

"No, you'll go right back to your office." Our mutual history with parking garages is too violent for me to consider walking through one with Nick unable to defend himself very well. I parked on the street, several blocks away, after dropping him at the front door. "I'll be okay. You need anything, make Constantine get it."

We part at the entrance to the break room, Nick to his office, me to the stairwell. His "hurry back" echoes in my head as I make my way down the stairs. I still feel like I'm missing something, or I lack the tools to understand where he's coming from when it comes to dealing with his family. Anyone sane and logical would know that any violence done to me would only succeed in bringing Nick and I closer together, not farther apart.

I push open the door to the street and step outside, scanning the sidewalk for anything out of the ordinary. Seeing nothing, I shift my grip on his keys and jog down the sidewalk to the car.

Chapter 11

There's something spectacularly creepy about slinking between great, hulking buildings while cars and slightly more terrifying noises play in the background. The warehouse district isn't one to walk around in after dark, but that's exactly what I'm doing. Nick always parked in a nearby outbuilding that was converted into a garage. It's a pain in the ass to open. I opted to park on the street several blocks away, choosing to risk my life walking through the deserted streets rather than risk someone driving by the warehouse and recognizing Nick's car parked outside.

Keeping to the shadows doesn't help my anxiety any, and it ratchets higher as I pat down my pockets, feeling for my phone. *Shit.* I left it in Nick's office, still plugged into the charger. I have no way of contacting anyone if something goes wrong.

Obviously, the solution is for nothing to go wrong.

I pause at the corner, clear of the light pooling under the streetlight. The streets are dead. No one's hanging around, not even bums, but I keep my head down and dart through the intersection as quick as I can anyway. Fishing the keys from my pocket, I clench them tight to silence their jangling and hurry for the door to the warehouse.

No light shines over the door. The shadows are darker here, making it difficult to fit the key in the lock. I finally manage and slip inside, locking it behind me. Faint light from the distant streetlights spills through the high windows, but the interior's pretty dim. I feel along the wall by the door for the light switch, but freeze when I hear the crunch of footsteps.

They stop right in front of the door.

Letting my breathing go shallow, I crouch down and slide my knife free of its sheath. The double-ended deadbolt eliminates the need for an actual doorknob. Nick opted for a U-shaped handle in its stead. I inch forward and to the side, away from the stairs. If the door doesn't hold for any reason, I'll be behind it.

The door rattles once in the frame as the person on the other side tries to open it. Another rattle, followed by a knock, then a slam, as though a body's rammed into the solid wood. I suck in a breath, feel the cold, calm detachment flow through me, pushing aside all concern for Nick and his leg and getting back to him as quickly as possible. My goal, my only goal, is to eliminate the threat outside.

Footsteps head away from the door, and I toe off my shoes as I count to fifty. At fifty-one, I dart up the stairs to the catwalk.

None of the furniture upstairs is tall enough for me to see out the windows. Which is good news, I guess, because that means no one can see *in.* Nick would have compensated for the lack of sight with surveillance equipment. I just have to find it.

I wake up the computer and scowl at the password screen. I don't have time to decipher it and, knowing my boyfriend, it's probably complicated as fuck and I'll never guess it in a thousand years. A quick tour of the room turns up nothing else of use, and I hurry back to the catwalk.

The door between the office and the bathroom taunts me. I've yet to see what's inside; Nick hasn't offered to show me and I haven't snooped, wanting to prove I'm not the immature brat he called me. But that was before someone was circling the warehouse, looking for a way in. I try the knob. It turns smoothly in my hand, and I open the door.

And immediately breathe a sigh of relief.

Here's the command center. The room is small, like it's an afterthought instead of an actual usable space. Four monitors are mounted on the wall, a table boasting a keyboard, a laptop, and a CPU under them. As I watch the screens, the green and white night vision pictures flit from one image to the next. It takes me almost a full minute, but I'm able to figure out the cycle. Except for the laptop, each monitor shows images from two different cameras. The laptop's screen displays an image of the front door, the occasional passing shadow the only indication the picture isn't completely stationary. A man strides into view and stops a few feet from the door, his face half obscured by the poor lighting. He appears to be studying the door.

I search the other screens, looking for a second man, a woman, dog, anything to indicate he's not alone. There's nothing. I go back to the laptop. I can handle one man.

First, though, I'm going to get what I came for.

I find a small duffle bag under the bed in the bedroom and stuff a couple changes of clothes in it, then take it into the office and do the same with Nick's clothes. I toss his prescriptions on top and zip it shut. I have no idea where we're going to sleep tonight, but once Nick hears about this, I doubt he's going to want to come back here.

In the tiny room, I check the monitors. The man is nowhere to be seen. I wait through two full cycles, but he doesn't reappear. I sit through another cycle, studying the images and mapping out a route away from the warehouse. The camera angles don't cover every foot of the exterior, so there are blind spots. Since I haven't had a chance to map the area around the warehouse, I'll be relying on instinct and skill.

I pick up the bag and creep down the stairs. No footsteps outside. I put on my shoes, slide my knife free, and grasp the bag by the handles. Easy to drop, easy to swing.

The lock clicking open is as loud as a gunshot. At least the hinges are well oiled. I peer into the dark, searching for the corner of the building. Nothing moves. I slip out, relock the door, and start for the dark end of the warehouse. It's the opposite direction from where I need to go, but I'll circle around. If I'm lucky, I might see our curious friend, and I can follow him.

Three buildings away, my luck runs out.

The crunch of gravel is the only warning I have before he strikes, but it's enough time. I swing the bag toward the sound and am rewarded with a grunt. Dropping the bag, I crouch low and spin around, knife at the ready.

He blends all too well. Dark clothes fitting close to his body to minimize noise, dark hair, dark shoes. I can barely make out his face. The shadows will work for both of us, concealing movements, hiding attacks, and it'll work against us too. Without light, I can't see if he's armed, so I'm forced to assume he is.

He takes a step forward, and I tense. "Put the knife down, Cassidy." I don't recognize the voice. "It's not necessary."

I straighten, but hold my blade at the ready. "You know, you're the second person to say that to me recently." Some of the tension leaves my shoulders. "If it's not necessary, why do you people keep sneaking up on me? Wait, don't answer that." If I've got another member of the family here at my disposal, I ought to take advantage of it. "Does Andreas really want me out of the picture that badly?"

"Yes."

The simple, one-word answer vibrates through me. According to Nick, I messed up, and I was slowly accepting that yes, I had. But as massive as my mistake was, he's giving me a chance to fix it, so I assumed the rest of his family would stay out of what is, ultimately, a relationship issue.

I tip my head to the side. "He does understand there's a high probability that hurting me will have the exact opposite effect, right? Nick's a grown man. If he decides he's done with me, that's his decision."

"Andreas is confident his son will eventually see reason. There's also the matter of you being responsible for the death of an LAPD officer. You turn yourself in, this all ends."

A chill races over my skin. I slammed my knife into Tris's groin in the heat of the moment, certain he was going to kill Nick. But I'm not walking into the precinct and surrendering. Tris wasn't just dirty, he was filthy. I'm not laying myself out over his death.

I shift the knife to my other hand and squint into the dark. "Can you do me a favor? Tell Andreas that if he wants to talk to me, he really ought to do it himself instead of sending a minion." I point to the street behind us, dimly lit by the streetlights. "You can go now."

"You *are* a brat," he mutters, and my muscles lock down. The only person who calls me a brat is Nick, because, let's face it, I am one on occasion. I frantically search my memory for every time he's said something. It's never around other people. So how does this guy know about it?

Or maybe I'm as paranoid as Nick, and it's a coincidence that someone else reached the same conclusion.

"Yes, and I'm *his* brat. Are you staying or going? If you stay, I'll just lead you on a really long hike back to the car, and then we'll take a nice, leisurely drive to Nick's office." This is *such* a waste of time. I could have stabbed him ten times over by now. I would except that it's another body to worry about, and I'm trying very hard not to add to my count.

This guy isn't making that easy.

"Why would you waste your time like that?"

"Because it's my time to waste, and until Nick decides it's safe, I'll do as he asks." I risk a few steps forward and pick up the bag. I'll have to circle back to the warehouse to clean out our clothing. We'll have to find someplace else to stay tonight, and every night after. Nick *definitely* won't want to come back after this incident.

I sling it over my shoulder and offer a little wave with my knife hand. "Have fun following me."

The man shifts forward, and I tense, squinting at his face. His expression is impossible to see, but there's no mistaking the frustration in his voice. "Cassidy. For your sake and for Dominic's, walk away."

"No, thanks. I'd rather eat glass." And I turn around and head for the lights.

There's several ways in and out of Los Angeles's warehouse district. There are fewer ways to get in and out of the warehouse without being seen, though. If I want to get our stuff out as quickly as possible, I could say fuck it and bring the car around to the door, especially since the guy came too close to discovering the warehouse's purpose for Nick ever to want to use it again.

Another safe house burned. Maybe he can sell this one so it's not a total loss.

The man who tried to attack me doesn't follow, and as I loop the car through the streets, I don't see anything suspicious. In the end, I decide to clear out the rest of our belongings. His injury makes it difficult for him to get around the warehouse anyway. Once inside, I pull the rest of my clothing from the cabinet in the bedroom, stuff it into a couple of trash bags, and throw them in the trunk of the car, along with Nick's duffle bag, the laptop, a couple of flash drives I find in the desk, and a gray tackle box full of first aid supplies. Overkill, maybe, but I'm not taking any chances.

The drive to Century City is uneventful, and I manage to find a parking spot a couple blocks away. I snag the pills and hurry to the office, aware that a lot of time has passed but no way of knowing how *much*. That phone's like a damn leash.

Nick and Constantine are in Nick's office, Nick on the couch with his laptop, Constantine at the desk. Nick has his leg propped up on the couch, his expression doing little to hide the pain he's in. He glances up as I enter the room. I dig the bottle of painkillers out and hand them to him. "How's it going?"

He snaps the lid off and shakes a pill directly into his mouth, dry swallowing it with a grimace. "Haven't been able to isolate the problem. Go home and get some rest. I'm going to be here all night."

I sit in the thin sliver of space next to his hip and wrap an arm around his shoulders to stop myself from falling off the edge of the couch. The way his body stiffens at my touch stings. Time. The only thing that will repair this damage is time. Time to show Nick that I'm listening to him, that I'm not just *trying*, but *doing*. "I'll be fine here." I lean in until my lips brush his ear. "We can't go back to the warehouse," I whisper. "Someone, I think it was one of your dad's men, was circling the place, and he caught up with me a couple blocks away." I don't tell him about the assertion that I should be the one to pay the price for Tris. We need more privacy for that.

Nick nods once. "Your phone went off while you were gone."

Can I kiss him? Will he let me? Given his reaction a moment ago, I don't think he will. "It might have been Denise. We're supposed to clean out our old apartment tomorrow. I'll leave you guys alone."

He stops me from getting up with a hand on my thigh. "Thanks for the pills," he says softly. "Leg feels like I stuck a hot fireplace poker through it." His eyes meet mine, dark and wary. "You sure you want to stick around?"

I'm surprised he's willing to consider letting me out of his sight. I don't want him out of *mine*. "I'm sure. There's this neat thing called the Internet, and it's full of cat pictures and K-pop videos. I'll just pull some of those up on my phone."

He groans. "K-pop? No. You can use my tablet if you get tired of such a tiny screen. But no K-pop videos."

The thread of relief in his voice is thick, and I force myself to hold his gaze. All that worry, all that fear, for *me*. I need to come back to him. Somehow. Somehow I'll break down the cold and stop running from the fear of what will happen once I do. I work up a smile. "I think I'll take you up on that."

Chapter 12

"It's clean. Like, actually clean." Denise stands with her arms wrapped around her stomach, studying the living room.

"Nick and I came in here a couple weeks ago to pick up a little," I lie. There'd been fingerprint dust all over the place when I moved back in, and I never bothered wiping it off. Nick must have scrubbed down the furniture one evening and I never noticed, though trace amounts of the black powder remain.

Cleaning off fingerprint dust was one of the many things I Googled last night. Apparently, it's a pain in the ass. The New Zealand police even made a handy PDF of instructions.

Denise shudders. "This place gives me the creeps." She drops her arms. "Bedrooms or kitchen?"

"Bedrooms. You've moved most of your stuff already, right?" I hand her a box.

"Except the furniture. We're trying to figure out where my desk will fit, but I'm getting rid of the bed." She starts across the living room. "What do you want to do with the couch and stuff?"

The couch was new when we moved in—a present from my parents. Her parents donated the TV. The rest of the furniture consists of a coffee table, a bookshelf, and a couple of lamps that we pooled our money to buy. "Do you want to take the TV?" I ask. "I'll take everything else, if that's okay."

She points at a lamp curved over the end of the couch. "I could use that lamp, but yeah, everything else. Don't need the TV. Charlie's is bigger."

I shrug. "Okay." I can always buy another lamp.

We split off into our rooms, and I bump my door closed behind me. There's more evidence of Nick's caretaking here in the neat stacks of books and papers on my desk, the lack of clothing littering the floor. The bed is unmade, and there's an ugly, jagged cutout in the carpet where Josef bled out after our fight all those months ago, but otherwise, it's relatively clean.

I set the box on my desk, grab a stack of books, and stick them inside.

I fill the box with books and papers, then go out and snag another box. I pack more books. Blankets. The few clothes left in my closet. I make piles of papers and texts I hung on to for some reason but don't actually need. I strip the sheets from my bed and carry them to the washer, only to discover we're out of detergent.

I always assumed when this day came, it would be much, much harder. There would be tears, maybe laughter, everything tinged with sadness. I can't feel anything. Certainly not sadness. And I know, *I know*, if Denise had any idea how remote and cold I am inside, she'd worry and ask how she could help. She can't. I can't tell her how to help if I can't figure out how to switch this off.

I fold up my comforter and try to stuff it back into the plastic wrapping it came in. I've had moments over the past few weeks where my emotions approached the expected range for someone who'd lost a loved one. All of them involved Nick.

That greedy, slippery need for revenge lurks at the back of my mind, waiting for a chance to rear its ugly head. But there's no one to take revenge *on*. And without that lust sated, it'll fester and spread, destroying everything.

I need to get out of my own head.

I leave the comforter half in, half out of the wrapping and hurry into the living room. The book case doesn't have much in the way of books on it—who has time to read with all the work to be done for classes?—but there's a few favorites along with a couple of DVDs, framed pictures, and a handful of random items. I pick up a snow globe and shake it. White flakes fall on the Statue of Liberty, swirl around its torch, and settle at the base.

"I can't believe you kept that thing."

I set it carefully in a box before I pick up the next item, a miniature Eiffel Tower. "I can't believe you kept *this*." The silver paint's chipped off in places, and the top point's long gone, a victim of an unfortunate incident involving Denise, Charlie, and a tickle fight.

She takes the miniature from me and cradles it to her chest. "Don't be talkin' 'bout my tower like that. You might hurt its feelings."

The snort escaping my lips is so goddamn normal, it brings shocked tears to my eyes. I blink them away and reach for a book.

"Cass?" She stops me with a hand on my arm, and I let the book fall to the shelf. "Can we take a break for a minute?"

Here it is. The *I'm worried about you, let me help you* speech. I drop onto the couch, my eyes on the blank TV. "How are things with Charlie? You guys ready for classes?"

"Charlie's driving me a little nuts. I guess he's not as far along on his senior thesis as he's supposed to be, and he's freaking out." The weight of her gaze is heavy and suffocating. "Truth, Cass. Are you okay?"

Truth. I am not about to tell her the truth, at least not all of it. "I don't know." Truth. "Do you think grief is supposed to look like something in particular?"

"No. And that's not what I meant. I don't expect you to be okay. I *do* expect you to talk to me about it. You used to, you know. How many times have you talked about your dad?"

Another truth. Denise is familiar with my ongoing problems with Turner, though she doesn't know what those problems *are*. "I don't know," I repeat. "I don't know how I'm supposed to feel about this." Something clenches tight and then shatters, deep inside. I suck in a breath and turn to her. Worry darkens her eyes, pulls her mouth down.

"I can't talk about something if I don't have the words for it." I push to my feet. "Let's take care of the kitchen."

Boxing up plates and glasses is painful because we don't talk. I try to get Denise to tell me about her post-graduation plans, but after a couple of pitiful attempts, she lapses into silence. We finish off by dumping the silverware into a box with a musical crash and hightail it out of the apartment and down to the street.

"Have you found a place to live?" she asks.

A car rolls by, bass thumping, and I wait for it to pass before answering. "Yeah, actually. A two bedroom on the south side of campus. So the furniture will come in handy."

She points down the block. "Did you... Did you still want to get coffee? I don't have anywhere else to be, and I could use some." I nod, and we start toward the coffee shop.

"A two bedroom? Who are you living with?"

I chew on the inside of my cheek. Denise's reaction to Nick has been all over the place. I think she likes him, to a point. "No one. Nick's paying for it."

"Whoa. Wait." She stops in the middle of the sidewalk and turns to me. "You're letting your boyfriend pay your rent. And you've been together how long? Three months?"

"Just about."

She blows out a breath in long stream of air. "Okay."

And she continues walking.

Once we've gotten our orders and made ourselves comfortable at a table next to the window, she cups her hands around her mug. "He's good for you."

He's better than I deserve. "Yeah."

"And you're happy?"

Before my life crumbled around me, I *was*. I nod, not trusting myself to speak.

"Okay." Her lips curve in a half smile. "If either of those changes, I reserve the right to go medieval on his ass."

* * * *

Nick's sprawled on the couch in his office, one arm thrown over his eyes, crutches on the floor next to him.

He doesn't wake as I shut the door behind me or when I move his crutches out of the way and kneel next to the couch. If this is the first sleep he's gotten since this whole mess started, I don't want to wake him, but he's bound to be more comfortable sleeping in a bed. He was glued to his laptop when I left to meet Denise and muttered an incoherent response when I told him I was leaving. He and Constantine worked through the night to pinpoint the issue with the app. They hadn't been close when I finally dropped off to sleep, curled up on the couch, and they weren't doing much better when I woke and dragged myself to shower in Nick's private executive bathroom.

Stretching up, needing the connection, I press a kiss to his jaw. "Nick?" I whisper.

His response is to grunt and shift onto his side.

The movement must trigger some pain, since he wakes on a muttered "fuck," face pinching tight. He slits open an eye. "Cass?"

"The one and only." I drop another kiss on his sleep-softened mouth. "C'mon. How about we go someplace with an actual bed?"

"You want to get me naked, all you have to do is ask."

"Ha ha." As gratifying as it is to hear him snarking about it, sex is the last thing on my mind. I don't even know how we'd accomplish it without causing Nick more pain. "You need more sleep."

Leather creaks as he pushes himself up, hissing in discomfort. "Quick nap. We're not done." He swings his legs off the couch. "Hand me my crutches?"

"Depends. Are you going to go back to your desk? Because if you are, then no, you can't have them."

He gives me his scary face, the one that's no longer intimidating. The expression fades slowly, resignation taking its place. "We don't have any place to go, Cass. I might as well keep working until I can figure something out."

"Who says you have to be the one to figure it out?" I get to my feet and hand him the crutches. "Does it matter if your family knows where we are any longer?" I help him up, and he tucks the crutches under his arms with a frown.

"Yes, but I'm out of safe houses, and our only other option is a hotel."

If he's worried about someone sneaking up on us, my old apartment isn't an option. The new apartment isn't, either, at least until we can arrange to have the furniture moved. Which leaves one place.

My father was as vigilant about personal security as Nick is, if not more so. The house has a security system, motion detectors, and a panic room. It's also in the middle of the block, the neighborhood peopled with middle-class families where anything remotely suspicious sticks out.

"My parents' house," I say at last. "Turner's security measures rival yours. They may still find us, but at least we'd have advance notice." And unless Mom cleaned it out, we'll have access to Turner's gun safe.

Nick must be more tired than I thought because he agrees without protest. He sticks his head in Constantine's office to tell him we're leaving, but quickly withdraws. "Sleeping," he murmurs.

"Did you guys make any progress?" I ask once we're in the car.

Nick tips his head back and shuts his eyes. "Some. We've run a slew of tests, and Constantine thinks he's figured out the problem. Sometime between when the virus ate away the code and a couple of days ago, someone logged in and deleted random sections. It's not anything huge, but it screws with the installation. So someone could download the app and possibly even get it installed, but it won't run."

I turn onto Sepulveda Boulevard. "Have you isolated all the sections?"

"Not quite. It took a while to figure out that's what's wrong, and then Peter assigned sections to the programmers. The three of us were running tests on the servers when we decided to take a break. I can run tests remotely, but any adjustments would need to be made at the source."

I blow through a red light. "Can I ask you something?"

"What's up?"

I tighten my grip on the wheel and swerve around a car turning right. "I feel like I'm missing something as far as your family is concerned. I get that your father doesn't want me anywhere near you, but that they'd go to, well, violent measures to ensure that seems weird. Also counterproductive, but definitely weird."

A horn blasts as a Mustang screams by, and I watch it weave in and out of traffic, zipping through a red light. I sneak a glimpse of Nick's face. He looks…done. Not exhausted, not worn out, just done. Like the fight's drained out of him.

"Dad and Uncle Anton agreed with the original plan," he begins. "They knew something needed to be done and were willing to allot the necessary firepower to ensure it would happen. Your decision to take action on your own meant they had no control. Control's huge. They couldn't predict who was going to be killed next because you didn't stick to a pattern. We had to scramble to clean up some of the sites. Families came to Dad, demanding retribution, and he had to tell them no because above all else, he *had* agreed that this needed to happen. They don't take kindly to cleaning up other people's messes, Cass. And because I didn't try to stop you sooner, he withdrew his support. He won't have someone with such volatile tendencies in his family in any capacity. It's jeopardized my standing within the organization."

Each word is a barb, piercing my skin and sinking in deep. I drive without thinking, without seeing, and have to slam on the brakes to avoid rear-ending the car in front of me. "Why aren't you angrier?" He said he was mad, and while he's withheld affection, he's still protected me.

"There's no point," he says simply. "You've damaged my trust. Part of me's waiting for you to run out and finish the job, even though Isaiah's gone. You took advantage of me, but when I knew I couldn't handle any more, I put a stop to it. Circumstances beyond our control took care of Isaiah."

Circumstances beyond our control. "I'm sorry." God, that sounds trite. As if an apology can make up for everything I've done. He was right to call me a selfish brat.

I can't do this to him.

"If I'm no longer around, there's no threat to either of us, right? I mean, Isaiah's dead. There's no one left for me to go after. At his core, Turner was a reasonable man, and so is your dad. Maybe living apart for a few months will allow things to calm down." When he doesn't respond, I take my eyes off the road and glance over. "What is it?"

He fists a hand on his thigh. "Someone has to be held responsible for Tris's death. I got a call from our guy in the department. A courtesy. He can't bury this one, even if he'd like to. Then I spoke with my father to confirm what you were told. He agrees that someone has to hang for Tris."

"I did it to protect you!"

"Doesn't matter. Tris is dead, and he's not supposed to be. Dad was waiting to find out for certain what the police would do before making a move, but now that he knows, he'll come after you. That's why you were approached last night. One attempt to ask you to turn yourself in before Dad moves on to other less diplomatic methods."

Just like that, the target's firmly attached to my back again.

Chapter 13

The house looks the same. The windows glint in the sun, the yard neat and tidy. Somehow I thought with both parents out of the house it would have fallen into disrepair, especially given how zombie-like Mom was the last couple weeks.

I step out of the car and dash up the front walk to the door, heart beating triple-time. The system's designed to send an alert within twenty seconds if one of the motion sensors is tripped, though Turner usually had them off if no one was home. A separate alert went out within fifteen seconds if one of the entry points—door, window, or garage—was triggered. I reset the codes myself the last time I saw my mother. Hopefully she hasn't changed anything.

The panel's beeping as I step into the front hall, and my fingers shake as I punch the buttons. The beeping stops, and I press the panel cover into place. It's a house. A place to stay. There are good memories and bad, like any other house. A car door slams outside, and I jump, stifling a whimper. A *car door*. Not a gunshot. No gunshots here. Nothing but my breathing echoing off the tile entryway. Nothing but Nick's crutches *thudding* on the front walk.

He swings through the door and stares up at the ceiling. I follow his gaze. The pendant light *is* kind of amazing. Mom saw a gorgeous piece of glass on a trip to Seattle but couldn't justify buying it. A slim, oblong shape, the blues and reds form a violent storm of color racing around the curves of the glass. Turner bought it for her and had it turned into a light.

"Pretty, isn't it?" I say.

Daddy!

I point to an entryway on the left. "Bedrooms are that way if you want to take a nap. Living room, dining room, Turner's office is to the right. Kitchen's off the dining room. I'm going to get our bags." Before Nick can respond, I escape outside and force air into my lungs, willing the panic to recede.

All those visits when Mom was still here, when I couldn't breathe and kept hearing Turner's voice in my head… I thought it was because of her. I thought she was the reason I felt on the verge of collapse the instant I set foot inside.

Coming here was a mistake. But Nick's right. We have nowhere else to go.

I pop the trunk and haul out bags, then carry them into the house. By our neighborhood's standards, the house is on the small side, boasting three bedrooms instead of four or five. I avert my gaze from the closed master bedroom door and drop Nick's duffle in the guest room.

My room hasn't changed much. Same dark green walls, same pine furniture, everything coordinated, thanks to my mom. It looks like she stripped the sheets before she left for Montana.

"This yours?"

I glance over my shoulder. Nick's leaning against the doorjamb, both crutches tucked under his opposite arm. "Yeah. The guest room's next door, my parent's is across the hall. Bathroom next to their room. I'll get you some sheets and make up the bed for you."

He limps across the room and lowers himself to the bed. "You're sleeping in here?"

"Yeah." Though I'm not sure if *sleep* will happen. The entire week before the funeral, I'd close my eyes and see my father die, over and over, until the blood was so thick I'd wake expecting to be engulfed in a lake of it. "You'll be in the guest bed. It's bigger."

He raises a brow. "I've heard you." His voice is quiet. "Do you know how many times you wake in the middle of the night?"

I sit next to him, careful not to jostle his leg. "They have to end at some point."

I can sense his hesitation, and it makes me curious. "The guest bed's big enough for both of us. You slept better when I was in your bed," he says.

We shouldn't. It's the opposite of what I asked for, what we need. But the need to say no is swamped and drowned by my desire to say yes. "Are you sure?"

"Positive."

Exhaustion washes over me. I want comfort. To be held. I scoot closer, releasing a breath when he wraps his arm around me. I tip my head onto his shoulder. "Guest room, then. I'll get some sheets in a minute. Hungry?"

"No," he murmurs. "Have to get back to work. I'll need to get on to your network."

I don't want to move. I don't think I *can*. Nick's immediate presence is the only thing keeping me together. Inside, everything's vibrating so hard I swear I've loosened some internal organs. I picture a countdown timer, complete with red, yellow, and blue wires, ticking closer to a line of zeroes. I want to brace for impact. I want to tell Nick to run as far as he can. The explosion will not be pretty. There may be nothing salvageable.

I let out a shaky breath. "It's been a while since I've needed to use it, so the password's likely changed. I can try, but if it doesn't work, you'll have to hack in."

He sighs and squeezes my arm. "Better get to it."

I retrieve his laptop and charger from the bag in the guest room and lead him to the living room. "Make yourself comfortable." I set the laptop on the coffee table and go to the kitchen for a glass of water.

There's no food in the fridge. I didn't think there would be, but I don't particularly relish the thought of going grocery shopping *again*. One day, Nick and I will be able have a place to live, and we won't be forced to leave it behind days or weeks later. Which, in theory, could eventually be our new apartment.

Dammit. Classes. Classes start next week. Target or no, I can't skip the first days of the new term.

"Cass?"

I fill a second glass from the tap and bring it with me. I hand him the water.

He fishes his pain pills out of his pocket and pops off the lid while I type in the last password I remember. It doesn't work. Turner never picked anything obvious for passwords, but I try a few possibilities.

"You're going to need to hack in," I say at last. "Um. I need to talk to you about something first." Rather than join him on the couch, I perch on the edge of the coffee table. "Class starts next week. I can't miss them. We need to come up with a schedule or a plan or something." Returning to campus, being around all those people, having to pretend that everything's all right, will be difficult, but it might be what pushes me forward.

When he doesn't say anything, I continue. "I'll call a moving company and see if I can get the furniture moved over the weekend. You're welcome to stay here if you don't want to stay with your parents."

"I don't have your schedule yet."

"I'll forward it to you. Do you have any moving company preferences? Anything I need to do before contacting someone?" I boost a hip off the table and pull out my phone. Tapping into my e-mail, I find my class schedule, then pull up Nick's name in my contacts. "I guess I don't have your e-mail address."

He holds out his hand, and I pass him the phone. "We have our own company do our moves," he says, thumbs flying over the surface. "Gentle Movers. So not them." Instead of giving me my phone, he sets it on his lap. "Are you sure about this?"

How many times are we going to have this argument? "Nick—"

He holds up a hand to cut me off. "I'm not talking about your safety. Putting you in the middle of a busy campus is smart. And if someone wants to get at either of us badly enough, they'll find a way."

I curl my fingers around the edge of the table. "Then what?"

"All you've done since your father's murder is kill people, Cass. When's the other shoe going to drop?"

It amazes me how well he understands me after such a short period of time. He's *right*. It will drop. "I don't know," I whisper, "but I can't sit around waiting for it to happen. Please don't make me."

He scrutinizes me like a trapped bug, his gaze flat and remote.

"You can't save me from this, Nick." The edge of the wood cuts into my hands. "You told me once I don't need permission to fall apart. I know it will happen. I also know there's nothing I can do to stop it."

Warmth seeps into his eyes and pushes away the distance. "You'll come find me when it does?"

I've been struggling with this for the past few days, ever since it became apparent my numb state wasn't going to last much longer. It doesn't seem fair to expect Nick to be there to keep me from shattering. If anything, I should be taking care of *him*.

"Cass." He snakes his hand around the back of my neck and brings me close. "Come find me," he murmurs.

I can't lie to him, so I kiss him and stand. "I'm going to make up the bed."

As soon as I'm out of his line of sight, I start shaking. Mom never bothered with a separate set of sheets for the guest bed. No point, she said. Whenever there was company, she'd just pull out one of their sets.

To make up the guest bed, I'll have to go into the master bedroom.

Standing outside the room, I shut my eyes, willing the trembles to stop. It's a room. I've been inside plenty of times, even after Turner died, and I was fine. I'll be fine this time too. I close my hand around the doorknob and push open the door.

The air is stale, a hint of Mom's perfume hanging around. I open my eyes and wait for them to adjust to the dim light. She stripped the sheets off the bed before she left and folded the blankets. Her closet door's open; most of the hangers that held her non-work clothes are empty. It doesn't look like she packed in a hurry. I take that as a good sign and step farther into the room.

Turner's side of the room looks the same as it always does, pin-neat and devoid of personal items. The sole exception is a picture of Mom and I on his dresser. Aside from the sheetless bed, everything's the same. Like it's waiting for Mom and Dad to return.

I can't remember what he smells like.

Panic squeezes my chest, coiling and tensing to spring. I walk around the bed to Turner's closet and slide open the doors. His shirts are lined up by purpose and color, shoes slotted neatly in their cubbyholes. I choose one of the shirts he'd wear on the weekend and pull it off the hanger. The soft, worn cotton bunches in my hands as I lift it to my nose and inhale the dark, musky scent.

He used Aramis for as long as I can remember. How could I have forgotten that? How could I have forgotten that so *soon*?

The panic tightens, pounces, and I break. *Hard.* I shove the shirt into my mouth to muffle the screams. The room vibrates around me, and everything is red. Dark red, the color of the blood dripping down Turner's face.

I love you.

He is *gone.* He is nothing but ash and memories, blowing away with each gust of wind. He will never tell me he loves me again. He will never sit at the head of the table and listen as my mother and I laugh and joke. He will never correct my grip, never spar with me.

He will never hug me.

Never see me graduate.

Never meet his grandchildren.

Never.

Never.

Never.

My eyes are burning, and the room's gone from red to hazy with water, my throat already raw from my muffled screams. I fall to my knees, curl into a ball, and land on my side. Tears stream down my face to soak into my hair. Pain sings up my arm as I pound my fist into the floor.

I can't breathe. Can't see. The tears and the screams won't stop. He should be here. *Here*, with his stone-faced disapproval, those quick, slight smiles that warm me from top to toe. My world is heat and fury and pain, then shatters so the splinters and shards slice through my skin. I wish my blood could bring him back. I'd cut myself open and give it all.

Muscles locked, lungs seizing, I struggle for air and shut my eyes, and it just gets worse. Isaiah with his gun, Turner stoic to the last. Turner telling me to leave, to take care of Mom, three words that rip me to shreds, over and over. I am never fast enough. Isaiah won by taking the one person he knew would destroy me.

My hands won't move. There's a small part of me that isn't crushed by the agonizing weight of loss. It says I have to move my hands, get the cloth out of my mouth because I'm not getting enough air.

The screams are these harsh, hoarse sounds, ripping at my throat, and my stomach churns as I try to suck in air through my nose. Another one builds, louder, harder, and I bite down on the shirt, punching my fist into the floor as the fabric absorbs the scream.

Pain streaks through my limbs, and I curl tighter, squeeze harder, the screams finally changing to whimpers and hiccups. I want my dad. I want the chance Isaiah stole from me. I want the father who gave me piggyback rides and taught me the cleanest way to kill a man twice my size.

Bombarded by memories, I slide into sleep, his shirt clutched in my hands.

Chapter 14

I feel sick. Sore and nauseous, my head as heavy as a brick and swollen as a balloon. My face is stiff with dried tears, and I desperately need a glass of water.

And I'm still holding Turner's shirt.

It's a sodden, snotty mess and no longer smells like him, but I don't want to let go. Not yet. I don't want to get up. I have no idea how long I've been on the floor. I tentatively stretch out one leg, wincing as the aches in my joints sharpen and drill into my bones. I roll onto my stomach and push to my knees. I manage to sit without falling over, the side of the bed propping me up.

Some people think of crying as a purge, a way to rid the mind and body of poisonous emotions. I wish that were true. I wish I could say I'm lighter, calmer, better prepared to handle what comes next. I'm almost dead certain it's a prelude to a long, dark spell, and I may never want to come out.

I stare at all the clothes Turner will never wear again, and the tears begin anew. I'm surprised I have any left. They burn my eyes and drip onto my cheeks. We lost so much time, me trying to be the child he wanted, Turner unwilling—or unable—to accept that I couldn't. I tip my head back to rest against the bed and let the sobs come.

"Cass?"

I bite my lip to keep from calling out. *Come find me.* He shouldn't have to deal with my mess, my problems. I've leaned so hard on him, and he should be leaning on *me* now.

"Cass? You in here?" Soft thuds from the other side of the room, and I hunch over to make myself as small as possible, body shaking as I swallow my sobs. "What are you doing on the floor?"

I turn my swollen, tear-stained face to him and watch as his expression softens in understanding and hurt. "Fuck, Cassidy. Why didn't you come get me?"

All I can do is shake my head and lower it to my hands, knees pulled to my chest in an effort to calm myself. There are some grunts and hisses as Nick sits next to me. "C'mere," he murmurs, wrapping an arm around me.

The barest hint of cinnamon drifts under my nose as I turn my face into his shoulder. "It's not okay," I mumble. "He shouldn't be dead."

"No, he shouldn't."

I sniffle back tears. "I always thought there'd be time. He'd get over himself one day. Maybe we never would have had a happy relationship, but…polite. He'd stop being so disapproving and I'd let go of my anger and we'd get along. Maybe grandkids would have changed him." None of this will ever happen. It presses on my chest, pushing all the air from my lungs, and I huddle closer.

My ass goes numb as we sit there, me curled into Nick's side, his heartbeat steady under my hand. Someday soon, Mom and I will have to clean out Turner's things and face the memories they hold. For now, I can shut the closet on them.

I untangle myself from Nick and stand. The closet doors are silent as I slide them shut. Nick takes my hand, and I help him to his feet. He brushes a stray tear from my cheek. "Go get some water. I'll deal with the sheets."

"You have work to do and—"

"Stop." A glimmer of anger sparks in his eyes. "Stop it, Cass. I'm not a fucking invalid, and you're hurting. Let me take care of you."

How is he going to make a bed when he can't—or shouldn't—put any weight on his leg? "Let me get the sheets, and I'll help you."

His scowl is fierce as he tucks the crutches under his arms. "It's a bed. I can stand long enough to make a damn bed."

When he gets that look on his face, I know better than to argue. The man's the most stubborn person I know. I find a set of sheets in the linen cabinet and drop them on the guest room bed, leaving Nick to wrestle with the covers.

My eyes are so swollen I can barely see, and my head is pounding in time with my heart. Full dark fell while I was asleep, and the shadows make it hard to see where I'm going. In the dim kitchen, I fumble a glass out of a cabinet and fill it from the pitcher in the fridge. Then I move to the sink and scan the backyard while I drink my water.

The yard is one of the few things my parents always did together. Weeding, planting, the general tending and cleanup of the flowerbeds was something that relaxed them both. Without the patio lights, it's hard to see how much of the winter yard chores they got through before Turner died. I drain the glass and set it next to the sink before walking over to the patio door.

I hesitate with my hand hovering over the switch for the patio lights. What if they didn't get very far, and the yard's a mess of dead annuals and weeds no one got around to pulling? Or what if it's the opposite, and it's all neat and tidy, waiting for Mom and Turner to come along and plant new flowers in the spring? Either way, I'm not ready for the pain it'll bring. I turn away as Nick enters the kitchen, the tips of his crutches squeaking on the linoleum.

"Bed's made," he says. He makes his way toward me. "Probably ought to eat something. You hungry?"

"Not really." I lean on the glass door, frowning when Nick narrows his eyes as he looks past me. "What?"

"Looks like something's moving." He jerks his chin toward the yard, and I glance over my shoulder. Mom planted a large, ornamental shrub in a corner of the yard. Turner argued against it, saying it was out of place, though I secretly always thought he didn't want the shrub there because it'd be a good place for someone to hide. Even with my compromised vision and the limited light, I see the branches shaking, moving in that way that has nothing to do with wind and everything to do with someone—human or animal—being someplace they're not supposed to.

"Might just be one of the neighborhood cats." My skin prickles with awareness, but I keep my casual stance.

"Too much of a coincidence for it to be a cat. Weapons?"

"In the gun safe. I can get them." My brain shuts everything out, focused on the potential intruder in the backyard. Grieving will have to wait.

He removes the crutches from under his arms and braces himself on the wall. "Silencers?" he asks quietly.

"He probably has some." Silencers are technically illegal, but that wouldn't have stopped Turner from having a few on hand. In addition to knife work and poisons, he used guns when necessary, though he didn't like them. Too inaccurate, he always said. A silencer would have been useful to him, though.

I wish I could take a moment to wash my face. I can't even risk blowing my nose. I run back to the master bedroom and slide open Turner's closet, shuddering at the sight of his clothes. I push them aside to get to the safe that is set into the rear wall. He reset the biometric system on my eighteenth birthday to allow me access to the safe if I ever needed it. After typing in the code, I press the ring finger on my right hand to the scanner and wait for the beep. The door releases, and I swing it wide. I grab the 9mm, check the magazine, and screw a silencer to the end of the barrel. Then I do the same with the .44.

Nick's standing next to the patio door rather than in front of it, turned sideways so he can still see out, but he's less noticeable to anyone looking in. I pass him the .44 without a word, and he flicks the safety off before undoing the lock on the patio door.

Turner always kept the sliding glass door well oiled, so when Nick slides it open a couple inches, the soft *sush*-ing sound is barely noticeable. Adjusting his stance to balance his weight on both feet, he lifts his arms, the silencer sticking out through the opening by an inch. "Go," he whispers. "Only way we'll find out what's hiding is to flush it out."

Aside from the patio door and the front door, the house has one other entrance—a door on the far side of the garage. I hurry through the house and let myself into the garage. The space is almost pitch black, and I stifle a curse when I bump into Turner's car. I throw out a hand and run it along the wall, feeling for the doorknob to the outside door.

The light over the door comes on at dusk, and there's no way to switch it off. It'll make me an easy target for anyone on this side of the house. I ease the door open and dart through the pool of light to the fence edging the side of the property, adrenaline pouring through my blood and clearing my mind. I still can't see very well, forcing me to compensate with my other senses. Back pressed against the fence, I stare blindly at the side of the house while I consider my options. Left, I'd approach the shrubbery straight on by cutting across the backyard and again making myself a target. Right, I have to go all the way around the front of the house, but I'll have more cover and I'm approaching from the side.

The extra seconds it'll take me to get around the front of the house are worth it.

I hurry to the end of the house and scan the street and front yard before running through the yard to the other side and around the corner. From here, I can hear the branches moving, a big fucking clue on a night with no breeze.

Nerves on high alert, I creep forward, fighting to remain focused on the task at hand. What are we going to do with a body? Will Nick call in a disposal team? Will we have to bury it in the backyard because he doesn't trust anyone in his family anymore?

The patio lights flash on, and I stifle a yelp of surprise. I see a dark-colored blob, the shrub branches shaking violently, and there's a muffled *pfft pfft* before a body hits the ground.

Great. Now there's a dead man in my backyard.

* * * *

"Please. Cass. Go. Take a shower. You look like shit."

I want to bang my head on the wall. "I *know* I look like shit. I *feel* like it. But there's a body in the backyard, and it needs to be dealt with first."

Nick's glare is so fierce I actually take a step back.

"All right. I'll let you handle this." I leave him standing next to the patio door and head for the guest room.

I pause in the doorway. The pillows are plumped and the blankets turned down, inviting me to crawl inside, and for a long moment, I consider doing just that. I can't deal with anything else today. The steam from the shower might help with my stuffy nose, though, and as growly as Nick is at the moment, I don't have the energy to fight him over something as trivial as a shower. I locate my bag, pull some clothes from it, and walk across the hall to the bathroom.

The moment I step inside the tub I lose the will to remain upright. I sink to the floor, uncaring the porcelain's still cold, and let the hot water pour over me. Tears well out of nowhere, and I don't fight them. They mix with the water and stream down my face.

Turner would tell me to get up, to keep going, to see this through to the bitter end. Strangely, I don't think he'd chastise me for letting Nick take control. Pushing my hair away from my face, I tip it up, the water rinsing it clean. Giving Nick the reins doesn't mean I can't help, though. I struggle to my feet and grab the soap.

Twenty minutes later I'm clean, dry, and dressed. While I won't say I'm ready to deal with what comes next, I'm not crying any longer. I open the bathroom door and follow the sound of Nick's voice.

He's in the living room, seated on the couch with his phone to his ear. When he sees me hesitate, he motions me forward. "I don't share your concerns, Dad. I'm not going to allow you to turn her over to the police."

Oh, no. Not going anywhere near this argument. I turn on my heel.

"Cassidy. Come here."

I glance over my shoulder. Nick has his phone tipped away from his mouth, his dark eyes furious. He waves his hand again, and this time I obey. His injured leg is stretched out parallel to the back of the couch, his other leg bent with his foot flat on the floor. Careful not to jostle him too much, I crawl between his legs and sprawl against his chest, shutting my eyes as his arm comes around me.

Andreas is saying something, but his words are too garbled and the volume's too low on Nick's phone for me to understand what he's saying. I'm cold. Ill. Exhausted. Something gnaws at my belly, and I can't tell if it's hunger or grief or anger. Nick cuts his father off with a curt "Good-bye," hangs up, and tosses the phone away. It lands somewhere at the other end of the couch.

"What's going on?" I mumble. "Your dad sending more goons after me?"

"Not if I can help it." He threads his fingers through my damp hair. "But talking to him did get me thinking."

"Wass dat?" Curled up against him, I could sleep for a month.

"LAPD's out for blood, and you turning up dead before they can get to you won't make them happy. I can't see him sending someone to kill you when so far he's been all about appeasing the department." He curls his hand around the back of my neck. "Crew will be here soon to take care of the body."

I'm too tired for this. "I thought you didn't want your family to know where we are?"

"The only other option is to get rid of the body ourselves. I'm not letting you do that." He strokes his other hand down my arm. "When was the last time you ate?"

The muffin I picked at while Denise and I talked is a distant memory. I can't believe that was just today. It feels like a week ago. "Been a while. I can order something. There's a good Thai place that delivers that's not too far from here." Ordering food means moving. Moving is at the bottom of my list of things to do. "Are you comfortable? I'm not hurting you or anything?"

"Stop it," he murmurs. "You're fine. What's the name of the place? I'll call them."

"Bamboo Palace. I want crab wontons and noodles." They make their own noodles, thick, fat ones smothered in peanut sauce.

"Wontons and noodles. Anything you want on the noodles?"

"Sweet and sour chicken." It's a dish usually served over rice, but their noodles are too delicious to pass up. "Want me to get your phone?"

The hand on my arm stills. "Huh. Shit. I threw it away, didn't I?"

"Yup." I sit up reluctantly, snag Nick's phone, and hand it to him before I cuddle up to his chest.

I don't remember falling asleep. The dream is full of half-formed images, Nick's face melting into Turner's, blood everywhere. Someone screams, the sound becoming a high, keening wail, and it's like it's coming from everywhere and nowhere. A shot's fired, followed by another, and then the house explodes in flames.

"Cassidy."

I jerk awake. Nick. I'm with Nick. We're lying on the couch in my childhood home. He shot someone, and now there's a crew on the way to clean it up. Nick's shirt is bunched in my hands. "Sorry," I mutter. I smooth out the wrinkles I made in his shirt, and he covers my hand with his.

"You're fine," he repeats. "I think the food's here. There's a guy carrying a bunch of plastic bags coming up the front walk." On cue, the doorbell rings, and I wince as it peals through the house.

"Can you take care of the delivery guy?"

I nod and slide off the couch. The floor's cold under my feet, and a hiss escapes as I walk across the tile in the front entry. I check the peephole and open the door, working up a half-hearted smile for the delivery guy. "How much do I owe you?"

"Already taken care of. Paid for when the order was placed." He hands me the plastic bags and walks back to his car, leaving me with more food than we need. As he pulls away from the curb, a dark-colored SUV turns into the driveway and parks behind Nick's car. Three men get out, each acknowledging me with a dip of his head before they start opening doors and grabbing tools and bags.

I leave the front door open and take the food into the kitchen. Nick's waiting, crutches once again tucked under his arms. I set the bags on the counter and begin pulling the containers out. "Plates are in the cupboard to your right."

He finds them and passes one to me. After piling food onto my plate, I retreat to the guest room, leaving Nick to handle the crew cutting up the dead man.

Chapter 15

The mattress shifts, and I reach out, half awake and wishing I wasn't. My hand connects with warm skin, and I drag myself closer. What side am I on? Nick was shot in his right leg. I deliberately took the right side of the bed, so there was less chance I'd accidentally hurt him. "Time is it?" I mumble.

"Late. Or early, depending on how you look at it. Go back to sleep, Cass."

Late or early. Disposal couldn't have taken more than an hour or two, and it wasn't that late when I closed myself in the guest room. "Work?" I lift my head, searching his face in the shadows.

"Crew's gone. Need a quick nap."

I lower my head to his shoulder and drape myself along his left side. "Won't get a quick nap in this bed." Especially considering he stripped to his boxers. Almost naked Nick is too tempting for me to ignore.

"Maybe more than a nap," he concedes. "Made some progress. Peter's reporting the app's installing 90 percent of the time, though once it's installed, it only works properly 50 percent of the time. May have to push the launch date back. Even if we manage to clear up all the issues and inconsistencies, it'd be smart to run it through testing again."

"Mmm." It's cozy here, lying skin to skin. We're not warily circling each other, questioning the other's motives. We're back to Cass and Nick, two black-hearted people who love each other. A perfect bubble, one that will pop all too soon, because that's what always happens to us. Our relationship so far is made up of moments, some stolen, some manufactured, but I want more than moments. I want uninterrupted bliss, days at a time where the only things that happen are the mundane routine of life.

I draw a heart on his chest with my fingertip. "What does this app do?"

"Parking app. This one catalogues all the available street parking in the city. It'll tell you if you need a permit to park on a specific street, or how long the pay parking is, or if there's a parking garage nearby. We're considering an add-on feature that allows users to report if they see an empty spot, or if they've just *left* a spot, but… I doubt it would be useful."

I snort. Considering parking's at a premium in this city, the service would be a waste. Any spots are gone within minutes, if not seconds. "I agree. So why consider it at all?"

He yawns. "Money. Add on this feature, we can justify bumping the price of the app." He trails his fingers down my spine and works them under the hem of my tank. "Why are you wearing clothes?"

"Random people in the house that didn't necessarily need to see me naked. Besides, you're more likely to get out of bed again if I keep them on."

"Maybe." The word comes out garbled, and his hand relaxes and falls away. "Don't let me sleep too long."

I resettle my head on his shoulder. I'll let him sleep as long as I feel is necessary. The last twenty-four hours were draining for both of us. I may have been asleep for hours already, but the soothing blankness of sleep beckons me back.

When I wake again, it's full light. Neither of us has moved, and when I try to roll away to stretch, Nick's hold tightens. I manage to wiggle my way free and slide off the bed. I dig a sweatshirt and my slippers from my bag and tiptoe out of the room. Whether he agrees or not, Nick needs more sleep. He's tired enough he could make a mistake, and then he'd get grumpy and broody. As much as I love grumpy, broody Nick, I can't handle him right now.

I detour by the alarm control panel out of habit and check the system. Alarm's on, as are the motion sensors. I frown. When I came out of the guest room to rinse off my plate, the men were still cleaning up the backyard, so I didn't bother activating the motion sensors. I didn't get up when Nick came to bed, either.

Nick must have figured it out. He's smart like that. After a moment's debate, I turn them off and backtrack to the kitchen and the coffee maker.

One sniff of the grounds left in the canister has me searching for the bag of beans I know Mom keeps in the freezer. The question is whether I can grind them without waking Nick. I end up wrapping a bunch of towels around the grinder and groping under them for the switch. It's awkward as hell, but my reward is the heady, bitter scent of fresh coffee.

While it's brewing, I wander to the patio door. The grass is flattened near the shrub, and before I realize what I'm doing, I flip the lock and open the door.

They did an excellent job. Aside from the grass, nothing appears out of place unless you look closely. A few broken branches, some ragged leaves, dirt turned and not quite smoothed out. I pad around to the back of the shrub and squat down. I shift a few inches until I have a good view of the door.

I hadn't bothered following Nick's driving protocol yesterday when we left his office. An oversight on my part, though I didn't see anything that looked remotely like a tail. So how were we found?

Better question. Who was he here for?

I plop down on the dirt and stare at the door. Nick says his father wants me alive, and I believe him. Several of Isaiah's men are still alive, but everything I've observed about them is they're followers, not leaders. And while Constantine's behavior in the last couple of days is odd, I'm not willing to leap to the conclusion he's behind this. Gathering the necessary information to confirm or clear will take time. I'm just not sure we *have* time.

The patio makes a good entry point into the house. With the solid wood fence concealing the backyard, an intruder would only need to be worried about being caught entering the yard through the front by a concerned neighbor or by the occupants of the house.

Exactly why Turner had motion sensors in addition to the alarm.

Whoever our would-be attacker was, he either knew about the sensors and counted on them being off, or he didn't know and got lucky. Until I had more information on who he was, I couldn't answer that question. I stand and brush dirt from my shorts. Coffee. I can't continue thinking without coffee.

I walk inside, and the rich, dark scent hits my nose, bringing with it one of my few good memories of Turner. Maybe I'd blocked it, or maybe I'd truly forgotten, but he was the one who gave me my first cup. I was fifteen. We hadn't completed training until very late the night before, and I was going to miss the first bell. Turner poured coffee into one of Mom's travel mugs, doctored it with milk and sugar, handed it to me, and smiled as I took my first cautious sip.

A smile. A real smile, one of quiet happiness.

I turn away from the coffee maker, tears stinging the backs of my eyes. How many of those smiles have I overlooked and locked away? Blinking rapidly to clear the tears, I shuffle down the hall to the guest room, no longer interested in staying awake.

Nick's still fast asleep as I crawl in beside him. He rouses when I press myself to his side to seek comfort. "Cass?"

"Go back to sleep," I whisper, trying to keep the sobs out of my voice.

His response is to cup the back of my head and guide me to him, his lips soft and seeking. On a whimper, I open for him, stroke his tongue with my own, ready and willing to use this as a distraction from the pain.

Little by little, the fierce ache of grief fades into the sweet warmth of Nick's kisses. His mouth never fails to amaze me. He teases me, seduces me, leads me exactly where he wants me, and I'll follow blindly because I know I'll get what he promises. I strain against him. I can't get close enough. When he strokes his hand down my side to clasp my hip, I hesitate. I want him. I want to drown myself in him and the chaos we create, but I'm afraid I'll unintentionally hurt him, and I'm afraid the intimacy of it will push us closer together when we're still so very far apart. It would be temporary, and all the more painful when it ends. Pressing one last kiss to his mouth, I try to ease away. He grips me tighter.

"Nick."

"Cassidy." He nips into my bottom lip. "You won't hurt me, love. Trust me."

Trust me. Odd choice of words, considering that's up for debate. His eyes never leave mine as he waits for my decision. And it *is* mine. This is one area I know, with bone-deep certainty, that he will never, ever do anything to hurt me.

I move over him. His hips come up to meet mine, the hard ridge of his cock pressing into my clit. "Oh, *fuck*." I need this. I need his hands and mouth on me, him inside me, making me forget that my world's in tatters. I rock on him, encouraged by his hands on my hips, and my lids drift shut. Spark after spark of desire flares outward, setting fire to my blood.

He works his hands under my tank, grips the hem, and pulls it off. Cupping my breast, he captures the nipple between his thumb and forefinger and pinches tight. The sharp sting draws a whimper from me, and he does it again, repeating the move with my other breast. He skims a hand down to my waist and around my back, urging me to bend forward for a kiss. Silly Nick. All he has to do is *look* at me, and I want to kiss him. I cover his mouth with mine, moaning at the back of my throat as the heat inside me surges.

It becomes a game. He trails a line of burning kisses along my jaw, I nuzzle the soft spot under his ear, the one that drives him insane. He scrapes his teeth down my neck, I flick a nail over his nipple. But I have the advantage of mobility, and I wiggle free of his hold, mindful of his injured leg. Limited as he is, he can't keep me from my destination, and for once, I have him at my mercy.

I grasp the waistband of his boxers and draw them down, helping him ease them over his hips. His cock lies heavy against his abdomen, the tip glistening with moisture. I run my tongue down the fat vein and close my lips around the head, pleased when he groans quietly. The more I focus on his pleasure, the easier it is to lose myself. I circle the base with my fingers and stroke up. Down, up, down, up, each stuttering breath urging me on, whispering *yes, yes, this is it.*

His cock grows slick, salt spreading over my tongue, his hips jerking in time with my movements. He pulses in my mouth, and I pull back, sealing my lips around the crown.

"Stop," he rasps, and shoves his hands into my hair, pulling free of my mouth. "Are you *trying* to make me come?"

I lick my lips and smile. "That was the general idea."

Hands sliding to my shoulders, he pulls gently, his eyes dark with lust. "C'mere. And take your shorts off."

For a second, I consider ignoring him. I was enjoying myself, high on the power I had over him. But my clit throbs, telling me it needs friction, and it needs it now. I shimmy out of my shorts and panties and crawl up his body, dropping kisses on his groin, his stomach, his chest, breath hitching as he strokes his fingers between my legs and plunges them into me.

That sound can't be coming from me. That...that... That *whining*, that greedy keening is not me. Yet I can't stop. I buck my hips, craving speed, incoherent mutters falling from my lips. Tension coalesces and spreads through my belly, and I dig my fingers into his chest.

He stops. He fucking stops and withdraws his hand, leaving me panting and wild-eyed, groping between my legs, hand closing around his dick. Our groans are loud and embarrassing as I sink down onto him.

It doesn't matter how many times we've done this. It feels new and amazing every time, his thick length stretching me perfectly. I rise and fall in slow, shallow movements, my eyes never leaving his.

We've come so far in a few months. The difference between fucking and making love can be long or short, and here, it's short. We've done it all, surrendered to our animal instincts, fought the other for control, stripped ourselves bare. He's ripped me open and given me everything, and it's there, in his expression, in the tenderness of his lips on mine. This is our world of stolen moments and, for now, it's enough.

He clamps his hands on my hips, thrusting up hard, and the change in pressure ratchets the tension higher. No fingers on my clit, nothing more than the angles of his strokes pushing me closer to the edge. I bear down, his hiss of pleasure lost to the pounding of my heart.

The orgasm is a shock, heat streaking up my spine and stealing my breath. The roaring in my ears renders me deaf. Nick pushes up one last time and mouths a single word—a curse, my name, I don't know—his face twisting in a rictus of pleasure.

I collapse on his chest, panting for air. I needed this on so many levels, this connection, this distraction. "I love you." Maybe he can hear it. Maybe I only thought the words. It doesn't matter. He knows.

He knows, and he loves me back.

Chapter 16

"Crane Movers had a last minute cancellation. They can take care of the furniture this afternoon." I set my phone on the arm of the couch and draw my knees up. It doesn't do much for the hollow sensation in my chest, but I do it anyway. "Do you need to go anywhere? I'll need to leave soon to let them in."

The five or six hours of sleep Nick got clearly weren't enough, but he insisted on going to work. He didn't bother to shave, which only adds to the fatigue evident in his expression. He drags a hand down his face. "No? I don't think so. We've repaired all the code, but Peter's still running tests on the servers, so I'm not going anywhere." He picks up his coffee cup and swallows the contents with a grimace. "Why are you the only person around here who makes decent coffee?"

I shrug. With the memory of Turner and the coffee still fresh in my mind, the thought of coffee makes me teary. I've succeeded in going twelve hours without crying. I don't want to break the streak now. "Did you recognize the guy in the yard?" We were too busy with each other earlier for that particular question to come up, but now that the haze of lust is gone, I want the answer before I leave to deal with the movers.

Nick frowns. "No. And that's...concerning."

Concerning is too mild a word for my paranoid and overtaxed brain. *Worrisome* is slightly better. I was counting on Nick identifying our would-be killer. Without that knowledge, we don't know who he was after—or who he was sent by. "Are you *sure* your dad doesn't want me dead?"

He sighs and motions for me to come closer. "Not everyone in my family is trying to kill you."

I get up and walk around his desk. He scoots his chair out to give me space to lean on the edge. "That implies that someone other than Isaiah is after me. So. Your dad?"

"It's a possibility," he admits. "If he thinks the danger to the family outweighs the need to placate the police, he'll do it. It would explain why I couldn't ID the guy, either. He's still holding some of the family secrets close to the vest."

Rubbing my hands over my face, I close my eyes and try to think through the possibilities. My brain doesn't want to work. It wants to shut down, leaving me to stare at nothing and curl into the fetal position.

I can't shake the pain. It's in my bones, my nerve endings, my cells. It's fat and clumsy and smothering, and I wish it *would* smother me. Then I wouldn't have to wonder what other happy memories I've buried are waiting to lunge forward and rip into me.

"I need to get going." I don't particularly *want* to. Moving into a too-large apartment I can't actually afford doesn't sit any better now than it did when Nick badgered me into signing the lease. Part of me is so tired of pushing him away that I want to throw up my hands and tell him to move in now. But another, much larger part, warns if I do that, I risk never truly forgiving him for what he did.

My mind finally wakes long enough to offer an additional angle I've danced around for the last few days. "Nick?"

"Mmmhmm?" He tips his head back and slouches farther in his seat.

I can do this. He needs to know. "What if... What if it's Constantine?" When he stiffens, I fight the urge to take his hand. He's an adult. He doesn't need handholding. "Wait. Please. Just listen." He dips his head once, and I let out a breath. "I don't have a lot to go on. I could be wrong. I *want* to be wrong. But I can't shake this feeling there's something he's not telling us. The night Isaiah died—" I squeeze my eyes shut. Everything about that night is wrong wrong *wrong*. "You had *just* hung up the phone with him when he showed up. When the virus was launched? Why wasn't he there for the interrogation? Then there are the failed acquisitions and the ones you stepped in to save. I overheard a conversation a few days ago that made me think he was telling someone not to kill me because it would only make you suspicious." I open my eyes and stand straight. "It's little things, Nick. Things that'd be easy to overlook or push aside. But I can't. I'm not built that way."

His mouth remains stubbornly shut, and new fears coalesce. I could be wrong, and voicing my doubts just widens the distance Nick and I are trying to bridge. "I'll see you later," I whisper. Wanting to hold on to some of the closeness we had last night, I kiss his cheek, heart sinking as he sits there stiff as clay. "I'll text you when the movers are done."

My tearless streak ends as I shuffle out of Nick's office and head for the stairwell. Even though I don't have time to waste, the first tears spill over as the door shuts behind me, and I slide down the wall and bury my face in my hands.

Someday, the pain will fade to a manageable ache. Someday, I won't automatically jump to the worst possible conclusion. Wishing that day is today won't make it easier to move on.

I wipe the tears from my cheeks and push to my feet. The movers said they'll be at my old apartment in about two hours. Denise and I packed up a lot of the apartment, but there are still odds and ends to sort out.

While I don't take a roundabout route to the apartment, I give myself a headache from constantly darting my gaze from the road to the rearview mirror and back again. I find a parking place two blocks from our apartment and call Denise as I walk over. She doesn't answer, so I leave a message about the rest of the crap that needs to be taken care of and stuff my phone into my purse.

Once inside the apartment, I stack the full boxes in a corner of the living room, then grab a rag and wipe down the furniture. Nick's efforts are appreciated, but a thin layer of dust has already settled, and I want to start my new life with clean furniture.

My phone rings in the depths of my purse, startling me from my thoughts. It stops ringing by the time I manage to dig it out. Denise's number flashes on the screen before it goes black.

This time, she answers on the second ring. "What's up?"

"I'm over at our old apartment." I wander through the living room to my bedroom. "I found a moving company with a last minute cancellation, and they're coming over in about an hour to move the furniture. They'll take the boxes, too, but do you have time to go through what we didn't pack? The more they can take, the better."

"Give me ten minutes, and I'll be there."

I stick the phone into my pocket and nudge the blinds aside to study the street below. I didn't notice anything out of the ordinary when I came in, and there isn't anything now.

Paranoia. Not a girl's best friend.

I'm in the bathroom, pulling half-empty bottles of body wash and lotion from the cabinet under the sink when I hear my name. "Cass?"

"In the bathroom," I call back.

"Wow." Denise stares at the counter. "Where'd all that come from?"

"Our habit of buying pretty-smelling things and then getting bored before we finish them?" I set several bottles of nail polish on the edge of the sink. "Do we just want to throw these out?"

"Seems kind of dumb to box them up and move them. They'll probably just end up under sinks again." She picks up a bottle, opens it, and sniffs the contents. "Oh, *ick*. Not to mention some of it's probably really nasty by now too."

"Probably." I shift from my knees to my butt, my energy and drive to get everything cleaned gone. "Can we throw everything else in the dumpster and call it good?"

"In the bathroom, or the apartment in general?" She extends a hand, and I take it, letting her pull me to my feet.

In general. The thought of packing away what's left in here is daunting, bordering on overwhelming. Who gets the pictures on the walls? Do we keep the battered posters that have moved from place to place? She leads me to the couch, and I collapse in a heap, ready for a nap.

"I don't know how I'm going to get through classes next week," I admit.

She curls up next to me. "You were okay yesterday. What's changed?"

No tears, thank God, but grief flattens me against the couch, and I tip my head back and shut my eyes. "The other shoe dropped." Bit by bit, I tell her everything: the incredible, debilitating sadness, the crying, the screaming, how even Nick's presence didn't help. "We spent so much time at odds with each other. We'll never get a chance to fix it." On cue, tears sting the backs of my eyes, and I sniff hard. "I can't stop crying, either, which is really annoying."

She pulls her lips down in an exaggerated frown. "Oh, yes, it's really annoying to have a perfectly normal reaction." I flip her off with a snort, but the tears recede.

"I know your relationship with your dad wasn't the greatest, but you're allowed to cry for him, Cass."

Stupid that I need to be reassured my reactions are okay even if they're out of character for me, but it helps. Neese has been with me through all the ups and downs of my relationship with Turner. Leaning on her feels right. So when she curls an arm around my shoulders, that's exactly what I do.

The lobby buzzer going off jolts us both out of our thoughts, and I rub a fist over my chest to calm my racing heart. "That'll be the movers."

"Where's your new place?" She pushes off the couch and walks to the intercom. "Hello?"

"Rory with Crane Movers. We're here for the furniture?"

"Come on up." She presses the button that releases the front door, then opens the apartment door an inch. "How'd you find movers so quickly again?"

"Last minute cancellation. New place is on the south side of campus." The faint *ding* of the elevator arriving drifts into the apartment, followed by heavy tread in the hallway. "You said I can take the TV, yeah?"

"Yeah."

A knock on the door, and it swings open, revealing three scruffy, broad-shouldered men in the hall. "Cass Turner?" the one in front asks.

I lift a hand. "Me."

They work fast. Denise and I are forced to move around the apartment constantly to stay out of their way, and after a while we give up on trying to pack anything else and huddle in a corner of the kitchen. We watch as they cart first the boxes, then the couch, coffee table, and my bed down to the truck blocking the street.

Denise and I crowd into the elevator with one of the men holding the last of the boxes from the kitchen. I turn to her. "Do you want to see the new apartment?"

She grins. "Thought you'd never ask."

The truck's already parked, the back door open by the time Denise and I walk up to my new building. But the movers aren't the only ones waiting for us to arrive.

Andreas stands off to the right of the front entrance, his expression cool and blank, phone in one hand. He's dressed casually in well-worn jeans and a dark blue sweater, but there's no mistaking his power and importance. It practically radiates off him, ensnaring everything in its path.

Denise leans in. "Who is that?" A tremor of something, fear or worry or awe, punctuates her question.

I bite off a sigh. "Andreas Kosta. Nick's dad." My keys clink against one another as I hold them out. "Would you mind letting the movers in? Fourth floor, apartment twenty-two."

A car rolls past, loud hip-hop blasting through the windows. The driver zooms to the end of the street, and we follow its progress until the car turns right. "Classy neighbors you got there, Cass." Denise takes the keys. "Which one opens the front door, and which one opens the apartment?"

I show her, and she waves to the movers to follow her while I continue past the truck to deal with Andreas. "Mr. Kosta."

He dips his head in acknowledgement. "Cassidy. Moving day?"

"Sure." I tuck my hands into my pockets. "Can I help you with something?" A gust of wind blows up the sidewalk, sneaking through the thick fabric of my sweatshirt, and I shiver.

"I've come to ask you one last time to reconsider. I understand you and Dominic have already signed the lease, and there may be some financial strain for you if you were to break it now. I'm willing to compensate you for the expense."

He's willing to compensate me. Anger, at once familiar and foreign, burns through my veins. "Why is it so difficult for you to accept that Nick loves me, and that he loves me enough he's not going to leave me just because you think it's for the best?" I suck in a breath, striving for calm. "He's a grown man. It's not like he's going to be living here anyway. Besides, he's been making his own choices and his own mistakes for years now."

The first hint of anger gleams in his eyes. "When his mistakes have the potential to ripple through what I've built, when there's the possibility those choices could severely damage everything I've worked for, it's my responsibility to ensure that doesn't happen."

I am *not* a mistake. I fist my hands, nails digging into my palms. "Isaiah is dead. His death was my one and only goal. I may have failed to achieve it, but that doesn't change the fact that Isaiah is no longer a threat."

"You killed a police officer without thinking."

I give him a baleful look. "You have no proof of that. Though if they were to run a ballistics report on the bullet pulled from Nick's leg, they'd find it's a match for the gun fired by Tris. The *only* reason the police know about Tris is because they arrived on the scene first. You can't control everything, Mr. Kosta." And I'll bet that chaps his ass like nothing else.

"Cass?"

I turn around. One of the movers stands next to the truck, and he waves me over. "Yeah?"

"Which bedroom did you want the bed in?"

The apartment's a corner unit with the doors to the bedrooms and the bathroom on the right side of the living room. One bedroom is right on the corner with two windows, and the other has a single window. "The room with one window." I really ought to go up and show him exactly where I want it, but I need to get rid of Andreas first. "Can you put it on the wall across from the closet? I'll be up in a minute."

His gaze darts past me, over my shoulder, and he shrugs. "Sure."

Why does Andreas think that being the head of LA's underworld entitles him to be, well, rude and pompous? Stifling another sigh, I turn my attention to Andreas. "Short of you inflicting bodily harm on me, I'm not leaving Nick. I wouldn't leave him even if you did hurt me, and you and I both know that will only serve to push him closer to me." Current troubles aside, every word I said is true. "I am sorry I've caused so much of a disturbance in your organization. But if I were you, I'd be more concerned with whoever tried to kill us last night."

He narrows his eyes. "What are you talking about?"

I narrow mine right back. I assumed Nick told his dad when they spoke last night. "Someone snuck into the backyard of my parents' house with a gun. Nick killed him. Nick is also fairly certain you want me alive so you can turn me over to the police. Is he wrong?" Andreas shakes his head. I wave my hand at the front door. "Okay. Good. Can I go tell the movers where to put things now?"

He rakes a coldly assessing gaze over me. "I will discuss this with Dominic. Immediately."

Oh, goody.

Chapter 17

Get your ass over here.

I check the text from Nick one more time as I push open the door to the ninth floor of his building. He didn't respond when I told him I couldn't leave until the movers were done. Dealing with them only took another half hour, since there was so little stuff and they were incredibly organized, but the time added to the drive meant over an hour passed before I arrived at the office. The chances of Andreas still being here are small.

I hope.

Constantine's office door is open, but as I walk by, I see the room is empty. Nick's door, however, is closed, and there's a low rumble of voices coming from inside. Gathering my faltering courage, I knock and turn the knob at the muffled "come in."

Of course I didn't get lucky. Of course Andreas is perfectly at ease, sitting in one of the visitor chairs on the near side of the desk. *Of course* Nick's expression is the same cold, blank one he uses whenever he's about to kill someone.

Which means I probably should stop Nick from doing exactly that.

Instead of greeting either of them, I round the desk and stop beside Nick. He doesn't hesitate to band his arm around my waist and pull me into him. Andreas will see the move for what it is—Nick's choosing me, and fuck whatever the family wants. I probably ought to feel guilty about causing even more discord between father and son, but I need Nick more than his father does at the moment, even with the distrust and hurt between us. I don't know if I would have made it through the last forty-eight hours with at least some of my sanity intact if it hadn't been for him.

Andreas doesn't need to know about our problems, though. I can put on a show for him, just like Nick. "Someone want to fill me in?" I trail my fingers up the side of his neck. The muscles are like stone.

"Dominic showed me the photo he took of the man he shot last night. His name is Rafe Moreno. He's not a member of the organization, though he is loyal. He's used for jobs too delicate for outsiders but too close for the family." Andreas doesn't move a millimeter. His control is amazing and a little scary.

The explanation doesn't quite make sense. Nick hisses softly when I accidentally dig my fingers into the side of his neck. "Sorry," I murmur. He squeezes my hip in response.

"I don't understand what Rafe does. Did," I correct. "Was he like Josef?" Josef was sent by Isaiah to kill me. The fight ended with Josef bleeding out on the floor of my bedroom.

Except...

Nick told me Josef wouldn't have taken orders from Isaiah because he wasn't placed highly enough. After Isaiah attacked me in the parking garage, we assumed Josef's loyalty had been bought. With my misgivings about Constantine rearing their ugly heads, though, I want to take another look at that. Later. First I need to know what Rafe did.

"Josef was a member of the organization, and his skills were much narrower." Nick loosens his hold, and I ease away as he tips his head back, his dark eyes intent on mine. "You familiar with gangs? Or at least fictional depictions?" I nod, and his lips quirk in a smile. "Instead of a company with different departments, think of the organization as a gang. You're going to have some people who aren't part of it but want to be, and then others who will claim an affiliation and do work for them when it suits, but may deny involvement at other times. Rafe fell into the latter category. When he did do a job, it wasn't always bloody or physical. It was something Dad or Uncle Anton didn't trust to someone in the family and was too sensitive for someone like your dad to handle."

A heavy weight forms in my chest at the thought of my dad, and I struggle to breathe through it. "So he's like Luca Brasi."

Nick's quick grin helps lift some of the weight. "Yeah. He's also more of a 'need to know' associate, and Dad didn't think I needed to know about him yet."

When Andreas clears his throat softly, I pull my gaze from Nick's.

"I did not send Rafe to your house last night, Cassidy."

His surprise when I told him about the attempt seemed genuine, but I didn't have much contact with him, either. "How do I know if you're telling the truth?"

"You don't."

Honesty. I can appreciate honesty. Suddenly tired, I lean into Nick's side. "Look, this is ridiculous. Your organization's already got a giant rift in it from Isaiah and his need for revenge. You know what's going to happen if you keep pursuing your desire to take me from Nick? That rift's going to get bigger. So let's pretend for a moment that I believe you, and Rafe wasn't there last night on your orders. And let's also pretend that you want to see me led away in handcuffs and not in a body bag." Nick's hand flexes on my hip, and I stroke my own over his fingers. I'm not going to die on him. Not if I can help it. "That means Isaiah wasn't working alone, and someone still wants your son out of the picture. What are you going to do about it?"

Andreas regards me coolly. The look is like so many Turner gave me over the years it hurts. Sad, pathetic even, that I'd give anything for my dad to look at me that way again. Nick shifts in his chair and pulls me onto his lap, my weight balanced on his good leg.

Something flits across Andreas's face. Surprise? Resignation? Did he really not believe that Nick would choose me?

The silence drags out to the point of awkwardness, until Andreas finally nods once. "You make a valid point. Additional security, to begin with. He will have a driver. I would ask that you remain at your house until I can arrange for the apartment next to yours to be rented and some of my men to move in. Your father's security is excellent, and there's space for additional men in the house."

Nick shakes his head. "Classes start Monday, and I'm not going to inconvenience her any more than I have. Cass will be at the apartment beginning tonight. What time's your first class?" he asks me.

"Nine." He's doing it. He's really going to give me the space I asked for. We're going to live apart. I don't know if I want to kiss him or yell at him. "I'll give you the codes to the security system."

"It's settled." Andreas stands and waits like he's expecting Nick to do the same.

"I'd like a minute with Cass." Something in his tone makes me wary, though he strokes a hand up my back. Andreas shoots me a look and steps outside before shutting the door behind him.

"How'd the move go?"

Seriously? He wants to have a normal conversation? "You mean before or after your dad showed up? They took everything that was packed. Furniture is more or less in the places I want it. I figured if you were working tomorrow I'd go over and put away the dishes and other kitchen things so I can use them. Were you fighting with your dad for the last hour?"

"About, yeah." He releases me, and I get to my feet. "But not before he ordered us to come to dinner."

I can't help it. I groan. Loudly. "It just gets better and better." I cover my face with my hands. "Your dad really has it in for me." When he doesn't disagree, I peek at him through my fingers. "What?"

He tugs my hand away. "I don't want to leave you by yourself."

Then he should have thought of that before he doped my coffee. Going home to an empty apartment and knowing Nick won't be sneaking into my bed in the middle of the night makes my chest seize. "I'll be fine," I say. "We need to fix this, Nick. I want the time you said I could have. More, I won't be the reason you split with your family."

He kisses me. "Don't worry," he murmurs against my lips. "They're doing that all on their own." He snags his crutches. "Come on. I made the mistake of telling Dad the server tests were delaying everything else, so we're having dinner with my parents."

Andreas stands outside Constantine's office, hands loose at his sides, chin up. I doubt the man knows the meaning of the word "fidget." I certainly can't see him pacing or idly playing Words With Friends on his phone. His dark gaze is direct and neutral. "Ready?"

In deference to Nick's injury, we take the elevator to the lobby. "Your parents are in Woodland Hills, correct?" Andreas asks as we exit the building.

"Yeah, near—"

Crackcrackcrackcrack.

There's screaming.

Crackcrackcrackcrack.

Tires squealing.

I'm on the sidewalk, pavement scraping my cheek, Nick half on top of me. Shot. We were shot at.

Panic roars through me, the world fading to white. Shot. Nick's been shot. I'm being smothered. I buck hard, banging my knees into the sidewalk. Warm hands cradle my head, and someone's shouting my name from very far away.

"Cass. Cassidy. Stop moving. Stop moving, love."

Love. Nick. He's okay enough to talk. I do as he asks, but I can't breathe. My breath comes in short, shallow pants, lungs spasming and shoving the air right back out. "Can't breathe," I gasp.

His mouth is right next to my ear. "Can you feel me?" When he takes a breath, his chest expands against my back. Is that what he means? I hope so. I'm starting to see spots. I nod. "C'mon. In and out." He draws in air, and so do I, then let it out when he does. In and out, in and out, our breaths synchronizing. His lips graze my ear. "You okay? Were you hit?"

The screaming hasn't stopped. People are shouting, someone's crying, and way off in the distance, there's sirens. I close my eyes and try to shut out the noise as I take inventory of my body. Cheek scraped from hitting the sidewalk. Palms feel a little raw too. Solid warmth where Nick's lying across me, pinning me to the ground. Knees throbbing. "I think I'm okay. Are you? Is the shooter gone?"

"Think so. Let's just stay down here to be safe."

Good idea. Fantastic idea. I work a hand under his, and he laces our fingers together. "You didn't answer my other question. Did you get hit?"

He hesitates before answering. "Dad pushed me into you. I'm fine."

Shooter be fucked, I need to see him. "Get off me."

"It's not safe."

"Get. Off. Me." I manage to push myself up, dislodging him, and I catch his grimace as he rolls onto his side. "Where is it?" Unable to wait for an answer, I run my hands over his chest and around to his back. When I skim down his right leg, he grunts.

"What?"

"Think I split some stitches."

It's been five days since Nick was shot. The danger of the skin splitting should have been past. The sirens are closer. I hope one of them is an ambulance. "Don't move. Do you want me to call Simon?"

He ignores the question and twists around. "Where's my dad?"

An excellent question. Andreas was on the other side of Nick as we hit the sidewalk, but I'm all turned around from being pushed to the ground. Street side is to my left, so I scan the curb first. Two other people are lying on the ground, but only one has someone hunched over him. Dread pools in my stomach as I crawl over. The man leaning over him looks up as I approach. "Can you put pressure on the other wound?"

I hover over the body and finally get a look at the man's face. It's Andreas, and he's still awake. Barely. His eyelids keep doing this weird fluttering thing. He was shot twice, once high on his left side, hopefully missing the heart, the other lower on his chest through the bottom of his rib cage from the looks of it. My hands shake as I pull off my sweatshirt and wad it up. I press it to the wound on his shoulder.

Andreas's lips move, and his gaze latches on mine. I lean in, barely catching his words. "Where's…Dominic?" His breath rasps out.

"Behind me. He's okay, thanks to you. Thinks he may have pulled some stitches. You're going to be okay too." He will be. He *has* to be. "Did you see the shooter?"

"Car. Dark…sedan. Dark…win…dows."

If he's having this much difficulty speaking, the bullet in his abdomen must have done some damage. Possibly nicked a lung. "Okay. Just hang on and don't talk." He rasps out another breath, and his eyes shut completely. I lean in and focus on the slight rise and fall of his chest, each breath reassuring me that, for now, he's alive and fighting to stay that way.

"Cass? Dad? *Dad*." Nick drags himself toward us. "How many times?"

"Twice. Once near the shoulder. Looks like the other might have gone through the bottom of his ribs." Nick can't stop the groan of pain as he stretches out his injured leg. I frown. "Hey. Be careful. Don't hurt yourself any more than you already have."

"Thank you," he says to the man applying pressure to the chest wound. He nods in response. Nick motions to my sweatshirt. "Let me," he murmurs.

"I'm good." Are the sirens louder? Please let them be louder.

"No, you're not." He points to my hands. My hands shake, even as I attempt to staunch the bleeding. His are steady as he takes my place, scooting on his ass to get into a more comfortable position.

The front of Andreas's shirt is almost completely soaked in blood. It spreads down his stomach to the hem, then up across his chest. The only unmarred spot is his right shoulder. I can't stop staring. The loss of that much blood doesn't bode well for his survival.

A siren shuts down with a *whoop*, the lights strobing over the people on the sidewalk. A car door opens, and I tear my gaze away from Andreas's prone form to see the siren belongs to an ambulance. I scramble to my feet. "Over here!"

One of the paramedics jogs toward me. "Two gunshot wounds, one to the left shoulder, the other to the abdomen." Nick's calm. Too calm. It's that glassy, dazed sort of serenity that comes from shock. Fear surges, and I shove it down. The paramedics need room to work, and any attempts to comfort Nick would only get in their way.

He'll have to hold on until we get to the hospital. We both will.

Chapter 18

Nick's hands look rusty. We've been here long enough his father's blood dried on his skin. We need to get to the hospital to get Nick's stitches checked out, but the wound isn't serious enough for an ambulance to take him right away, if at all. For now, the paramedics are letting Nick sit on a gurney while they check the remaining victims.

And ever since Nick pointed out my hands are shaking, they won't stop. The second I think I have it under control, I get another glimpse of all that dried blood, and it starts again.

"He's not answering his phone?"

"Huh?" I struggle to focus on Nick. He looks at my hands, and I glance down. I called Constantine a moment ago to see if he might be able to drive us to the hospital, since neither of us are capable at the moment. It went straight to voicemail. I scrunch my brows together. Reaching his voicemail immediately when he's preparing for a product launch trips all the wires and alarms, especially since he's been on Nick's ass about remaining in contact. "Oh. No. Straight to voicemail."

"Try him again."

I dial without thinking and get the same result. Some of the fog clears away, and I pull up the number for a cab company. When the dispatcher answers, I step away from the ambulance. "I need a pickup at the corner of Century Park West and Constellation Boulevard."

"Century Park West?" Some clicking, and the dispatcher's tinny voice comes through. "Ma'am, that entire area is blocked off. Emergency responders only."

Great. We're stuck here unless we can convince an officer or a paramedic to get us out. I mumble a "thank you" to the dispatcher and hang up. When I turn back to the ambulance, one of the paramedics is shutting the doors. "Wait! What are you doing?"

"Taking him to the hospital. The wound on his leg's reopened." She moves to shut the other door, and I catch a glimpse of Nick seated on the stretcher inside.

They're taking him? How am I going to get there? They've already checked me over and confirmed I wasn't injured. The scrape on my cheek and the ones on my palms were cleaned but not bandaged. They wouldn't have stayed on anyway.

I stand there like a dummy, unable to move or form the words to ask if I can ride in the back with Nick. The ambulance pulls away. I drop my phone. The screen cracks, and I stoop to pick it up, stumbling back and forth as my legs start shaking as badly as my hands. I sit on the curb and rest my head on my knees, waiting for my strength to return.

I want to curl into a ball and wait for my mommy to make it all better.

Mom's in Montana, though, checking in at four PM like she said she would. I didn't answer yesterday, and when I didn't answer today, she called again. Just a few minutes ago, actually. I should call her back. Tell her everything's all right. I don't want her walking into this fight. Not when she's finally starting to sound better.

"Ms. Turner?"

Who knows my name? I raise my head and find Officer Gregory watching me with a bland expression on his face. "Hi." The word comes out steady, surprising me, since I haven't managed to stop trembling.

He holds out a hand, and I stare at it, not sure it won't bite. We don't have the best history, and I'm pretty certain he thinks I had something to do with the break-in at my old apartment.

He's not exactly wrong.

Since I doubt I can get up under my own power, I take his hand and let him pull me to my feet. "Do you know when they're going to open the streets again?"

"Likely in a few hours, once they've cleared the scene." I forgot how tall he is. Officer Gregory is a moose of a man. Nick's taller than me by a solid couple inches, but the officer towers over me.

"Cabs aren't doing pickups." If I thought I could drive without crashing the car, I would have followed the ambulance, provided they allowed the car *out* of the cordoned-off area. I'm clutching Officer Gregory's hand hard enough to fracture bones, and it takes a lot of effort to keep my teeth from chattering.

His expression softens slightly. "Do you need a ride somewhere?"

It occurs to me he might just want a chance to talk to me further about the shooting. I don't care. "I don't think I'm okay to drive, and I need to get to the hospital. The ambulance that just left had my boyfriend in it. His dad was shot."

Both brows shoot up. "Andreas Kosta?" I nod, and he mutters, "Should have made the connection earlier."

Well, yeah. We *are* standing outside Nick's office. "I don't know what hospital they were taken to."

Someone hails Officer Gregory, and he calls out a response. "Most likely Cedars. I'll call into dispatch and double check." He shifts his hold to my arm and starts toward a patrol car. "Surprised they didn't take you in the ambulance as well."

The remaining ambulance inches away from the curb, lights flashing over the darkening street. The streetlights came on some time ago, and for the first time since the shots were fired, I take a look around.

Dark stains mar the concrete. Yellow crime scene tape is strung around a large section of the sidewalk, little plastic placards scattered here and there. Evidence markers, I think. They're emblazoned with bold, black numbers, and I automatically count them. Ten. Ten shots. Ten shots fired. How many people were hit besides Andreas? A sheet-draped body is sprawled on the pavement. I suck in a breath and turn my head away.

I've lost it. I've lost the coldness, the edge, that calm under pressure I've relied on for weeks to get me through each day. Before Turner's death, the sight of a dead body wouldn't have bothered me in the least. This one will give me nightmares.

He opens the back door to the car, and I duck inside before my legs give out completely. Andreas was breathing when they left. It was labored, and he needed an oxygen mask, but he was breathing. He's not going to die. They'll stitch him up, and he'll be good as new. Better than. He'll be pissed that someone shot him and finally stop treating me like I'm the enemy.

My fingers are fat and clumsy as I poke at my phone, and dried blood flakes onto the cracked screen. I need to call my mother back. I don't want her to worry. It refuses to light up, and I press the power button to restart it.

"Ms. Turner?"

Startled, I drop the phone on the floor between my feet. "Yes?"

"Is there anyone you want to meet you at the hospital?"

Liana might already be on her way, and I don't want to drag Denise into this. "No. What hospital are you taking me to? Did you find Nick and his dad?" Shit. Dinner. "Has someone called Malena? That's Nick's mom. We were going to have dinner with her. Her and Andreas. We tried to reach his cousin because he works in the building but his phone was off." I pause for breath and realize I'm rambling like Denise when she's nervous. Officer Gregory just waits patiently for me to finish.

"Dominic and Andreas Kosta were both taken to Cedars-Sinai. Someone likely has already reached out to Malena."

"Oh." Of course they would have. She's next of kin. I tuck my hands between my knees, uncaring that I'm transferring blood onto my jeans. "Okay."

I spend the short drive to the hospital staring out the window to avoid Officer Gregory's increasingly skeptical looks and trying to wedge myself into the emptiness I've inhabited so easily in the past. As we pull up to the doors, I think I've succeeded. My hands no longer shake. They're not even trembling. I scoop up my phone from the floor and wait for the officer to open the door.

"Thanks for the ride," I say, climbing out of the car. "Can you tell me anything about the shooter? Did anyone see him?" Cool evening air washes over me, and I suppress a shiver.

The skepticism is gone, replaced by the bland expression he had when he first approached me. "We have a description of the car. Only a vague description of the shooter. I understand the car windows were quite dark."

I shrug. "I didn't see anything. I was in the middle of telling Andreas where my parents live when the first shot was fired, and then I was on the ground." My phone vibrates in my hand, the screen lighting up. A notification pops onto the screen, fractured by the crack running through it. Voicemail. Probably my mother. I lift my gaze and meet Officer Gregory's straight on. "I need to get inside."

After another long, considering look, he steps aside. "Take care, Ms. Turner." He gets in the car and drives off.

I listen to the voicemail as I walk toward the entrance. The sign for the emergency room is weird; some of the letters are yellow, while others are red. It's also small. If it weren't for Officer Gregory and all the other exterior signs pointing in this direction, it'd be easy to overlook the entrance.

"Hi, Cass. It's Mom. You didn't answer yesterday…or today. I hope everything's all right." Mom leaves it at that, short and simple, and I wonder how much more she wanted to say and chose not to. Besides, what would I have said if I *had* answered? Sorry, I was in the middle of a breakdown? I was trying not to get shot?

I have to press twice as hard to get the touch screen to recognize my request, but the call rings through just fine. I lean against the wall several feet away from the entrance and wait for Mom to pick up.

"Cass? Is everything all right?"

Strangely, the concern in her voice helps me center, holds me firmly in the middle of the emptiness. "I'm okay. I'm sorry I missed your call yesterday. I was taking a nap, and Nick didn't want to wake me." Lie. I was passed out from crying. "There was a shooting outside Nick's office this afternoon." Truth. "I left my phone in his office and couldn't get to it when the building was on lockdown." Lie. A complete, total, bald-faced lie. Mom might hear about the shooting, but there's absolutely no reason for her to know I was on the street when it happened.

"There was a shooting?"

Shit. Shit shit *shit*. I hate the smallness of her voice, the hesitant question. "Yeah. Nick and I are fine. A drive-by. Police are searching for the car and the shooter, but we had an escort out of the area." Sort of true. "How's Montana?"

She doesn't respond for the longest time, and when she does, I can tell she's retreated inside herself. Rather than drag the conversation out, I tell her I love her and end the call.

The check-in desk blocks the view of the emergency room. The desk is manned by a smiley-faced brunette, who cheerfully informs me that yes, Dominic Kosta was brought to the emergency room and points to a hallway behind her.

It should be illegal for someone that chirpy to work in an ER.

The hallway leads to the main part of the department. A set of sliding double doors is to my right, and I stumble back when they *whoosh* open and a gurney powered by a paramedic and three scrub-wearing people races by. They run down a short hallway separating the waiting area from the double rows of beds partitioned by curtains. Someone starts barking out orders, calling for blood bags.

Only about a quarter of the beds are full. I twitch aside a couple of curtains searching for Nick, and then back away quickly before anyone can notice me. I finally find him halfway down the row. Someone brought him one of those open-backed hospital gowns to change into, and it gapes around his neck like he can't be bothered to tie it properly. The same dazed look covers his face, and it takes a second for him to recognize me. "Cass."

I shove my phone into my pocket and hurry to his side. The coldness dissolves as I take his face in my hands and kiss him hard. He curls his hands around my wrists, holding me in place as he breaks the kiss. "I'm sorry," he murmurs. "I shouldn't have let them leave you."

Leave me? Oh. I press a chaste kiss to his lips. "I don't know that they would have allowed me to ride in the ambulance with you anyway. It's not like I was badly injured or anything." He releases my wrists, and I climb up on the bed beside him.

"How *did* you get here? I know the streets were blocked off. Did you talk to Con?"

I shake my head. "When I tried him the second time, it still went straight to voicemail. I got a ride over with one of the officers at the scene. Officer Gregory? The guy who questioned me about the break-in at my old apartment? He dropped me off a little while ago." I gesture to his right leg. "What's up with your leg? Stitches split?"

He flips the blankets aside. A thick white bandage covers the wound, dotted with bright red blood. "The ones on either end are fine. The ones in the middle came apart. I'm waiting for them to come back with a suture kit. The doctor went to see if he could get any information on my dad's condition."

My hand trembles as I take his. "He was awake when the paramedics arrived."

He squeezes hard enough I think my bones might break. "He's tough. He'll make it." It sounds like he's trying to convince himself, so I keep my mouth shut. If Andreas is anything like Turner, he won't give up easily.

So much blood.

I shut my eyes, and that only makes it worse. Turner's face going slick and red as the shot rings out. Andreas's shirt turning dark and damp as blood seeps from his wounds. "It could have been you," I whisper shakily. It so easily could have been Nick. I open my eyes, see all my worry and fear mirrored in his. "Nick... Where's Constantine? Where's your cousin?" *Why isn't he answering his phone?*

Nick opens his mouth, shuts it, opens it, shuts it again. The fear's replaced by something I don't recognize, something hard, something reluctant.

I don't think we're going to like the answers to those questions.

Chapter 19

I hate waiting. I hate the not knowing, the helplessness, the hope that rises and falls each time someone looking vaguely authoritative approaches and then passes me by. I hate the doubt that creeps a little closer with each passing minute.

I squirm in the hard plastic chair. A doctor who didn't look old enough to be practicing medicine came and mumbled something about redoing Nick's stitches, then stared at me until I moved to the other side of the bed. No one's stopped to give Nick an update on his father, and when I tried to ask the doctor, he gave me a blank look and went back to snapping on his gloves.

So there's nothing to do but wait. Wait and worry and take a trip down the paranoia trail.

Constantine's radio silence stabs me in the side like a thorn. Thorns can't sink very far below the surface, but they can still do plenty of damage. They can tear the skin as effectively as a knife and leave you exposed to further threats.

Just because he had his phone turned off doesn't mean he's behind the shooting. But the random spray of bullets is the third one of its kind that's happened since I met Nick. Two times is a coincidence. Three is a pattern, and it's one I can't ignore.

I lower my head to my hands. I don't know how to do this. I don't know how to find the clues I'm looking for, and I'm afraid I'll look too hard at Constantine and miss something huge. Like the actual killer. To top it off, what information I do have is shabby and pitiful and not nearly enough to confront him with. He'd get all insulted, and if I'm wrong, I'll have ruined our friendship for no reason.

I start with the list. The fucking bullet-point list I made for Nick, back when I was far more certain Constantine was behind everything. It was a list of the deals that Nick had to step in to save over his cousin's protests or they would have ended up in the toilet. It was a good enough reason for me to want to dig deeper. Just how far is that *deeper*, though?

A noise from the bed catches my attention, and I lift my head. Nick's pulling the covers back over his legs, and the doctor's beating a slow retreat from the bed. Nick must have taken the time to adjust his hospital gown, since it no longer looks like it's going to fall down. "You look ready to keel over," he comments.

"Gee, thanks." He's right, unfortunately. With the adrenaline high gone and my shock under control, I'm tired. I want food and a bed. "What'd the doctor say about your leg?"

"To stop putting so much stress on it and let it heal." He rakes a hand through his hair. "No word from Con?"

I guess my doubts must not be very important to Nick if his cousin is still one of the first people he calls when there's trouble. "No. Not yet, anyway. I can try calling him again." In the background, an intercom squawks, calling Doctor Raleigh to the ER.

The moment we can leave this hospital can't come soon enough.

Nick frowns. "Don't bother. If he's not with my mother, I'll call him then. Someone will be by soon with discharge paperwork and another set of crutches, unless the paramedics brought in the pair I was using." He glances at his lap. "Can you pull the curtains shut? I think I'm allowed to get dressed."

"Aw, you don't want your ass hanging out?" I tease, and his grin is surprised and quick and bright.

"Only person I want staring at my ass is you, love. Curtains?"

I get up and tug the curtains shut, then find his clothes neatly folded on a chair on the other side of the bed. "Have you spoken with your mom at all?"

He shifts his legs over the side of the bed and reaches behind him for the ties holding his gown together. He yanks at them, and they snap. "Phone's busted. Had it in my front pocket instead of the back, and it cracked when I went down. Won't turn on." He pulls the top of the gown to his waist and picks up his shirt. "Soon as they spring me, we're going upstairs. I think the OR is on floor five."

When he slides off the bed and lurches forward, I dart around to the other side and catch his shoulders. "Wait a second, okay? I just got you back in one piece. I'd really like to keep you that way." He lifts his right arm, and I duck under, bearing his weight as he struggles to pull his bloody jeans on with one hand. When he gets them to his knees, I grab the waistband and drag them up to his hips.

The curtains part as he's settling on the bed, turned sideways and ready to leave the moment the doctor says *go*. It's the same nurse who tracked down a doctor to fix his stitches, and praise the tiny baby Jesus, he's come bearing forms and crutches.

"Andreas Kosta is still in surgery," he says, passing over the forms. "Fifth floor. Please stop by the desk before you leave."

Nick signs the paperwork without reading it and grabs the crutches. He tucks them under his arms as he gets to his feet. He jerks his chin to the paperwork lying on the bed. "They're all yours." And he swings out into the corridor.

I offer a pained smile to the nurse, mumbling my own "thank you" as I go after Nick. Even on crutches, he's fast, and I have to lengthen my stride to catch up. "Nick. Slow down. He's in surgery. He's not going anywhere. You've got time to take care of the paperwork."

Nick stops abruptly and glares at me. "I know that. But my mother's up there, my sisters are probably up there, and someone else has got to be able to give me more fucking information than *that*." I stare after him as he hobbles toward the elevator.

He's jabbing impatiently at the elevator button when I walk up. I keep my mouth shut as we board the elevator and trail behind him when the doors open seconds later.

The waiting area is nicer than a hospital waiting area should be. Situated next to a large window, table lamps provide extra light rather than harsh fluorescents, and the couch and chairs are covered in a soft dark blue fabric. Lia jumps up from her chair and runs over, bypassing Nick to throw her arms around me. The air in my lungs huffs out in surprise, but I hug her back tightly.

"You're okay?" she whispers.

My surprise increases. "I should be asking *you* that. Are you okay? How's your mom?"

Lia releases me and pulls me aside, and I watch Nick's other sisters fuss over him as he lowers himself to the couch next to his mother. "Mom's... I guess she's okay. She hasn't said much." She glances over her shoulder. "Nicky's okay? You're okay?" she repeats.

"Nick pulled some stitches. We were down in the ER getting him patched up. I'm fine. Some scrapes from where Nick pushed me down. Are you *sure* you're okay?" She hadn't actually answered the question.

Tears well and spill down her cheeks. She swipes her fingers under her eyes. "If I'm not thinking about it, yes, I'm okay. Dad was stable when they took him in. That's good. It's good, right?"

The pleading note in her voice hurts. *Hurts*. It's a knife in the heart, and I almost lift a hand to rub away the pain. "Yeah, it is." Better than Turner got. I nudge her toward her family. "Go sit down." I need a minute alone. Several minutes, to be honest. The worry and fear for Andreas is quickly being replaced by jealousy. *He's* still alive. *He* has a fighting chance.

Nick needs me, and he doesn't need my anger over something he can't control. Lia's brows draw together, and I work up a smile for her. "I need to call my mom," I lie. "I'll be there in a bit." Expression still uncertain, she wanders over to her family, and I walk down the hall in search of a quiet, secluded spot.

I find the exit for the stairs and scan the door for an alarm. Finding none, I step into the stairwell and let the door shut behind me. Then I slide down the wall. My butt hits the polished concrete hard enough I wince.

The human mind can take only so much stress and chaos before it starts developing coping mechanisms or shuts down higher thought. How much more can I take? What other horrible things have to happen before my mind and body finally say *stop*?

I stretch my legs out in front of me. The coolness of the concrete seeps through my jeans, the sensation traveling up my spine to wind its way around my head. I'll do this as long as I have to. Because my only other option is to give up, give it all up, and that's no option at all.

* * * *

Someone's murmuring my name and shaking me awake. *Ow*. There's a crick in my neck, a bad one, and I wiggle my jaw to work out some of the stiffness. "Hmmm?" Falling asleep with my head on Nick's shoulder *sounded* sweet and romantic. Really it's just painful.

Nick's expression gives away nothing of what he's feeling. "Dad's awake. We're going to see him."

Relief that Andreas survived the surgery wars with a resurgence of jealousy. "Oh. Good." I stretch away from Nick and tilt my head back and forth. "I'm going to walk around a little." Without waiting for an answer, I kiss his cheek and stand, then hurry for the stairwell. A couple flights of stairs will wake me up and give me a chance to work out the residual anger.

I want to hurt something. Punch it, strangle it, rip it apart. I shove open the door and sprint up the stairs. I push my rage into a corner with each step, my mind calming even as my heart rate climbs. Whining and crying over the unfairness of life won't do me any good. Maybe someone would have caught up to Turner eventually. Maybe the outcome was inevitable.

Six flights later, I no longer want to smash my fist into the wall. I turn around and walk slowly to the fifth floor landing. I'll call a cab to take me back to the car. It'll give Nick a little more time with his family and me more time away from them.

The waiting area isn't empty as I expected. Constantine has his back to me and his phone at his ear. I quiet my steps, hoping to hear something that might convince me one way or the other that he isn't behind the shooting this evening.

"No, we need to finish the server tests first." A pause. "I don't fucking care how long it takes, Peter. They need to be done before the launch." Another pause. "We're not pushing the date back again. We already did it once. We do it again, we'll lose consumer confidence." His shoulders tighten, and I hold my breath. "Get it the fuck done and stop bitching to me about it. You can sleep when the launch is over."

He disconnects the call and shoves the phone into his back pocket. Point about consumer confidence aside, Constantine's attitude just then strikes me as…off. Harsh and unbending. Not something I'd normally associate with him, but then Nick *did* say he's impossible to live with in the weeks before a product launch.

"More sleepless nights ahead, huh?" I ask.

He whips his head around. Icy fury races across his face, followed by a weary smile. "More like we can sleep when we're dead." He steps toward me, arms outstretched, and I stiffen involuntarily. He doesn't notice and hugs me as tight as Lia did. "You're okay?" he murmurs.

"Some scrapes and bruised knees. Nothing I won't recover from." I wiggle free of his hold as discreetly as I can. "Since you're here, can you tell Nick I went to pick up the car and I'll be back soon?"

"Wait until he's done. I'll drive you both over."

I'm already backing away. "No, it's okay. I'll take a cab." The elevator pings off to my right, and I jog to catch it before the doors close.

Leaving Nick alone with his cousin—well, alone with his cousin, his mother, and his sisters—is a calculated risk. If Constantine *is* the one behind the shooting tonight and the attempt at the house the night before, he likes a plan. I'm counting on that need for a plan to hold off the spontaneous urge to get rid of Nick as soon as the opportunity presents itself.

Besides, all three mass shooting incidents had a certain amount of anonymity. Whoever ordered the shootings wants some distance between him and the killing so it would look like an unfortunate accident, though I wouldn't call murder an accident.

The elevator opens onto the first floor. I dig my phone out of my pocket and call for a cab, pleased when the dispatcher tells me one will be here in two minutes. I leave through the ER and walk to the curb, eyes glued to the street out front.

Motive. I need a motive. Coming up with a motive will give me—us— something to work with. It could be as simple as wanting the power Nick has, or revenge for a deal gone wrong. It could be something obscure neither of us could guess in a million years.

I stick with the simple and move power and revenge to the top of the list. Greed, lust, fury… They're strong emotions, strong enough to push a person to do something they normally wouldn't do. Revenge rode me *hard*. It makes sense that whoever's after Nick is being chased by the same nasty demons.

The cab pulls up, and I climb in and give the driver the closest intersection to where I parked the car. My phone buzzes in my hand. I squint at the name on the screen as I try to accept the call. "Neese?"

"Who else would it be?"

"I dropped my phone and the screen cracked. Think I need to replace it. It doesn't like it when I try to do, well, anything on it. Anyway, what's up?"

She murmurs something unintelligible, and a lower voice answers. She must be talking to Charlie. "Our semi-annual tradition. Pizza? Bad movies?"

Crap. Denise and I always start each semester with a large pizza and the worst movie we can find on Netflix. The harder our classes get, the more important it becomes. Spring semester junior year, it turned out to be one of the few nights we actually got to do something fun. It was like the moment we set foot on campus, our profs threw weeks-long projects and fifteen page papers at us. "Right. Sorry, it's been a crazy couple of days." The cab rounds a corner. "My place isn't really ready for company. Can we do it at yours?"

"I was going to suggest that. I was also going to suggest you bring Nick with you."

Our relationship has been all over the place recently. A night of doing nothing together might bring us back to a level playing field and repair some of the damage. As I open my mouth to say yes, Constantine's conversation echoes in my head. *We can sleep when we're dead.* "I'll ask, but he's been swamped at work. I don't know that he'll have time."

Literally? Or figuratively?

The cab rolls past Nick's office, the crime scene tape gone, the bloodstains still visible, even in the dark. I turn away from the window. "I gotta go. I'll see you tomorrow? Around six?"

"Six it is. I'll order the pizza." We hang up, and it occurs to me this is the first time in weeks she didn't ask me how I am.

Chapter 20

I've been here before. The familiar hazy, languid heat cloaks me like the blankets on our bed. I know those hands, that mouth, the sweet whispers where the words don't matter, only the intent. His intent is to wake me enough I swear I'm dreaming, and it's working.

I'd know his kisses anywhere. Pre-Nick, I had good kisses and bad, a few fantastic ones that left me dizzy and breathless. Nick took what I knew and destroyed it. He's my high bar, my impossible achievement, and if he knew his lips on mine had the power to short circuit my brain every time, he might take advantage and turn me into a pleasure-craving zombie.

Something about the way our lips fit together makes me absolutely certain I will never find this connection with anyone else. Tonight, there's an urgency in his kiss, pushing me closer to the frantic surge and swell of lust and farther from dreamland. It washes away the strain and mutual mistrust we've been operating under and tears it down to basics: him, me, fucking. He's not toying with me. Using teeth and lips and tongue, he devastates my mouth, and I claw at his shoulders in an attempt to get closer.

He skims a hand down my side, hooks his fingers under my knee, and props my leg on his hip. The move traps his cock between us, and I want to stroke it to bring him some relief. He rolls onto his back, bringing me with him.

And I finally open my eyes.

The room isn't so dark I can't see his face or the need expressed there. "Cassidy," he whispers.

I trace his lips with my finger. "What do you need?"

His gaze focuses on my mouth. "You."

"Then take me."

But he doesn't. He doesn't even move. I let my finger drift away from his mouth and trace the line of his jaw. "Nick? Is something wrong?" His jaw tightens under my hand. "Talk to me," I say softly.

The words come haltingly, his eyes never leaving my mouth. "I was dreaming. I *knew* I was dreaming." He walks his fingers up my leg to my hip. "We were being shot at again. Only instead of the bullets hitting my dad, they hit you. They hit you, and you wouldn't open your eyes." He lifts his gaze, and I see the wild desperation in them. "I keep coming too close to losing you."

It's a big fear of his, and it's one I've heard before. There also isn't much we can do about it. The life he leads invites danger to stalk him. Fuck, it practically knocks down his door.

He's not done talking, though. Hands running over my skin, gaze roaming my face, he continues. "I was glad it was him. For a good, solid minute, I was glad my dad was the one who was shot. Because it wasn't you."

He threads his fingers through my hair, pulls my head down to his, and takes my mouth with all the fury he'd shown earlier. The heat shoots through me and I groan. We'll talk later about this fear of his. Right now I need him as much as he needs me. Feeling daring, I suck his tongue into my mouth. My reward is a hard, firm jerk of his hips, the thick length of his cock rubbing my clit. I rock on him, his length growing slippery with my arousal. He can't keep his hands in one place. They're everywhere, stroking, gripping, teasing. They pause at my hips to encourage my rhythm, to speed it up, and I do.

His injury keeps him somewhat immobilized, making him more demanding. My head must tilt *this way* to give him access to the sweet spot under my jaw. He works his hand between us so he can tug and pull at my nipple. "Sit up," he rasps.

I don't. I trail my tongue up his neck and suckle a kiss to the soft skin over his racing pulse. He grabs my hair in a loose ponytail and tugs my head away. "Sit up, love."

I try to bring my mouth back to his and get my hair pulled for my trouble. "I don't want to," I whisper.

"One more time." The hand on my breast slides lower. "Sit. Up." I let out a stuttering moan as he presses firmly on my clit. "Or I'll stop."

I sit up.

He immediately follows. I swallow my whimper as my hardened nipples brush against his chest. The change in position doesn't do much to widen his range of motion, but he doesn't let that stop him. Bunching my hair in his fist again, he tips my head back, scraping his teeth lightly down my throat to my collarbone. I squirm on his lap. I feel trapped with his hand holding my hair and the other gripping my wrists behind my back. Trapped, but not scared. The opposite, actually. I'm eager, nerves buzzing in anticipation.

"Let me touch you," I beg.

"No." The words are muffled on my skin, and I squirm, redoubling my efforts to touch him when the head of his cock slips inside. "Stop moving," he growls.

I don't stop until he's all the way inside me and he clamps both hands on my hips. I need to move. I need friction. When I tighten my inner muscles, he shuts his eyes and hisses out a breath. "Cass."

"*Please*." We're just *sitting here*, his cock pulsing inside me, my clit throbbing, and while I don't think I'm anywhere close to orgasm, *I don't care*. The connection that comes alive whenever we have sex is about more than release. I feel him everywhere, like he's invaded my soul, like he's become a part of me and turned me into a sappy, gooey love-struck mess. Heat crawls up my neck to my face, and I wind my arms around his shoulders. "Make love to me."

Such cheesy, clichéd words. Words I'm embarrassed by. They're so out of place, yet they're the only ones I can think of that describe exactly what I want to do, and what I want him to do to *me*. It won't change things between us, but I can't ignore that we both need it. I kiss him slowly, coaxing his lips apart with my tongue. Pressed together from mouths to groins, nothing can break us apart.

One kiss leads to another, a string of them growing hotter and hotter, and I start rocking. Not hard, not fast, just tiny, shallow strokes that inch me closer to the edge. Another stolen moment, one that spins out as our breathing synchronizes and our hips move in counterpoint. I want to crawl inside him. I want to fuse us together.

"Fuck, but I love you," he murmurs. "Bear down. Can you do that?"

"I d-d-don't know." What new thing is he going to show me? I slow almost to a complete stop, breath hitching in my lungs as I try to do as he asks and clench around him. I must do something good because he groans, and the building tension increases tenfold. "Nick?"

"Like that." Hands on my waist, he encourages me to roll my hips. The pressure becomes a weight, and I strain against it. "You're incredible," he whispers.

I don't know what's happening. I am so *lost*, lost to this raging inferno scorching my veins. I tremble and kiss him. Kiss him hard, hoping he'll ground me because I'm about to fall apart. "I love you." I repeat the words against his lips, over and over again, as the trembles become shakes and the heavy weight low in my belly blooms and spreads.

Ever since I discovered what an orgasm was, I've had all kinds. Never this. Never this slow roll consuming everything in its path, climbing gradually to a peak and shimmering there for ages. I'm vaguely aware of Nick grinding out my name and the bruising grip of his hands on my hips.

My head is spinning.

I remember I need to breathe to live, and I drop my head to his shoulder, panting for air. His chest heaves and brushes mine. "Fuck," he gasps out. "*Fuck.*"

I turn my face into the crook of his neck. "Mmmm." He smells like... mine. Cinnamon and sweat and...home.

A cramp spasms in my hip, and I grunt at the sudden pain. "Back in a minute." I lift myself off him and crawl from the bed, then limp my way to the door as my muscles unlock.

Nick joins me in the bathroom as I finish cleaning up. Even in the soft glow of the bathroom nightlight, I can make out the weary lines digging into his skin. "We need to talk."

Cold rushes over me. *We need to talk.* The four most hated words in the English language. That doesn't change the fact that he's right. Shivering, I hurry to the guest room and pull on the first thing I find, which is unfortunately Nick's T-shirt.

I walk into the living room. He's slumped on the couch, crutches propped against the arm. I pull the throw off the back of a nearby chair and wrap it around me before curling into the opposite corner of the couch. "I'm not going to like this, am I." It's not a question; whatever he's about to say is sure to be displeasing at best and soul-destroying at worst.

"Probably not," he says. "We can't keep doing this."

I don't want to speculate on what *this* is. "You'll have to be more specific."

He waves his hand toward the hallway. "What just happened shouldn't have."

The cold seeps through the blanket, creeping into my limbs. "We shouldn't have what? Had sex?" Once the words are out of my mouth, I realize he's right. Sex, or at least sex where we're at, only complicates matters.

"You can't tell me you suddenly forgive me for what I did. You do, I'll know you're lying, and I'll want to know why." He sighs. "We both need some space, and circumstances are ensuring we don't have any."

I pull the blanket tighter as the cold penetrates my core. I asked for this, and as badly as I need it, it still hurts to hear. "There's furniture in the apartment now. Since class starts on Monday, it would be easier for me if I was there. You're welcome to stay here until you find a place to live." A shudder wracks my body. "You're still angry."

A car drives by, and Nick cranes his neck to try to see out the window. "Not angry. Anger's a useless emotion." I cringe, the unintentional insult burning. Anger fueled my need for revenge, and while I knew he didn't approve of my methods, I thought he appreciated the end result, same as the rest of the organization. "Trust is a two-way street, and you damaged mine. A few days of behaving like the mature, methodical Cass I know helps, but it's not enough."

Just like his acquiescence to my request to live alone and take a step back isn't enough. We both have needs that aren't being met, and they deserve equal weight. "I know."

"We'll stay here while we figure out what to do next." He picks up his crutches and struggles to his feet. But my brain's awake, and it's already thinking of possibilities.

"No," I say slowly. "We can do this apart. We can make this work. You can stay here until you find a place to live, and I'll move into the apartment like we planned."

"Cassidy—"

"Don't," I warn. "Do you really want to have this argument? Because I don't."

Somewhere down the street, two of the neighborhood cats start fighting, their screeches filling the silence. I struggle to keep the tremble out of my voice. "Please. I need this. So do you. We can't keep putting it off because the timing isn't right."

He growls low in his throat. "You're right."

"So we do this? Like we agreed?" He nods once, and I let out a breath I didn't realize I was holding. "Is there anyone left that you trust to handle security?" I tuck the blanket more securely around my shoulders. "Turner installed the system here himself. Anything you can't figure out, I can explain, except for the gun safe. It's a biometric lock, and I don't know how to program it to allow you access. But you should have someone you can call if something goes on the fritz here."

He remains on his feet, hovering over the end of the coffee table like a shadowy mountain. "I'll take care of the security at your apartment. I'll need a few days to get everything together. Until then, I'd like you to stay here. It's safer." His voice softens to a plea. "Please, Cass."

Is he scared? As scared as I am? And he's still letting me move out before this is over? I don't deserve him. I stand and pad toward him, trailing the blanket. "Go back to bed."

He shakes his head. "Only if you come with me."

I arch a brow. "Doesn't that defeat the purpose of this whole conversation?" I would race him down the hall right now. I'm not ready to sleep alone. Not again.

His lips brush my forehead, and I lean into him. "One more night," he whispers.

One more night. To comfort. To say good-bye, at least for now. "Okay."

* * * *

"Where's Nick tonight?" Charlie asks, reaching out to take the crust Denise hands him.

"Spending time with his family. His dad's in the hospital, so he wanted to be there." I lick sauce from my lip. "Can you turn it up a little?"

Charlie glances over, remote in hand. "Hospital? Everything all right?"

"Yeah. He'll be fine. Just some surgery." Surgery necessitated by a couple of bullet wounds, but if Denise and Charlie haven't heard about the shooting from the local news, I'm not about to enlighten them. I work up a grin. "Volume? Please? We're missing some epic whining right now."

"I think this may be the worst one yet. *How* did you hear about this movie?" Denise leans forward and selects another slice of pizza.

"Some entertainment site was talking about a remake. And it's not that bad."

Charlie groans. "It's called *Mother, May I Sleep With Danger*. Cass, how does that not equal a bad movie?"

I shrug and reach for another slice of pizza. "I could have chosen, oh, *The Amanda Knox Story*. Or that one about Wills and Kate." My phone buzzes from its place on the arm of the sofa. After a glance at the screen to assure myself it's not Nick, I decline the call.

Our talk in the early morning hours resulted in a daylong awkward silence, broken only when he told me he'd texted Lia to drive him to visit his father. I've spent most of the day assuring myself this is normal, that everything will work out the way it's supposed to.

So far it's only sort of working.

"We should all try and get together for dinner or something." Denise picks up a glob of cheese and pops it into her mouth. "Provided there's actually *time* for a life this semester."

"Sure." It's a few steps back. We'll still go on dates. I pick up the slice on my plate and put it down again. "We're... I dunno. I guess kind of taking a break?"

Denise and Charlie's heads whip toward me in unison. Charlie recovers first and picks up the remote. The image of a much younger Tori Spelling freezes on the screen. She's in the middle of crying or yelling or something, so her face is all wonky.

Denise puts her plate on the coffee table and scoots across the couch. "Did you guys have a fight?"

It's not quite accurate, but it's the safest description I can think of. "Sort of." The pizza doesn't look the least bit appetizing anymore, so I set my plate next to Denise's. "And it's not a break*up*. We're still together."

My phone buzzes again, and I glance at the screen. I have no idea what Constantine could want with me. I decline the call, then turn my phone off. "We both realized we've moved awfully fast, so we're slowing down, taking a few steps back."

Denise chews on her lower lip, and Charlie says her name. At his low warning tone, she releases it with a guilty look in his direction. She shifts on the couch so she's facing me. "You're okay with this?"

I slump back into the cushions. "Yes? No? I'm the one who brought it up. We *do* need some space."

Before our talk, I figured Nick would spend most of his downtime at my—our—apartment, leaving me on my own for a night or two every couple of weeks. It's basically the opposite of what I told him I needed, and the realization I could be spending weeks on end alone in an apartment I can't actually afford is strangely painful.

Ever since Nick came along, the loneliness that's followed me around for years has disappeared. I'm not looking forward to experiencing it again.

But I think I need to.

I push my hair behind my ears and reach for my plate, determined to enjoy the rest of the evening. Charlie hasn't spoken a word, and Denise is watching me carefully. I force a smile. "It'll be fine. Like I said, a break, not a breakup. We're not going to stop talking or spending time together. He's got a project that's been eating up a lot of his time recently anyway, and he needs to focus on that and his family.

"He was there when I needed him," I say quietly. Nick sticking by my side through the aftermath of Turner's murder is more than I deserve. "We're not going to throw this away just because we've finally decided to be smart."

I point at the screen. "I'm a little afraid to find out what's going on. Judging by her face, it's either scary, sad, or she's just discovered that she really can't act and she has no idea how she'll get through the rest of this movie."

Denise snickers and picks up her plate, and Charlie restarts the movie. I glance at my phone and contemplate calling Constantine to see what he wants.

Nothing good, I figure. And I bite off the end of my slice.

Chapter 21

I've used this mug countless times. The silver's scratched in places, and the black lid doesn't always want to screw on properly on the first try, but it still works. Steam wafts over the rim, and if I dip my head a little, I can see the deep brown liquid.

It's the one familiar object in a sea of unfamiliarity. New clothes, new bag, hell, new kitchen.

Though I haven't had a chance to use it or my new bedroom. I won't until the security system's installed at my new apartment. We stayed at my parents' house last night, Nick in the guest room, me in my old room. I thought sleeping apart would be hard, but I was out the moment my head hit the pillow.

Nick darts his gaze from the lid lying next to the cup to my face. "I think that round thing is supposed to screw into the cylinder."

I stick my tongue out at him. "Funny." I pick up the lid and twist it into place. "You want some toast?" I point to two slices smothered in grape jam, a single bite taken out of the corner of one of them.

His crutches *thunk* on the linoleum floor as he rounds the counter. "No, because you're going to finish it."

My stomach cramps, and I suck in a breath. "I don't think so."

He leans the crutches against the counter and nudges the plate toward me. "You need to eat, Cass," he says quietly.

Needing is so far away from *able* in this instance, and I am nowhere near able to eat. "They'd call me," I whisper. "First day of the new term, Mom and Turner would call me. Mom always told me to learn." I smile despite the tears stinging the backs of my eyes. "Turner wouldn't say much. Usually a terse 'good luck' and a reminder to stick to a schedule so I could get my work done in a timely manner." The lump in my throat aches something fierce. "I don't think he approved of my choice of major. Or maybe he just didn't care." A tear sneaks past my defenses, slides down my cheek, and I dash it away. I fist my hands on the countertop and concentrate on my breathing, pushing away the rising need to fall apart. Nick winds an arm around my waist and turns me into him. I rest my head on his shoulder. "When does it stop hurting?"

He sighs and holds me tighter. "I don't think it ever will. I just think it fades into the background." He brushes his thumb across my cheekbone. "Are you sure you're ready to go back to class?"

"I don't have much of a choice." If I withdraw now, I risk having to drop out completely, forcing me to reapply to the college in order to finish my degree. While it's not the end of the world, it *is* a major inconvenience, and there's no guarantee there'd be room if I have to reapply.

I lift my head. "Come on. We need to leave now if I'm going to get to class on time." With Andreas in the hospital, his thoughts for increased protection for the two of us never became an actual plan. I'm driving Nick to the office, then re-parking the car near my apartment and walking to campus.

He gives the plate of toast a final pointed look. Sighing, I pick up the piece with the bite out of it and take another one. The sweetness of the jam triggers my gag reflex, and I swallow convulsively. I manage to get the bite down. "No more. Unless you want it, I'm dumping it."

"I'll eat it in the car." He tucks his crutches under his arms while I transfer the toast to a paper towel. We grab jackets and bags, and all too soon we're out the door, ready to start the day.

Nick's new phone rings the moment he's settled in the passenger seat. Balancing the toast on one leg, he growls at the phone before answering. "What?" he barks. I ease the car out into the street. "Fuck's sake, Con. We're on our way." The volume on Nick's phone is loud enough for me to hear his cousin's voice, though I can't make out any of the words. "I don't fucking know. A half hour?" I stifle a wince. I didn't bother calling Nick's cousin back last night because I didn't see the point. And other than the brief moment in the emergency room, I haven't brought up my renewed concerns about Constantine. Nick's a captive audience now. I might as well get it over with. I turn left and check the rearview.

"Fuck," Nick mutters. He picks up a piece of toast and crunches into it.

I scrape my teeth over my top lip. "So, um. I wanted to talk to you about something."

"Yeah?" The word comes out garbled, spoken around a mouthful of jam and crunchy bread, and I smile in spite of myself. Nick's maturity is usually miles above the college boys I've dated. But he still talks with his mouth full. Stupid, but it makes me love him more.

"Nice to see you smiling this morning," he says softly. "What did you want to talk to me about?"

The smile drops abruptly. "Constantine." I stop at a red light and check the rearview. Was that black SUV behind us a few blocks ago? Nick remains silent, and I sneak a quick look at his face. Closed off. Does some part of him suspect what I'm about to say? "I think he's behind the shootings." The light turns green, and I swing a quick right. No black SUV in the rearview.

Out of the corner of my eye, I see Nick pick up the toast. "Explain."

I can do this. I've done it before. But that was before Turner's murder and the attempts on Nick's life, and finding that blank, remote detachment is a struggle. I flex my hands on the wheel, speed up and pass another car, blow out a breath and draw in a new one.

For Nick to take this seriously, I have to start at the beginning. "You remember the list I gave you."

"The deals."

"The deals," I confirm. I dart my gaze from the road to the rearview. No black SUV, though the silver sedan looks familiar. Or maybe I'm being paranoid. "I said it then. It's enough to warrant a closer look. Revenge can be sparked by petty things, Nick. It doesn't take a lot to fuel the beast.

"When we returned from Thailand, we were so busy looking for Isaiah that Constantine wasn't even on my radar. And for the most part, he didn't do or say anything that stuck out at me. I might not have noticed it anyway." My fault. My fault for slapping on the blinders and lulling myself into that false sense of security. Isaiah was smart. Very smart, and we underestimated him. While he could have pulled off the firebombing of Nick's house and Scott's shooting without inside knowledge, having help would have made it far more efficient. Help that Constantine could have provided. Since those will be much harder to prove, I set them aside for now.

"My birthday. Who knew what your plans were?"

"No one."

A siren wails behind us, and I whip the car through a left turn, narrowly missing an approaching truck. "No one? It doesn't have to be literally. Did you tell anyone it was my birthday and you'd be celebrating with me? Anything like that?"

He hisses out a breath. "I did tell Con. We were at a critical stage in the app testing, and he needed to know I'd be harder to reach for the evening."

So his cousin may not have known *where* we were, but he did know Nick would be otherwise occupied. "Would Constantine have any reason to sabotage the app?"

Nick's response is to pick up the remainder of the toast and eat it slowly. I have to admit it's a stumbling block in my reasoning. A really big stumbling block. More like a barricade. Why would Constantine willfully and willingly demolish his own hard work?

"The add-on I told you about was his idea." It takes me a minute to remember what he's talking about—the add-on that would tell a person searching for a parking space when one just opened up. "When we were halfway through development, he came to me with an offer. Another company wanted to buy the existing code. We fought about it. We'd agreed during the initial development stage that we would launch the app ourselves in order to grow that side of the company. But he eventually backed down and agreed our original plan was the best course of action. Otherwise, no, I can't think of a reason for Con to work against us."

I chew on the inside of my cheek. It's the one piece that doesn't want to fit, no matter how hard I try. In the short time I've known him, Constantine's been fairly laid back when it comes to business. Except...

In the files I searched, Nick's cousin did protest—regularly—that there was no need for Nick to step in. "It's kind of out there, but what if... What if Constantine did it so he could, I dunno, swoop in and save the day? Demonstrate you're not the only one capable of bringing in the money?"

"Constantine has nothing to prove. He's closed deals before."

There's no mistaking the stubbornness in his voice, so I move on. "The day Mom and Turner were taken."

"He helped us find them, Cassidy."

"And after? He let Isaiah walk right out the front door. He could have gone after him, and he didn't."

"We needed help getting your mother out of the house." But I hear the first note of doubt, and I pounce on it.

"He found the house in Pasadena so we could keep an eye on Isaiah, and then Isaiah shows up in the backyard. Not only that, he sneaks in minutes after he gets off the phone with you? When he supposedly should have been at the office? And don't tell me he could have been in the car on his way there," I say, anticipating Nick's point. "It would have been ten times harder for him to have the sort of conversation the two of you were having if he was away from his computer."

Nick sighs. "Cass—"

"No. Let me finish. He's been weirdly insistent on knowing where you are. You can't tell me you don't suspect *something*. Otherwise we'd still be staying in his guest room. What if he found out about Rafe somehow? His father would know who he is, right?"

"You're bringing Uncle Anton into this?" he growls.

"I'm saying that just because your father didn't tell you about Rafe doesn't mean Anton felt the same. He may have told Constantine for his own reasons. And the shooting the other day? Constantine wasn't in his office. For all we know, he may not have been in the building. He had his phone off when he's been on your and everyone else's asses about the app launch for the last week. Something's not adding up, Nick."

I double park in front of Nick's office. "Whoever's behind this isn't waiting around. Two incidents in two days? I don't want it to be Constantine. But the longer it takes to figure it out, the bigger the risk to you," I whisper. "I can't lose you too."

His scowl softens. "You won't," he says. "Let me think about this. It might be Con. It might be someone else." He opens the door and gathers his crutches. "Don't be late for class."

My heart sinks, but I work up a smile for him. Stupid to believe I could convince him in one thirty-minute drive. "I'll see you this afternoon." In addition to my morning class, I have back-to-back afternoon classes. The plan is to come to his office and hang out for a few hours while he works.

"Don't worry about picking me up this afternoon. I'll call Dad's driver, have him chauffer me around." His grin is humorless. "It's what Dad would have done."

The extra time will allow me to do more unpacking, even though I won't be staying at my apartment until Nick has the security system installed. "Are you sure?"

He leans over and kisses me hard. "Go to class. Call me when you get home. Don't text."

Home. Not the apartment he rented for me, but my parents'. I wait until Nick's safely through the front doors, then drive to the apartment, taking a long, circuitous route. It leaves me with less time to get to class, and I walk as fast as I can through the streets to campus. After almost dribbling coffee down my chin despite the mug's covering, I opt to wait until I'm seated to take another sip.

Campus is already crowded with returning students, and the first hint of discomfort rises. I hear my name a few times, and I wave in the general direction of the sound. Unease creeps higher. So many people. A prime place to pick someone off. Hard to find the shooter in a crowd. Sweat breaks out along my hairline. I grip my travel mug so hard my knuckles ache.

My legs are weak. Breathing is difficult. Each step forward is like wading through rapidly setting concrete, and the unease morphs into panic. This doesn't make *sense*. I'm not the target. So why do I feel like there's a bull's-eye on my back?

"Cass?" Scott appears by my side, and I blink to clear my vision of the double Scotts. "You all right? You're kind of pale."

"I'm fine." I sway slightly, catching myself before I can stumble. "Actually, I'm not fine."

He takes my elbow and guides me off the walkway. We stop under a tree. "Maybe you should stay home today."

I drop my gaze to the ground. The grass is green and springy under my feet. Clean. Alive. I suck in a breath, then blow it out. "No. I can't miss the first day of classes. I just didn't expect it to be this hard." My phone rings in my bag, and I fumble it out, avoiding Scott's concerned eyes. The cracked screen displays Mom's number, and I almost drop the phone.

I stab at the accept button until it connects. "Mom?"

"Hi, dear." The words are hesitant, not nearly as strong as they've been the last few times we talked. "It's the first day of classes, isn't it?"

I sag against the tree. "Yeah. On my way to class now, actually."

"Well, that's good. It's good you're back in school. Your father would have wanted that." He would have? "Don't forget to learn." My lips wobble into a grin as I bite back a sob. There's a tremor in her voice when she continues. "I'll be home in a few weeks."

I swallow hard. "You should come over and see my new place. Stay for dinner."

"I'd like that. How's Nick?" she asks. She draws in a breath. "Does it matter that I'm still not sure I approve of him?"

I can practically *hear* the frown in her voice, and I snort out a laugh. "Not really." Scott shifts on his feet and glances over his shoulder. The walkway's less crowded, and I mouth *time?* at him. He pulls out his phone and holds it up so I can see the clock. "Mom, I have to go. I'm already late for my first class. I love you."

"I love you too, dear. I'll call you this afternoon, and you can tell me about your first day."

I hang up and stuff the phone into my bag. Scott jerks his head to the walkway, and when I take a shaky step forward, he slings his arm around my shoulders. Some of the panic recedes, and we join the flow of students heading toward the north side of campus.

He squeezes my shoulder. "Mom doesn't approve of the older boyfriend?"

"Some days. Others she doesn't seem to mind. You still seeing Tori?" We dodge a group of chattering girls standing in the middle of the sidewalk.

"Yeah. I'm meeting her for lunch if you want to join me."

"Sure. You guys should have dinner with me and Nick." We *will* get through this. We'll learn to trust each other again. I push the depressing thoughts aside. "That is, if you can handle Tori's fangirling over Nick." I shoot him a teasing grin, and he scowls, working his hand under my shoulder to my armpit. He digs his fingers in, and I dance away. "Hey! It's not my fault!"

He scowls harder. "I'm going to get you for that fangirl comment."

And as we hurry down the sidewalk, trading playful insults, the last of my panic drains away.

Chapter 22

"Which port does it go in?" I tug on the cable to get more play in the line.

"Any of the top three will be fine." There's amusement in his voice, and I glance over my shoulder. Nick's staring at my ass with a delighted grin on his face. When he notices my glare, his grin widens. "You didn't really expect me to not appreciate the view, did you?"

"I knew there was a reason you wanted me down here," I grumble. The giant U-shaped desk arrived shortly after Nick was dropped off this evening along with several boxes of computer equipment. When I took the apartment, I knew the second bedroom would be an office. I just figured it would remain empty for a while. My desk doesn't take up nearly as much space and fits nicely in the corner of the bedroom, so I didn't actually need the extra room.

"You do realize I may only be here for a couple months, right?" *You do realize you may never move in here, right?* I keep the question to myself because he *does* know. I have no plans to apply to graduate school at UCLA, and provided I actually complete my degree by the end of summer term, I don't know where I'll end up. I wiggle the end of the cable into place and back out, keeping my head down so I don't hit it on the desk.

"Doesn't matter if it's a couple of months or a couple of years. If I have this set up, I can work here or at the office. Probably end up working here while you're in class some of the time." He hands me the mouse. I stifle a sigh and crawl back under the desk to plug it in.

He leans forward and grabs the mouse as I shove it over the back edge of the desk. I'm conscious of his gaze locked on my ass, and the cable slips through my fingers. I fumble it into place. Heat sweeps through me. It's like his gaze is setting my skin on fire. "Seriously. You can stop staring any time now."

"When I do that, you'll know something's horribly wrong," he murmurs.

We finish plugging in the various computer parts without incident. The fans come on with a near-silent *whirrr*, and soon Nick's lost in the flow of data and programs and networks.

That's my cue to fix dinner.

Even though we're not living together, Nick said to order whatever groceries I wanted, whenever I wanted. I might hate the idea of him paying the majority of the rent on a space he won't get to use, but I have no qualms about taking food from him. It actually gave me an idea of how to work our way back to each other—standing dinner dates. One or two nights a week, he comes over for dinner.

In the meantime, I *may* have gone a little overboard with the groceries. Everything was delivered this afternoon, along with a new phone for me. If the zombie apocalypse were to happen, we'd have people breaking down our door to steal our provisions.

I opt for easy and tasty, and forty-five minutes later I set a bowl of sesame turkey and green beans next to Nick's elbow. He grunts in acknowledgement, and after a minute, I return to the living room and my own dinner.

Balancing a bowl full of ground turkey and rice while simultaneously reading a large, heavy textbook takes practice. Lots and lots of practice. Since I hate my desk and only use it when I need to write a paper, my balancing skills are pro-level. I read about obscure British authors while shoveling food into my mouth, then surprise myself by going back for seconds.

Not eating all day will do that to you, I guess.

I come up for air two long and boring chapters later. The apartment's silent. No clicking of keys from the office, no muttered curses. I check my phone; it's going on nine. He can't have been working all this time.

Is this what life with nick will be like? Quiet evenings with me on the couch, alone, and Nick chained to his computer?

Silly. It wouldn't be like that *all* the time. During certain phases of a project, sure. Or when the family business takes precedence. But it won't be silent and lonely. It can't be.

I pick up my bowl and carry it into the kitchen, rinse it out, and stick it in the dishwasher. I push up my sleeves and wash the cutting board and the knife. The rice pot still has bits of rice stuck to the bottom, so I fill it with water and set it back on the stove to soak.

Out of things to clean and unwilling to read ahead, I wander into the office. The bowl's empty. Nick's slouched in the chair, legs stretched out under the desk, and he's toggling back and forth between two of the three screens.

Needing to touch him, I loop my arms around his neck and rest my chin on top of his head. "What're you doing?"

The third screen flashes to life. "There's something off...." He clicks to the middle screen. "I went into the project server to do some cleanup work. Someone's been moving things around."

"And that's a problem?" I ask. He tips his head back, dislodging my chin, and his expression is properly chastising. "Okay. It's a problem. Is anything missing?" I follow the movement of the mouse and giggle when I see he has an actual mouse instead of an arrow. "Please tell me you can install that on my laptop."

"What? The mouse?" He lets it idle, and the mouse sits up and nibbles a piece of cheese.

"Yes, the mouse. Also, why do you have something so stupidly cute and adorable in your programming?"

He sends the mouse scampering up the screen, and I squeak loud enough Nick cringes away from me. What? *It's cute.* Stupidly cute, to be exact. Stupidly cute equals high-pitched annoying noises.

"Created it for Lia, originally. And next time you make that sound, please do it in another room where it won't hurt my eardrums as much."

"Oh, hush."

He right clicks, and the mouse becomes a boring arrow.

"Anyway. Are you missing anything?" I ask.

Text blurs as he scrolls down at hyper speed. "Not that I can see. So far," he amends. I'm surprised he can see anything given how fast the screen's moving. "Peter mentioned he would be doing a reorg and purge. Fuck knows it needs it. But he wouldn't be doing it now. He's got enough to handle." He takes his hand off the mouse, and the screen stops moving.

The screens blip. Nick leans forward. "It shouldn't be doing that, either," he mutters. He gropes behind one of the monitors, and the cord wiggles slightly. "In tight. Can you check the connections to the tower?"

He scoots the chair back, and I crawl under the desk. "Wiggle the cord again. I don't know which one it is." A cord off to the left shakes. I close my hand around it and follow it to the tower. "Plug's secure." We repeat the process for the other two monitors. Both are firmly plugged into their respective ports.

"Shit." He rolls the chair farther away from the center of the desk. "Connection's secure." I crawl out from under the desk and brush my hair away from my face. He's staring at the monitors like he's afraid if he looks away, he'll lose data.

And as we're both watching the monitors, they blip again.

He swears, and I scramble to my feet and out of the way, allowing Nick to attack his keyboard with vicious speed. "If this is a server issue, we're fucked."

A thought pops into my head, and my stomach cramps in response. "Nick?" He continues to mutter to himself, running searches and inputting commands. The screens blip, and blip again, and I put a hand on his shoulder. He snarls at me, and I jerk away. "Jesus. I have an idea, all right?"

The chair creaks as he sits back. "Sorry." He blows out a breath and scrubs his hands over his face. "What's your idea?"

He won't like it. He hasn't said anything about our discussion in the car. If Constantine really isn't behind all this chaos, I need more information. Someone else to pursue, a direction to go in. I wave a hand at the keyboard. "Can I...?"

At his nod, I hunch over the keys and type in a search request, hoping I spelled it correctly. If someone's actively deleting data while it's streaming, that might explain the blips we're seeing. While the search runs, I step aside and cross my arms over my chest, avoiding Nick's eyes.

The computer emits a soft *duhn-duhn* to indicate it's finished searching. Nick squints at the monitor. "Sager?"

I nod. "I think I spelled it right. I remember the first time I saw it I thought of that scientist, Sagan?" One side of his mouth quirks up in a reluctant smile. He nods, and I continue. "Anyway. Sager was on that list of deals I gave you. It's the only one I can remember off the top of my head, other than the Nautilus project. Do you still have the list somewhere?"

"At the office. In one of my desk drawers, I think." He sighs and pulls his phone from his pocket. "What does the missing Sager file have to do with your idea?"

I hug myself tighter. "What if Constantine's the one who deleted it? Just now."

He shrugs. "Sager ended up not being worth the money we would have spent, so it's kind of a moot point if the information's gone from the server."

Is he being dense on purpose? Or am I just not explaining myself well? "That's not why I brought it up, Nick. The folder on Sager held everything having to do with the deal. The contract drafts, negotiation points, the offer, the counter offer. And all the correspondence relating to the deal. *All* of it."

When I was searching through the files, the correspondence was what I paid the most attention to. There were some heated e-mails exchanged between the cousins. A few were downright nasty. For as close as they are, Constantine and Nick didn't hesitate to throw down when it came to their shared business holdings.

Makes me wonder if it's the same with family business.

"Those e-mails and memos are the closest thing to evidence there is. If Constantine is the one deleting it, it's all the more damning." Nick's expression is coated in an inches-thick layer of ice. God, I want to slink into a corner. "Am I paranoid? Maybe. Am I accusing your cousin for no reason? Possibly. Give me someone else," I whisper. "Give me another suspect. Please." I will do *anything* to get Nick to stop looking at me like that. Anything except the one thing guaranteed to tear down this wall rising between us.

I can't ignore my suspicions about Constantine any longer.

I swallow around the sudden lump in my throat. "How do you delete files off the server? Can anyone do it?"

"Anyone with access. Remote access will leave the files cached, though." He's so distant. He might as well be on the other side of the world from me. "To truly delete the files, you have to access the server directly."

I take a step toward him, flinching when he arches a brow. Does he know how much this hurts? I've told him. I *know* I have. He knows Constantine is my least favorite choice. "Who has direct access to the server? Everyone?"

"Not the server room. It's pass coded, and the terminals on each server have several passwords that are changed weekly. There's an activity log, again password protected. Con, Peter, and I have access to the server, as well as a few other key employees. Cory's assistant has been given access for the duration of the app launch with the understanding it will be revoked once the project is finished."

Okay. A list. We'll make a list, like we did with Isaiah. "Who has access to the activity log?"

"Me, Peter, and Con." His other brow shoots up, challenging me to bad mouth Constantine.

But I'm not taking that bait. I lower my arms. "We should get moving then." Any further delay could result in more deleted files, and I *need* those files. Hard copies, yes, but digital ones, and their timestamps. If I can't get my hands on a smoking gun, so to speak, I'll take that information to someone who may listen to my far-out theory.

Who that person would be, I don't know.

Nick lifts his phone.

"Wait. Who are you calling?" *Please let it be Peter. Or his sister. Or his mother.*

"Con. To ask him to meet us at the office. This is his business too, Cassidy. If there's something wrong with the server, this affects him as well."

I want to pry the phone from his hands. I link my fingers together to keep from doing that. "Would you humor me for a little while? Just until we get to the server and check the activity log."

From the way he stares me down, I'm certain he's not going to do as I ask. I'm prepared to beg when he lowers his phone. "Get your coat."

Legs weak with relief, I shuffle out of the office and through the depressingly bare living room. I snag my jacket, the hanger falling to the floor in my haste. I grab Nick's and pass it to him after he props his crutches against the wall.

The car ride is painful. Every topic of potential conversation I think of sounds trite or otherwise unimportant. I don't *want* to talk about anything important, though. Not with Nick doing his best impression of a snowman in the passenger seat.

But even the unimportant feels important right now. As though this next conversation could change the dynamic between us, and I can't afford to screw up.

I don't know how to get him to understand that I wouldn't accuse Constantine of murder on a whim. If Nick came to me and said he thought Denise was trying to kill me, I'd laugh in his face. I'd keep laughing and insist he's delusional as he calmly lays out his suspicions and what he says is evidence. Because there's no way in hell my best friend would want me dead.

"Is that it?" I ask suddenly. "Is this whole thing like you telling me Denise is trying to kill me?" I double park in front of the office and turn to Nick.

His brows draw together, his expression dark despite the streetlight shining down. "What the fuck are you talking about?"

I ignore the car horns behind us. "I'm trying to figure out why my suspicions about Constantine piss you off so much. You don't believe me. You also know him a lot better than I do. The closest I can get is Denise. I wouldn't believe *you* if you said she's the one shooting at us. I've known her for years. She's my best friend. Closer than that."

Another blast from a car horn, and I flinch. Nick doesn't move to get out of the car, though. He studies me for so long we both flinch at the next car horn. "Yeah," he says. "That's close."

He gathers up his crutches and gets out of the car. Bending down, he sticks his head inside. "That's close enough, Cass." He shuts the door and makes his way across the sidewalk to the front door of the building.

I have no idea what to do with this new understanding.

Chapter 23

I've never noticed how loud the eighth floor is until I'm standing outside the elevator, listening for extraneous noise. Since a good portion of the floor is taken up by the servers, it's cool, bordering on cold, and there's a constant hum, like hundreds of refrigerators running. No voices as I approach the cracked-open door to the server room, though. It took longer than I expected to find a parking spot on the street. Nick's been up here on his own for a good twenty minutes. He should be talking to himself, or swearing, or…or…*something* to let me know he's here.

Apparently, paranoia makes me selfish.

Cold air washes over me as I step inside. Nick's standing in front of the server terminal, crutches propping him up and a frown marring his face. The frown spurs a cautious hope. Will he take me seriously now? I shut the door behind me and walk over, my footsteps muffled by the humming. "What's up?"

"Someone's fucking with us." He pokes a few keys, and his frown deepens.

I peer around him at the monitor. Names and timestamps are laid it out in neat rows. "Why do you think that?"

He points to the most recent entry. "Cory supposedly accessed the server from the terminal about an hour ago."

The temperature in the room plunges from cold to freezing. "Cory's dead."

"Exactly."

I shiver once and resist the urge to rub my hands up and down my arms. "Wasn't Cory's access deactivated after he died?"

Nick shakes his head. "It was easier to allow Loren to continue using Cory's password than set up an entirely new set of permissions." Loren must be Cory's assistant. Nick's fingers race over the keyboard, and the activity log disappears. "The first step is to enter your individual password. If it's recognized, it'll take to you the next screen where you enter the first of the rotating passwords. There are four in all."

"Anyone who knew Cory's password *and* the terminal passwords could have gotten in." I lower my arms and tuck my hands into my pockets. "Do you think it was Loren?"

"No," he murmurs. "Loren's been out of town the last two days. Family emergency."

Constantine wouldn't be happy about that. I add it to my mental list. "Why would someone want you to think Cory was the one accessing the server?"

Another fan kicks on somewhere in the room, and I shiver again. Nick adjusts his crutches and returns his attention to the keyboard. "Someone wanting to play a joke?"

"A sick one," I mutter. *Wrong* doesn't even begin to cover it.

"Most likely it's to cover his tracks. The activity log isn't un-hackable, but neither Peter, Con, or I have the permissions to edit or alter it."

I shut my eyes. It's there in his tone; he still doesn't want to believe his cousin could be behind all this. I might as well beat my head against a brick wall. I'd probably get further. "Who has access to the server?"

He starts rattling off names, and I hold up a hand to stop him. "Hold on." I don't have anything to write with—or on—but I take out my phone. It's newer than my old one, and it's got so many fucking apps it takes me a few seconds to figure out where the notepad one is. By the time I've got it open, Nick's struggling not to smile. "Shut up."

"Wasn't saying anything." He gives in, and the smile spreads across his face.

"No, but you were thinking it. Rather loudly too. First name?"

"Terry Schneider." He lists three other employees in addition to him, Constantine, Cory, and Peter.

"Any of them have a connection to the Sager deal?" I slip the phone back into my pocket. Several fans click off, the noise level in the room decreasing significantly, which makes it really easy to hear the footsteps in the hall. I tense and press my back against the server. The footsteps grow louder, and I scan what I can see of the room, ready to bolt. Best cover is to round the server, then skirt the edge of the room to get to the exit.

Nick shoots me a look that says I'm being ridiculous, and I glare at him. We've been shot at twice in the last couple days. His father's in the hospital because of it. I will be on edge and on guard until whoever is fucking with us is either dead or behind bars.

It's kind of shocking to realize I'd prefer dead. Dead people can't escape from prison or bribe police into dropping charges.

The beeping from the door lock is fainter than the footsteps were, but I can still hear it. The lock releases, and the door swings open. Because the server we're next to is off to the right of the entrance, whoever just entered isn't visible.

We don't have to wait long. Constantine stops at the end of the aisle, both eyebrows shooting to his hairline. "Hey. Something wrong with the server?"

"Files moved around, a few of them were deleted. Nothing important."

I clench my jaw at Nick's casual explanation. They damn well are important. If the other missing files are the ones on that list, I'm left with nothing but Constantine's odd behavior. Even I have to admit it's not enough.

Nick jerks a thumb at the monitor. "I know Peter mentioned wanting to clean it up. Did you assign that to Loren?"

Constantine frowns. "No. Why?"

"Cory's password was used to log into the server."

Either Constantine's an Oscar-worthy actor, or he's genuinely shocked by the statement. I watch him closely. Deep frown lines, lips parted, a flash of hurt in his eyes. Did he like Cory? Was that a move Isaiah made that Constantine didn't approve of?

He recovers and waves a hand at the terminal. "Can I...?" Nick hops aside, and I fold my arms over my chest, looking at Constantine rather than the screen.

He's good. He is *good*. So good doubts trickle in. His expression grows harder and harder as he scrolls through the log. It could be someone else. Peter. Or maybe there was someone in Isaiah's crew we missed.

"Loren has no reason to go in and delete files. As far as I know, he wasn't around when Peter brought it up." There's a soft *crack* as he slides the keyboard into its slot. "What's missing?"

Nick swings around Constantine and heads for the door. "Not sure. That server became disorganized to the point I don't remember everything that was on it. Regardless, whoever was in here deleting the files is gone."

"Ought to run a virus check on all the servers. Just to be safe." Constantine passes Nick and holds the door open for him to get through. I trail after the two of them, uncertain what my role is. Constantine does have a point. After the earlier virus scare, they can't afford to slack off now.

"Good idea." Nick's voice floats through the door, and I hear his crutches *thunk*ing in the hallway.

I stifle a sigh. Guess I know where I'm spending the night.

* * * *

"You all right?" Denise pauses with her hands half in the box. The bookshelf behind her is only a quarter full. By the time all the boxes are unpacked, I suspect it will still have plenty of room. After all, Nick doesn't have anything to put on them.

I twist my head back and forth, and a small whimper escapes. "Yeah. Slept wrong." The couch in Nick's office isn't nearly as comfortable as it looks. I woke up with a stiff neck, and my mood's been shitty as a result.

That's not entirely true. Nick's continued refusal to agree that we should be taking a closer look at Constantine's actions has driven a wedge between us, and it's getting bigger and harder the longer we don't talk about it.

Neese returns her attention to the box. "Where's Nick staying?"

"He's at his parents' house for the time being." The security system Nick ordered for the apartment was installed the same day his computer equipment arrived. Once it was in place, there was no need for us to remain at my parents'. The adjustment to living alone has been…interesting.

She huffs out a breath and sets a stack of books on the shelf. "What's all the computer stuff in the other room for?"

"It's Nick's." I shouldn't have let Nick help me put away the groceries. I can't find half the stuff I swear I ordered. I empty the cupboard onto the counter below. "He's using it like a second office."

She arches her back. "Ow." She stands and stretches her arms over her head, then wanders to the kitchen. "Weird. And he's not living here?"

"No." The cereal is supposed to all go together. Simple logic. I line up the boxes by height, ignoring her snickers.

She *has* accused me in the past of being anal retentive about the kitchen.

But her question pokes at me, and as I continue to put the food back in the cabinet in the proper order, it gets louder and louder until I have to address it in order to get it to shut up. "He might move in eventually. I don't know. Before my dad died, we were talking about it like it was a given."

She opens the cupboard above her head, rummages through it, and pulls out random items. A bag of flour. A tiny bottle of vanilla. A bottle of red wine I don't remember ordering. "Do you think this break might end up being permanent?" she asks.

I motion for her to switch places with me, and she flips me off before stepping away from the counter. "I don't really know. When it first came up, I figured that's all it would be. A step back." The heightened tension between us coupled with our mutually agreed upon desire to slow down has brought all my doubts rushing to the forefront. "Now… I have no idea where I'll be once I graduate. I don't even know how much longer I'll be at UCLA. Can I finish up during summer term? Or am I going to have to finish next fall? It's not like Nick can just pick up and move, either. His businesses are here, along with his family." Despite everything that's happened over the last couple of months, I doubt Nick's considered leaving the family business behind. And I can't ask him to. He's comfortable with his role, and I think he *wants* to take over for his father someday.

"I take it you haven't spoken with him about any of this."

"No," I admit. In my defense, we've been trying to stay alive. Discussing the future of our relationship isn't a priority. "There hasn't been a good time. He's got a project launching soon, and there's some family problems he's been dealing with too."

Denise holds up a hand. "Whoa. Family problems? Is he okay?"

"I think so." A bald-faced lie. He's nowhere near dealing with the issues plaguing his family. "Anyway, I thought maybe we could, you know, let things settle a bit before we break open the huge relationship discussion that we kinda sorta shoulda had a while ago." I shut the cabinet as my stomach rumbles. "You hungry?"

She grins. "I spotted an Indian place a block away. Feeling adventurous?"

The last time we ate at an unknown Indian restaurant, we both ended up with food poisoning. "Um…"

She grabs my wrist and pulls me to the door. "No 'ums.' We're trying it."

Fifteen minutes later, we're seated at a small table with plastic-covered menus in front of us. The place doesn't *look* sketchy. "Hole in the wall" would be a more appropriate description. The room is narrow, barely wide enough for the two-seater tables and an aisle. A long counter wraps around the open kitchen. From where I'm sitting, I have a clear view of the chef, and it's kind of fascinating to watch him work. Flames leap from the burners. He moves with the grace and precision of a dancer, from counter to stove and back again. There are several skillets and pots on the burners, and he somehow manages to keep them all in check without looking frazzled.

"I think this may be my new favorite place," Denise declares.

"You haven't tried the food yet."

"Don't need to. That dude is awesome." She jerks her head toward the chef.

We turn our attention to the menus, and a server stops at our table to take our orders. Once he's gone, she leans her elbows on the table and studies me. "Are you sure you're all right? Because you don't look like it."

I swallow a sigh. Denise in full-on worry mode is like playing tug-of-war with a particularly stubborn dog. She won't drop it until she's satisfied. I should have recognized the signs. "It's an adjustment," I admit. "I didn't count on it being as hard as it's been." The time I spent living with Nick was mostly out of necessity. That didn't make it difficult. When I wasn't driving myself nuts wondering if he was only doing it to ensure my safety, I liked it.

The first night sleeping apart from him, with him in the guest room of my parents' house and me in my old room, ended up being an anomaly. My brain doesn't care that the new security system will alert me to any intruders within seconds of a breached entry point. It knows Nick isn't beside me. "I keep waking up in the middle of the night, expecting him to be there, and when I remember he's not, it takes a while to fall asleep again."

She opens her mouth and closes it again as the server deposits the *naan* in the middle of the table. "Are you having second thoughts?"

"No." Though if it turns out I'm wrong about Constantine, and Nick can't forgive me for questioning his motives, I'll have to move out of the apartment. He shouldn't have to pay for something when he no longer has any connection with me. "And if it ends, it ends."

"You know, that's the second time you've said something like that." She rips the paper off her straw and pokes it into her soda.

"Like what?"

"Like you're already thinking it's over."

I glance up at the server as he sets our food down. "It's not intentional." I don't want to lose Nick. I want to believe this break is just that—a break, a way for us to backtrack and build a stronger foundation.

Breaks have a sneaky way of making themselves permanent, though. I pick up my fork. "We'll work it out."

If we don't, I'll just have to find a way to survive.

Chapter 24

Several hours later, I let myself into my dark apartment. The dark is expected, as is the disappointment slinking in as I shut the door. And as I stand there, the loneliness slips in and makes itself comfortable.

I toss my keys on the kitchen counter, flip the deadbolt closed, and wander over to the couch. A sense of déjà vu washes over me as I flop down and tip my head back, shutting my eyes. I've done this before. Days blended together as I killed or stalked my next target, unaware of how close I was to the edge. I came home to a dark, empty apartment, worn out, ready but not ready to give in. I crawled into bed alone.

The difference is when I went to bed, I knew I wouldn't stay alone for long.

I rouse myself and track down my phone. Then I hesitate, thumbs hovering over the screen. Something that gets the point across, yet isn't clingy. I hate clingy. I refuse to be the clingy girlfriend. *Made it home. Let me know when you're at your parents'.* I send the text before I can talk myself out of it. It's a reasonable request. He wants to know when I get home; I should be able to ask the same of him. It'll keep me from worrying.

It's early still, about eight, but the few hours of sleep I got last night were restless. And while today wasn't particularly strenuous, I spent too much of it inside my own head. I don't know if I'll be able to sleep, but right now, it sounds better than being awake.

I drag out my bedtime routine, though, take my time washing my face and brushing my teeth. I spend far longer than necessary debating whether to put on my usual tank top or sleep naked. I double-check my schedule for tomorrow, then waste ten minutes on Facebook and YouTube, watching a video of a baby panda crawl around when it's supposed to be napping.

No answer from Nick.

Time drips down until it's 8:30, and I'm out of excuses. Either I'm up and studying or I'm in bed attempting to sleep. I grab my e-reader and trudge off to bed. Compromise. I need to get started on *Howard's End*. I might as well do it in bed.

One of my favorite parts about being an English major is the surprises. The amount of reading I do each term can be overwhelming, and by the end, I swear I'm never picking up another book. But every semester, I manage to find myself enjoying at least one of the assigned readings, and *Howard's End* proves to be just what I need for the night. The story of the Wilcoxes and the Schlegels is engrossing, and it's almost eleven when I get up for a glass of water.

I hurry out into the living room and snatch up my phone. Nick texted back an hour ago. An *hour* ago. *Two* hours after I texted him to begin with. His answer is brief and less than satisfying. He's still at the office and probably won't make it home.

My stomach twists and cramps, and I continue to the kitchen for my water. I doubt he's alone at the office. If he's been working since last night, that means Peter and the rest of the team are with him, along with Constantine. He's not completely alone, and something tells me Constantine won't do anything with the rest of the team around.

I refill the glass and carry it with me into the bedroom. The rumpled blankets and the single light burning on my bedside table look lonely. Strange how a few months of living with Nick can have such a huge impact.

I turn out the light and lay in the dark, familiarizing myself with the shadows and sounds. With the windows closed, the street noise is muffled, but I can still hear an approaching car from the end of the block. Someone walks by the door. The building creaks and settles, and there's a shout of laughter from the street below.

I dream in fragments. Denise and I grinning like idiots on the giant Ferris wheel on the Thames. Scott chasing me through campus, like he did on the first day of classes. Nick, his arms around my waist, threatening to throw me into the brilliant turquoise water of Phuket.

Cinnamon drifts under my nose, and I roll over, groping blindly for the source. Hands curl around mine, stilling them, and I scoot closer. I don't want to open my eyes. I don't want to find out I've been dreaming Nick into this bed.

"Cassidy."

On a moan, I slit my eyes open. Broad, hard chest, stubbled jaw. I do my best to lunge toward him and bury my face at his throat. "You're not supposed to be here," I mumble.

He smooths a hand down my back. "I know."

"Don't go." It's a step in the wrong direction, but we're allowed a few missteps, aren't we?

"Not going anywhere tonight," he says. "Why are you wearing clothes?"

"Didn't realize we had a rule about clothing in bed." He smells so *good*. Feels amazing. "'Sides, what does it matter? You need sleep. I need sleep. Early class tomorrow, and I really need to get a run in." The reminder draws a groan from me. I'll have to get up earlier to fit that in before class. Which means resetting my alarm. Which means letting go of Nick.

I pull away reluctantly and feel around for my phone. After adjusting my wake-up time, I roll back to Nick. "You get everything done?"

"Retested all the servers for viruses. Nothing. Since the file deletion isn't relevant to our current project, we've put it aside to handle after the launch."

I stiffen, and his hand pauses in the middle of my back. The rest of the files could be gone by then. With the entire team called in, I wasn't as concerned about deletion—they'd be otherwise occupied. I understand the decision to focus on them later too. But someone's already deleted at least a couple of them, and on the heels of the shootings. Any normal person would be suspicious.

"Cass."

I can't talk about this with him. Not now. "Go to sleep, Nick." I pull out of his arms, and though it hurts, I roll over, putting my back to him. "We can talk about it in the morning," I say quietly. Or never. Never works. If he won't believe me, I'll figure it out on my own.

I just hope I can put it all together before Nick's taken from me permanently.

For the first night in a long time, he doesn't make an attempt to hold me. I've become used to the heat of him behind me, or the warmth of his chest under my cheek. Facing away from him, I listen to the sounds of him settling in for the night. Because of his injury, he's taken to sleeping on his back. He tugs the covers up. They end up covering the lower half of my face, and I bat them away. His legs brush mine. He sighs. "You're being a brat."

"How is trying to sleep being a brat?" To prove how un-bratlike I am, I turn around.

"Fine." He drags me across the half a foot separating us. "You're mad."

Might as well admit it. "Yup. I'm also smart enough to realize that we won't end this standoff tonight. You need a big, glaring declaration of intent. You want irrefutable proof that your cousin wants you dead. I can give you the pieces. I can relay snippets of conversation I've overheard or point out his odd behavior. But I can't give you that. I think Constantine wants you dead. You can't, or won't, see it. I get it. The horse is dead. We should stop beating it." I tip my head back and press a kiss to his jaw. "You probably haven't slept much in the last two days. Go to sleep, Nick. You want to talk about this tomorrow, we can."

He's like a fucking security blanket. My head on his shoulder and his arm holding me close, I fall asleep immediately. I sleep deeply, soundly, and when my alarm goes off the next morning, I don't shut it off and curl back up for more sleep.

Nick doesn't wake. Heat creeps over my face as I study him. It always hits me when I least expect it—*how* is this man in my bed? He's mine, for however long I want him. I know this much. I kiss him softly and slide out of bed, careful not to wake him.

I'm not the only one with the idea of a run before class. I make turns at random as I pass a couple of other students, spotting someone I remember from my American Playwrights seminar last year. She waves, and we keep going in our respective directions.

My tour of the neighborhood uncovers two coffee shops, a convenience store, a yoga studio, plus half a dozen restaurants. Two delis, a pizza place, a bakery-cafe, a Mexican restaurant, and the Indian place Denise dragged me to. The streets are lined with cars, not an inch of space between the bumpers. A few boast parking tickets, and one has a giant pink checkmark on the windshield. I grin. Someone's about to get towed.

The apartment is empty when I let myself in sweaty and a little out of breath. There's a bright orange sticky note on the fridge, and my heart squishes a little as I read it.

Come by the office when you're done with class. You can download the remaining files.

Nothing makes my heart go pitter-patter like Nick's faith in me. It's not a total acquiescence, but it's enough to spark a flicker of hope. I'll take that flicker. Flickers can become flames. This one will. I just need to be patient.

Determined to hang on to my good mood, I take my time getting ready and end up running out the door, in danger of being late. I hit campus with ten minutes to walk to the north end for my first class. Head down, fingers clutching the strap of my messenger bag, I run smack into a hard chest.

Hands close around my upper arms before I can jerk away and mumble an apology. "Thanks for making this easier, Cassidy."

I snap my head up. "What are you doing here?" *Why* is he here? He should be at the office with Nick, pretending he's not plotting to kill him.

Constantine smiles. That previously charming expression makes my skin itch. "I came to get you." His tone is pleasant. The gleam in his eyes is not.

Some passing students give us curious looks, and I try to free myself without drawing any more attention. I back into another hard chest, and I glance over my shoulder at a man I've never seen before. He's built like a brawler, sunglasses hiding his eyes and a short, trim beard covering the lower half of his face. I yank hard on my arm.

"You don't want to do that." Constantine tightens his grip and pulls me closer, slipping his arm around my shoulders and his free hand going to my waist. A pinprick of pain surprises a gasp from me, and I glance down. I can't see anything, but as I move my hips, I feel it again. A knife? The bastard's got a knife on me?

"Unless you want to add to your collection of scars, you should stop." He digs the tip of the knife in farther. Warmth trickles over my skin.

"Oops. I did suggest you stop moving. Come on. We'll be late."

Conscious of the other man's steps behind us, I stumble alongside him, the trickle steadily spreading over my hip. "Could you move the knife? I'm bleeding."

"That's kind of the whole point." He guides me down a path leading to Sorority Row. The sun shines in my eyes as we break free of the trees covering the walkway and causes me to veer into Constantine, the knife stabbing into my side. A whimper escapes, and he actually adjusts the knife, the pain lessening. It's still poking me in the hip, but not as deeply, and I think—*I think*—I may have a shot at disarming him. We're exiting close to Sorority Row, which means there should be people out. In theory, anyway. People equals possibility of distraction, and that's all I need to get away from Constantine.

We reach the street, and the moment a bus rumbles past, I grab Constantine's wrist and jam my elbow into his stomach. As far as defensive maneuvers are concerned, it's not the greatest, but he's got me pressed so close to him it's the only one I have.

He grunts and digs his fingers into my shoulder. "Dumb move," he hisses.

I slide my hand up his forearm and drill my fingers into the meaty underside, hoping he'll drop the knife. It clatters to the ground. I drop into a crouch, Constantine following me down because he *won't let go.*

His hand is firmly attached to my shoulder, and he's hugging me into him. "Cooperate, Cass," he growls. "You know you're safe."

No, I don't know that. I *know* I'm not his intended target. I'm a means to an end, and I will not be that means. We both dive for the knife. I scrape my knuckles on the pavement when Constantine yanks me up. The fucker actually lifts me off my feet, his progress hindered by my bag, and I kick out, wiggling around, not caring if I draw attention to us.

Click.

Lips brush my ear, my skin flushing hot, then cold. "Now will you stop moving?"

His silent companion has a gun trained on my head, heedless of the danger of being seen. "From this distance, he won't miss," Constantine murmurs. And he's right. Headshots are easy to screw up, but there's less than three feet separating me from the man holding the gun. The likelihood of him missing is slim.

Constantine's arms tighten around my waist, causing the edge of my bag to cut into my lower back. "Get in the car."

Eyes on the gun, I do as he says and get into the black SUV parked at the curb. He climbs in beside me, takes the gun from the bearded guy, and shuts the door. "You couldn't have come up with something more original?" I ask, jolting forward as the car pulls away from the curb.

He shrugs. "Why would I when this is basically fail-proof? Nick will come running to save you. Isaiah was good for a lot of things, but failing to kill you was an unexpected bonus."

Unfortunately, he's right. Nick's proven multiple times he's downright obsessive about my safety. Constantine will call; Nick will come running. If I don't come up with a plan, we'll both end up dead.

The leather seats make it easy to slide away, and I press my back into the opposite corner. Constantine left my hands free. He probably assumes with a gun pointed at my head, I won't attempt opening the door. And I won't. The move's too obvious, and if I don't end up with a bullet in the head, I'll still end up injured. But Constantine didn't take away my bag, and he has yet to insist I keep my hands where he can see them. My phone's in the side pocket of my bag. Nick's number is the only one I've programmed into speed dial. I can't tell him not to come. I *can* tell him to come armed.

The gun hasn't wavered, and neither has Constantine's gaze. I inch my hand into the side pocket and draw the phone out, letting it fall onto the seat beside me. "Where are you taking me?" The position of my bag does a good job of hiding the phone from Constantine's view. Rather than try to slide it clear, I leave it where it is.

"The warehouse you holed up in a week ago. Didn't know Nick had that place." He glances at my hip as I try to unlock the screen without looking down. He frowns. "What do you think you're doing?"

I hit speed dial as Constantine lunges for the phone. As Nick's voice plays through the speaker, Constantine brings the gun around, and I shoot my hand up to stop him from smashing it into the side of my face. "Nick! The warehouse!" I throw myself forward, aiming for Constantine's chest.

The gun goes off.

Chapter 25

The world stops. Constantine's eyes are locked on mine, fury marring his handsome face. The shot might as well have been a cannon blast. And he's got a firm grip on the gun. We're caught in a game of chicken, and whoever blinks first is the one who dies.

Focus, Cass. Go with your gut.

Turner's voice drowns out everything else, nudging me into the cool, empty efficiency I've been so desperate for these last few days. The gun's pointed at the ceiling, my hand on Constantine's wrist. He hasn't moved since it went off. My bag's hanging around my shoulders. There's not a lot of room to work with in the backseat of the SUV, but if I can get enough momentum, I can smack him with my bag.

Unfortunately, if I miss, he'll shoot me. Which means I can't miss.

Without breaking eye contact, I grab the bag and swing it around. The bag makes a loud *smack* as it connects with Constantine's arm. I ram my elbow into Constantine's nose and go for the gun, twisting around on the seat so my back is to his chest. The car swerves, throwing us both against the front seats.

Focus. I can't use this. Constantine's arms are longer than mine, so in order to actually touch the gun, I have to lean forward. I'm safer with no space between Constantine and me.

The strap of my bag bites into my neck. Constantine yanks it hard, pressing on my windpipe. Shadows form and crawl in from the edges of my vision, and I can barely hear his labored breathing in my ear. "Stop. Fucking. Moving," he rasps. The strap's too tight. Ducking my head won't shift it off my neck. I fight off a wave of dizziness and suck in a breath. I wish my nails were longer. They won't do a lot of damage, but fuck, I have to try.

I rip my nails down the inside of his forearm and drive both elbows into his chest. He lets me go with a surprised *whumph.* I pull the bag off and go for the hand still holding the gun. Another shot rings out, the bullet narrowly missing my foot.

A burst of rage surging through me threatens to shove me off balance, both physically and mentally, and I take a few seconds I don't have to shut my eyes and breathe. He will not win. I won't let him.

Constantine's curled over me, chest flush against my back, blood from his broken nose dripping onto my cheek. I have one hand hanging on to his wrist, the other tucked in against my stomach to keep him from grabbing it. If I can elbow him in the ribs a second time, I might be able to reach his balls.

No one ever said I had to fight fair.

He'll be expecting the elbow, though. I've already hit him twice. He won't let me connect a third time. Second best option—snap my head back and hope I hit his nose. The risk of a headache is worth it.

The car swerves again, and I crash my head into his face as we smack into the back of the seat. His left arm loosens enough I can snake my hand between my ass and his groin. From the way he's sitting, though, all I get is a small handful of loose fabric.

He chuckles. "Nice try, *love.*"

Fighting desperation, I twist around and thrust my knee toward his crotch, missing when he wraps his arms around me in a hug. My arms are trapped against his chest, hands inches away from his throat. Blood coats his upper lip, congealing around the nostrils. The beginnings of a bruise shadow the inside corner of his left eye, the earlier fury replaced by cold amusement.

"Don't worry," he says. "You'll live to see Dom one last time."

I curl my fingers into claws and grip the front of his shirt. "Thanks. I think." I drop my head to the crook of his neck, adrenaline pumping hard and fast. If I can get the gun from him, there's still a chance I can overwhelm Constantine before we get to the warehouse.

As close as we are, though, he'll feel any move I make. I have one option left, and if it doesn't work, it's sure to piss him off to the point where he may decide to kill me now.

"It's nothing personal, Cass." His arms are iron bands.

Nothing personal. Why is there nothing personal in this business? "Sure as fuck feels like it," I mutter.

"Not my fault you keep getting in the way."

What was it Nick told me? Loose ends don't get tied up; they get snipped. "Am I a loose end?"

"If that's the way you want to think of it." We round a corner, slower than the last couple we took. "Almost there."

I picture the streets surrounding the warehouse like a grid. Plenty of cover, and it'll be busier during the day. I turn my head and rub the tip of my nose up the line of his neck, clenching my teeth against the urge to gag.

"What do you think you're doing?" he murmurs. He doesn't let go, doesn't relax his hold, but I didn't expect him to. "You can't seduce your way out of this."

I have no problems robbing cradles.

Motherfucker.

My gag reflex kicks in full force when I place my lips on his skin. A growl sounds low in his throat. A warning. I have a few seconds. Less than. Opening my mouth, I bite as hard as I can, breaking the skin.

He curses and jerks his head away, his arms relaxing slightly. Planting my hands on his chest, I push back, ram the heel of my palm into his jaw, and free my other arm enough I can reach up and grab his hair. I slam his head into the window. The gun fires. This time, though, the SUV speeds up, the driver cursing long and loud. I slam Constantine's head into the glass once more and throw myself backward. Constantine drops the gun on the floor. I dive for it right as the car lurches to a stop.

Pain races up my neck as I'm thrown into the back of the driver's seat. I ignore it and close my hand around the gun. Weakness sneaks down my other arm, spreading from the pain in my neck. Something to worry about later. Preferably when I'm not trapped in a car with a man who wants to kill me.

The gun shakes as I point it at Constantine. To be expected, I guess, since I spent most of the car ride fighting. "Why," I pant, "can't your family leave me *alone*?" I flick the safety off. The grip is bulky and awkward, and my finger slips off the trigger. "Do you have something against talking through your problems?"

He groans softly. "I could talk myself to death, Cass. It won't do any good." Wincing, he sits up and slits open an eye. "Get out of the car. Now."

Click. I guess the last gunshot didn't do much damage because the driver's pulled a gun on me. Turning my head to the left hurts. My neck's growing stiff, limiting my range of motion. Before I can shift and shoot the driver, he presses the barrel to my temple.

Constantine pries the gun from my hand. "Out of the car. Dom should be here soon."

We make an odd and stumbly group of people. Thanks to being slammed around in the car, I hurt in weird places. Constantine's mouth is covered in drying blood, and the driver has a dark stain running down his lower back. From the placement, it looks as though the shot may have gotten him in the kidney. The bullet must have gone through the seat. He'll collapse if he doesn't get medical attention soon.

Several cars are parked along the narrow street in front of the warehouse. A few men are leaning against them and the wall near the door to the building. No visible weapons. No sign of Nick, either. I hope he doesn't come. He will, but until he shows, I'll hope he won't.

The number of people waiting for our arrival surprises me. If this is indicative of how the organization as a whole feels about Nick, he's screwed, whether he lives through today or not. "Do you really all hate Nick that much?" I ask the group at large.

"They're all ready for a change," Constantine replies.

"And you're *such* a good example of that." The snarky remark gets me a slap across the face. Tears well, and I blink them away, let them drip down my cheeks. "What kind of 'change' could you represent? Huh? You're one of *them*. You're a fucking *Kosta*." I raise my voice. "You want change? Then maybe someone who isn't a Kosta should run the organization."

I get a punch on the jaw for my troubles. "Shut the fuck up, Cassidy." Constantine jerks his head toward the entrance. "Get her inside. When Dom gets here, let him through."

"No need."

I drop my head to my chest and let the pain settle in. Dammit. He had to come riding to the rescue. One of the things I love the most about him will be the thing that gets us both killed. The ache in my jaw is nothing compared to the one in my chest.

Footsteps crunch on the loose gravel scattered across the road. I inhale sharply as fingers brush the underside of my chin, tipping it up. The small smile on Nick's lips is at odds with the rage in his eyes. "Ready to go home, love?"

"I was ready before they got me in the car." He has a plan. He's too steady not to have one. I search his expression for anything that might clue me in on what he's planned. "Nick?" There's nothing there. Nothing but his absolute fury that I'm here, and there are a bunch of guns pointed at us.

"Enough." Constantine yanks me to the side, out of Nick's immediate space. "Inside."

Nick reaches out, snakes an arm around my waist. "Sorry, Con." The warehouse explodes.

My back hits the ground with a sharp smack, but Nick's hand cradles the back of my head to keep it from connecting with cement. Fire rains down around us, pieces of wood and glass like shrapnel. I hear screaming. Smoke stings my eyes and clogs my lungs, Nick heavy on top of me.

A blast of heat surges over us. He lifts his head, gives my face a cursory scan, and pushes up on his hands. "You okay?"

"I think so."

"Good." Pain twists his face as he gets on his knees, then his feet. Aside from the bruises I'll be sporting on my face, hips, and back tomorrow, I'm uninjured. Constantine lies beside us, his face white with ash, eyes shut. Blood streams from a cut on his temple. The dark red carves rivulets through the layer of ash to disappear into his hair. When I poke him, he doesn't so much as twitch in response.

I scramble to my feet, eager to be gone before he wakes up. I get a quick look at the warehouse before Nick pulls me down the street away from the fire. It looks like someone cut through the middle with a flaming sword. Both ends are more or less standing, though quickly becoming engulfed in flames. The men leaning on the section of wall that's now missing are fiery, charred lumps. More bodies are slumped in the street, some moving feebly, some not at all.

"What did you do?" He's limping badly, and I glance at his leg. A dark stain's spreading along his thigh. "You know, your leg's never going to heal at this rate."

"Thanks for that. And what I did was lay a well-placed explosive and took out the two men Con had on the other side of the warehouse. Couldn't risk blowing the whole building. Too many people around, buildings too close together." His voice is strained, and I move into his side to take some of his weight. We round the corner of a neighboring warehouse and turn onto a sun-dappled street. It's empty except for a pickup truck parked in front of a loading dock. "Don't have a lot of time." Nick tries to pick up the pace and stumbles.

A bullet zips past, and we both dive for the ground. Nick shifts his weight so he's on top of me. "Nick."

"Don't move," he grits out.

"Stop trying to protect me!"

"I'll stop trying to protect you when the sun explodes."

Someone kicks my foot. "How touching. Get up. Both of you."

Nick rolls off me, and I crane my neck to see Constantine standing behind me, gun trained on Nick. Every bone in my body is crying in agony, but I shift onto my back, then sit up. "Seriously. If you're going to kill us, could you just get it over with already?"

Nick never takes his eyes off his cousin. "Why?" The question is quiet, barely audible over the roar of the fire and the shouts of the warehouse workers.

"You're in the way," Constantine says simply. "You don't fucking trust me to finish the job. You're on my ass, hanging over my shoulder, so certain I'm going to screw up."

"The Nautilus project," I murmur, and Constantine nods.

"Nautilus, Sager, a number of others that I could have saved without your help." He sneers at Nick. "There's more to it, though. You're Andreas's son. You know if my father had been born first, everything you have would be mine. The organization needs to change. Needs to trim down, consolidate. No one fucking listens. He won't even listen to you. You're gone, he has no choice."

Greed. One of the most basic of human emotions and the driving force behind so much.

"Why Isaiah?" I ask.

Constantine cuts his gaze to me. "Isaiah's needs meshed with my own. He wanted you dead. If the first hit had gone off like it was supposed to, we wouldn't be here today." He motions for us to stand. "I can't shoot you like a couple of fish. Get the fuck on your feet."

Gravel digs into my ass, but I remain sitting, contemplating the gun. It's currently pointed at Nick. The street's otherwise deserted; no one's run around the corner to help Constantine. I risk a glance over my shoulder. A couple of men dash through the intersection. None of them think to look down the street. Everyone's distracted by the flaming building one block over.

Nick's struggling to stand, and Constantine's watching him with impatience. Honorable bullshit aside, he might get trigger happy. Of course, if neither of us does anything, we're basically just waiting for Constantine to shoot.

No more reacting.

I curl my legs under me slowly, like it hurts to move. Considering it *does* hurt to move, I barely swallow the hiss of pain trying to escape. Once I'm on my knees, I sneak a glance at Nick. He's on his knees as well, and he's not moving. Blood's spread out from the wound in his thigh. I swear on all that is holy, I am chaining the man to the bed for a week.

Somehow I need to get Nick's attention without drawing Constantine's focus away. Shifting my weight onto my right hand, I lift my left, dislodging a few pebbles in the process. Nick's in my periphery, but I can't actually *see* his face. I'm running on hope and adrenaline now. Keeping the movement as small as possible, I point with my left hand toward Constantine, swinging my hand forward like I'm going to push, telegraphing my intent as best I can. He's close enough I can throw myself at his lower legs and knock him off balance.

Muscles burning with tension, I spring forward. My shoulder smashes into Constantine's shin. Through the shock of pain, I fight to wrap my arms around his legs. I guess I ought to be grateful I succeeded in knocking him off balance. He takes a giant step back, and I scramble backward, only to fling myself to the left as a shot rings out. Body screaming in agony, I slowly stand up, swaying back and forth.

"Fucking cunt," Constantine spits out. I drop to my knees as he squeezes the trigger, narrowly avoiding the bullet. I should stay on the ground. Every time I get up, I end up flat on it anyway. This will save time. I fall forward and press my cheek to the pavement.

Over the continued shouts and crackling wood from the fire one block over, I hear a string of curses and the sounds of flesh smacking flesh. I lift my head. Nick's standing. He's standing and pounding his fist into Constantine's face, heedless of the gun clutched in his hand. Guy must have super-glued it to his palm, because I don't think he's let go once.

As I watch, head fuzzy with pain, Constantine brings the butt of the gun down, missing Nick's head and hitting his shoulder. Nick grunts, locks both hands around the back of Constantine's neck, jerks his right knee up, and slams it into his solar plexus. Constantine doubles over and drops the gun at his feet.

That gun has become my holy grail. I push up to my elbows and belly crawl forward. I snag the gun as Nick rams his knee into his cousin's face. Constantine collapses in a groaning heap.

Dead people can't come after me. Dead people can't kill Nick. I sit up and aim the gun at Constantine's head. My hands are shaking. How many shots has he fired? Four? Five?

Dead people will finally leave me alone.

"Cass." Nick limps over and gently pulls the gun from my hand. "It's over."

Over. I fall back and stare at the sky, smoke scudding across the faded blue, bits of gravel digging into my skull.

It's over.

Chapter 26

I look like a prune. I study the puckered, wrinkled pink skin of my fingertips as water drips down my forearms. The heat and the Epsom salt helped with some of the aches, exactly like the nurse said they would. The pills in the orange bottle on the sink should take care of the rest.

Nick knocks on the door and pokes his head into the bathroom. I scowl. "Get back on the couch." He promised he'd stay off his leg as much as possible for at least a week. Some promise. It took him only a few hours to break it.

"You've been lying in there for close to a half hour, love. Time to get out." He withdraws his head, and I hear his crutches *thudding* against the carpeted floor. Water sloshes close to the rim of the tub as I sit up. He's right. Dammit. I've refreshed the water twice to keep it warm. Gritting my teeth, I stand and reach for the towel I placed on the closed lid of the toilet. I dry off and pull on a pair of sweats and a hoodie, then pad out of the bathroom to find Nick.

He's on the couch where he's supposed to be, injured leg stretched along the length of the cushions. I wander over and squish myself into the corner of space he left me. "I'm out. *Now* will you stay off your leg?"

"Bossy," he murmurs. "Bath help?"

"Some. Not as much as the pills, though." The directions say to take one every six hours. Based on the time I took my first one at the hospital, I have two more to go. "Know what you want for dinner?"

"Cass."

I shut my eyes at the warning note in his voice. He's done nothing but apologize since the police and fire crews showed up at the warehouse. He's sorry he didn't listen to my concerns. Sorry he put me in danger. Sorry, sorry, sorry. If I hear that word one more time, I'm going to kick him.

"I'm—"

I jab at his uninjured leg with my foot. "You say you're sorry one more time, the next thing I kick won't be your leg."

His mouth curves into a smile. "You're cute when you're trying to be intimidating."

I sigh. "I know you're sorry. You didn't want to believe me, Nick. I get that. It hurts, I won't lie, but I understand why you didn't want to listen." Constantine's betrayal sliced through us both. He sheltered us. He shared food with us. I liked him. A lot.

His expression sobers. "I hate that I hurt you. I hate that I could have prevented it from happening at all."

I chew on the inside of my cheek. "I hope we never have to face anything like this again, but... If I'm bringing my concerns to you, it's for a reason. Will you listen? That's all I want. Next time I try to talk to you about something, you listen."

"Deal." He darts his gaze to his leg. "Motherfuck."

"Don't you dare move it."

The cushions bounce as he shifts on his ass, the movement forcing me from my spot. He nestles into the corner, injured leg still extended, but he bends his uninjured one and places his foot flat on the floor. A vee of space opens, and he holds out a hand. "C'mere."

With Isaiah and Tris dead and Constantine in police custody, the danger is gone. We should be going our separate ways, falling back into the routines we've tried to create since we agreed we needed to spend time apart. For all his apologies, his refusal to listen and *pay attention* to my misgivings succeeded in widening the gap between us. But today's standoff was exhausting on several levels. One or both of us could have died, several times over. The need to feel Nick around me, warm and solid and *real*, is overwhelming.

Careful of his leg, I scoot into the space he created. I sigh when his arms come around my waist and he nuzzles my temple. For the first time since he limped to my rescue this morning, I relax. "What's going to happen to Constantine?" I murmur.

His hold tightens, and silence descends. "I don't know," he says at last. After Nick got patched up in the ER, he went up to see his father and filled him in on what happened. Whatever was said between them, he hasn't seen fit to tell me. "He's in jail, being held without bail. Dad still isn't quite willing to admit that change needs to happen. He wants to speak with Uncle Anton first."

The lack of answers doesn't bode well for the future. "What's going to happen to me?"

"You?"

I nod. "Your dad's been quite insistent that I need to be held responsible for my actions. Is he still planning to have me turned over to the police?" If I'm going to be arrested, a heads-up would be nice.

Nick surprises me by laughing. "Fuck. I forgot to tell you. You're safe."

I lean away and scowl. "And you didn't think I should know this?" I push at his chest to get him to release me, but all he does is tighten his hold.

"With everything that's happened in the last few days, it got lost in the shuffle. He's still unhappy with how you chose to deal with the issue of Isaiah, but he won't be turning you over to the police."

The news should make me happy. Knowing I can finish my degree without constantly looking over my shoulder, without waiting for that knock on the door? There's security in that. But Nick's laughter has faded, leaving behind a weariness I feel in my bones. "What else?"

"Nothing you—" He stops when I glare at him and sighs. "I told him if he didn't drop his vendetta, I'd walk."

Shock races through me. Nick has been adamant about remaining in the organization. "You're not serious." I study his expression, note the mule-like stubbornness of it. "You *are* serious. Nick, *why*? This is what you want. You've told me a few times. Why change your mind now?"

He frees one of his hands and shoves it through his hair. "This has been building for a while, Cass. Peter, Constantine, even Isaiah have all gone to my dad, alone and together, to tell him we're spread too thin. It's the one thing my cousins and I agreed on." Sadness flits across his face. Is he wondering what might have happened if they'd all worked together instead? "Constantine and I have been having difficulty keeping track of the day-to-day operations because they've grown so large. I've been handing jobs off to Peter that technically he shouldn't be doing, but I don't have the capacity to handle them myself. The family needs to undergo a major change, and with Con out of the picture, I need to reorganize the companies too."

He drops his head back onto the back of the couch. "It's one shitstorm after another," he says quietly. "Nothing's going to happen quickly, but if Dad doesn't start listening when others speak, the ship will continue sinking. It might be time to bail." He lifts his head. "I don't like the idea of continuing to operate within boundaries I can't see."

I frown. "How big a part do I play in this? Because if you're basing your decision on what's happened—"

He cuts me off with a finger to my lips. "Yes, it will factor into my decision. Anyone who says otherwise is a fucking liar." He replaces his finger with his mouth, the kiss soft and chaste. "You matter, Cassidy. If you didn't, you wouldn't have been able to hurt me. Give us time. We could surprise each other."

Forever. I want you forever.

Forever is a long, long time, and it's a step I know I'm not ready for. That doesn't stop me from craving it like a drug. I let out a shaky breath. "Okay."

* * * *

Clouds chase each other across the sky, wind whipping through the twisted, spindly limbs of the Joshua trees the park is named for. Mom stares at the view spread out before us. "This is it," she says quietly. "We're here."

She makes no move to get out of the car, though. The four weeks she spent at Aunt Carol's were good for her. The dark circles are gone, and she's regained some of the weight she lost. But sitting there, her hands clenched on the wheel and a frightened, haunted look in her eyes, it's as though she's regressed in a matter of minutes.

I don't want to be the strong one. That's her job. Someone has to get us both through this ritual.

We're here alone. No one but us, and that's how it should be. And if Mom doesn't have the strength to start down this path, then I'll have to do it for us.

I pop the button on my seatbelt and open the door. The movement seems to kick her into gear, and she unhooks her seatbelt and follows suit, climbing out to continue her study of the park. I retrieve the canister containing Turner's ashes from the back seat and round the hood of the car.

It's not all of him. The minister at the funeral home suggested we may both want to keep a small portion. Mom has hers in a little ceramic box Turner bought for her on some random weekend trip they took years ago. Nick surprised me with a Chinese porcelain jar the other day. It's sitting on the bookshelf in my living room.

The lump in my throat makes breathing difficult. Mom holds out a hand, and I take it like a child. Together, we start down the path into the park.

Turner's directions are detailed. Follow the main trail for half a mile and veer to the left toward a cluster of boulders. We trudge along, not speaking, the sun peeking through the clouds. Mom finds the rock formation he mentions and points to it. "Up there."

It's not large or high, which is good. Neither of us are climbers. We scramble up the boulders to the top, my progress hampered slightly by the canister. I pass her the metal container and take a minute to wind my ponytail into a bun.

Mom sits, canister clutched in her hands, eyes on the scrubby desert sprawling around us. "He'd come here after every job. There'd be sand in his clothes. He tried to shake it out so he wouldn't track it into the house, but he always managed to bring some of it with him."

I squint against the brightness. "How do you know?"

Her smile is soft and sad. "He'd tense up. Walk around like there was a steel rod in his back for days. When the job was over, he relaxed." She turns to me. "He did it whenever you took a job. Or at least the ones he knew about."

Every new thing I learn about Turner pulls the wound open a little bit more. I study the desert, trying to see what he saw. "It's constant, and it's constantly changing." Like the ocean. "You look at it often enough, you won't see it, but you know it's different."

Her eyes widen. "You're right."

It's my turn for the soft and sad smile. "I use the ocean. Constant and constantly changing." I didn't know that Turner needed a place to take himself apart and then put himself back together. I don't like thinking he did. It makes him…human. Vulnerable.

Tears well, and I don't fight them. They spill down my cheeks, falling faster when Mom folds me into her arms. I cry for all the missed opportunities, for all the times I held my tongue when I could have told my father I loved him and missed him. I cry for all the moments I overlooked. If we'd just had more time, we might have been able to compromise.

"The night you got your acceptance letter to UCLA." She strokes a hand down my back, and I sniffle, trying to quiet the sobs. "He put it in the safe. Right next to his guns and our passports. Said it was important to keep it safe in case we needed physical proof you were going to be a Bruin. He was proud of you, Cassidy," she whispers.

I love you.

Three of the most important words in the English language. They have the power to heal, to give hope, to decimate and destroy. With those three words, Turner became the dad I wanted. I never took *I love you* for granted, and he's reminding me even now how precious they are.

"Mom?" I blink away the last of the tears. "I love you. I don't think I tell you that often enough."

She sniffs wetly. "I love you too, dear. And there's never 'enough' when it comes to that."

I sit back and scrub my cheeks dry, then get to my feet. "What were his directions? Just sorta...fling them out into the open?"

Mom looses a very un-Mom-like snort. "Hardly. They are to be scattered on the boulders in a gentle but firm manner."

"He did *not* say that. Gimme." I snatch the paper from her and scan the directions. Sure enough, Turner wants his ashes scattered in a "gentle but firm manner." "I've never heard him speak like that."

"He had his moments." She twists the lid off the canister. "Ready?"

How can anyone be ready for something like this? I step close to her and slide my arm around her waist, her arm coming around my shoulders. Mom tips the container sideways and shakes it, a line of ash floating to the rock beneath our feet. She passes it off to me, and I finish the line.

Another tear tracks down my face as the wind kicks up some of the ash, carrying tiny pieces of Turner out to the desert. "Bye, Daddy," I whisper.

I love you.

Epilogue

The air in the apartment is stuffy and hot. "Air conditioning's turned off." The landlord, a growly, scruffy-faced middle-aged man, shuffles over to one of the windows and shoves it open. "Apartment's been empty for several months."

I nod and continue my perusal. The place is clean, but it's a few steps down from my current apartment in Los Angeles. Worn carpet, small rooms, plus a smaller kitchen than I'd like. I leave the landlord leaning against the half wall separating the kitchen from the living room and duck into one of the bedrooms. The lone window faces the narrow street, the building across the way blocking most of the sunlight into the room. It'll do for a bedroom.

The second bedroom isn't much brighter, and it's even smaller. It doesn't help that Nick dwarfs the room just by standing in it. Hands tucked in his pockets, the sleeves of his slate blue dress shirt rolled up to his elbows, he's every inch the dark, intimidating man he was when we met almost a year ago.

"Well?" he asks.

I scan the room. "It's the best I can afford." My pulse is rabbiting. "I don't need pretty or spacious. Just safe and clean, and this is both." He nods, and I move to the window, avoiding his gaze. I'm nervous. For the first time in a long time, Nick's making me nervous. Or more accurately, the question I have for him is making me nervous.

My mouth has gone dry, and I run a fingertip along the windowsill. The words come out in a rush. "Would you be okay in a place like this?"

We've been oh so very careful these last nine months, both of us speaking about the future—*our* future—in broad terms. There's never been any doubt we *have* a future together. While it was bumpy at times and we still fought over Nick's obsession with my safety, we stuck with our promise to slow down and fix what we'd damaged. But as the weeks became months and I threw myself into completing my degree, we never got around to having an actual conversation about what comes after graduation.

And Nick never moved into the apartment, despite paying for most of it. He gets plenty of use out of it, choosing to work in the office there several days a week, but his clothes never migrated to my closet, and while he has a toothbrush in the bathroom, the apartment is very much mine.

San Diego isn't far from Los Angeles. If we have to, we can make this work from our separate cities. I'm selfish, though. I'm tired of being apart from him. Now I want him. *All* of him.

That he has yet to respond to my question does not bode well.

His expression isn't any help, either. No one does bland neutrality quite like Dominic Kosta.

"If you have something to say, now would be a fantastic time to say it." Seriously. He needs to say something before I start babbling like Denise.

He glances around the room. "You can do better."

I throw up my hands. "No, actually, I can't." The offshore account holding all of my ill-gotten funds has been donated to charity. I haven't touched the life insurance money from Turner's policy. It'll come in handy when I need to pay for grad school. Assuming I get in. Moving to San Diego before I've even applied to graduate school is a risk. I need to get away from LA for a while. Charlie and Denise are moving to Cambridge, and Mom's actually considering moving to Montana, something I never thought she'd do.

Nick walks out into the living room, and I trail after him, trying to shrug aside my hurt. When he keeps going through the front door, I offer the landlord a pained smile. "I need to think about it."

He shrugs. "Don't think it's likely to get rented any time soon. You decide you want it, I'll knock a hundred off the monthly rent."

Great. Now I'll have money for groceries. Or other bills.

I squint against the San Diego sunshine as I scan the street for Nick. He's already in the car, seatbelt on and the engine running. I climb in and snap my own seatbelt into place. "You know, if you don't want to live with me, that's fine. You don't need to be an asshole about it."

"I didn't say I didn't want to." His mild tone is almost as annoying as his refusal to answer the question. "I want to show you something first."

The last time he wanted to show me something, the item in question turned out to be a brand new Mazda 3 hatchback. No amount of threats or protests that a used car would suit me just fine could change his mind. The car was mine, and when I tried to pay him back for it, he got pissed.

Over the twenty-minute drive, I fire question after question at him. Each one is met with silence, and I finally give up and stare out the window. We pull up to what looks like a duplex, the sand-colored building set back from the sidewalk with a small patch of grass in front. The beach is across the street, waves gleefully smashing into the sand.

I get out of the car and study the duplex. One side looks occupied; there are curtains drawn across the front windows to block out the afternoon sun. As Nick rounds the car to join me on the sidewalk, the possibilities start to sink in. "What did you do?" He holds out a hand, a silver key dangling from his fingers. I stare at the key. "Nick, what did you do?"

He takes my hand and folds my fingers around the key. The edges bite into my palm. "Yes, I want to live with you, Cass. Someplace safe and clean and with more space than the little box you just looked at." Snaking an arm around my waist, he leads me up the front walk and unlocks the door with his own key.

I should probably say something, but I'm stuck on *yes I want to live with you*. We could live in that box for all I care, as long as he's with me. The hardwood floor echoes under our feet as we step into the living room. "You know I can't—"

He cuts me off with a kiss. "Don't," he murmurs. "Don't say it. You're not paying for this, love. I am. You want to pay for something, pay for the food. Gas for your car."

I pull away and wander to the far side of the living room. The walls are painted a pale, soothing blue. "You rented this place without me seeing it? How did you know I'd like it?"

"The ocean's right across the street and the kitchen's huge. And I didn't rent it. I bought it."

Of course he did. Why rent when you can buy? "I don't even know if I'll be here in a year." San Diego State and UC San Diego are among my top choices for graduate school, but there's no guarantee I'll get in.

The kitchen's as large as he promised. The gas range is a gleaming black, matching the shiny side-by-side refrigerator. Glass-front cabinets stand empty, and it's all too easy to picture them full of brightly colored plates and cups.

I trail my fingers along the edge of the counter. *Own* signifies an even greater permanence than *rent*, and I'm okay with that. I turn around as he enters the kitchen. "How many days a week will you be in LA?"

"Maybe one or two at the most. The new company will be taking up a lot of my time." He bought a start-up in San Diego when I first started talking about moving. Then? It made me shake my head. Now? It means he'll be closer.

"And your dad's okay with this?" I hold my breath, half afraid of what he'll say. Andreas has proven reluctant to embrace the necessary changes for the Kosta organization to remain viable—and that reluctance drove a wedge between father and son. It's growing wider every day.

Nick's taken several steps back, as has Peter, the two of them choosing to focus on the businesses Nick owns. The longer he stays out of the day-to-day operations of the family, the more hopeful I am this will be permanent.

He leans on the counter. "No."

A single word, and it says so much. That part of Nick's life, and my life with him, isn't behind us. It may never be.

I slip my arms around his waist, my lids drifting shut as he kisses the top of my head. "Okay."

We'll figure it out. It's what we do. Figure it out.

Together.

Amanda's second book in the series, Game of Vengeance, is a must read for more of the same sexy, edgy thrills.

On sale now.

Game of Vengeance

An eye for an eye, blood for blood.

UCLA student Cass Turner was hoping to move on from the family business—but when the business is professional assassination, that's easier said than done. And sleeping with the man she was supposed to kill only complicates things. Her relationship with Nick Kosta, a lieutenant in LA's largest crime family, was supposed to be no-strings-attached fun. But if the two of them want to stay alive, they'll have to keep each other close.

Nick's traitorous cousin, Isaiah, is out for blood, so Cass can't afford any distractions as they try to hunt him down. Yet she can't help puzzling over Nick's motives—does he really share her deepening feelings or does he just feel responsible for her? And if their relationship is for real, will they even have a future? Because with their enemies several steps ahead of them, one false move could bring disaster for everyone Cass holds dear... and in this game of cat and mouse, no one will leave unscathed.

Chapter 1

"No."

I huff out a breath. "What else am I supposed to do? Sit at home, twiddling my thumbs?"

"Nah. You'd be sitting on the couch in my office twiddling your thumbs." Nick's trailing his fingers over the scar on my stomach as if he's trying to reassure himself it won't split apart at the slightest provocation.

"You can't force me to come into work with you every morning. Unless you're planning on handcuffing me and tossing me in the trunk of your car." I try to scoot away from his touch and almost fall off the bed, biting back a sigh when he tightens his hold.

I liked my little beach hut when it was just me, and I could walk around in my underwear because it was too damn hot to wear any clothing. For the last three days, I've liked it even better, but two full-grown adults crammed into a double bed isn't exactly my idea of a good time. There's not a lot of action happening in said bed, though I have to admit I've slept a lot better tucked against his side. My libido's taking a vacation while I recover, and Nick hasn't so much as hinted at sex.

"You remember the handcuffs?" he asks, a lazy smile on his face. It's distracting, that smile, causing my brain to misfire even as I want to smack him for it.

I shoot him a death stare. "Do *I* remember the handcuffs." He cuffed me to the door of his car with a set of fuchsia fuzzy handcuffs a few days after we'd met. It's pretty hard to forget those things. "You're not seriously saying you'd use them?" I pull his hand off my waist. "I can't keep the rest of my life on hold, Nick. I want to go back to class."

He slips his hand free and glides it over the curve of my hip. "It's only for a little while longer."

A little while longer could easily turn into *not just yet*, and the next thing I know, I'm a college dropout, forced to either work a dead-end job or continue killing people for money. I struggle to keep my annoyance in check. He's worried. I can work with worried. I roll off the bed and pad across the room to the miniscule kitchen for a bottle of water. "You can't know that. I'm not made of glass, and I can't live in a bubble."

He gets to his feet and stalks toward me, brows lowered as he glares. He nicks the bottle from my hand and drains it. "You died. Twice. I don't want to find out if the third time's the charm."

Point to him. I stroke a hand up his chest, his enticingly bare chest, and curve it around the back of his neck, letting my fingers play through the ends of his hair as I consider my words. Isaiah hasn't been found, and as long as he's out there, Nick and I both have targets on our backs. At the same time, though, forewarned is forearmed, especially in this case. "Isaiah took me by surprise," I say softly. "He's not going to be able to do that again. Campus is crowded. If I'm not on campus or with a friend, I'll come straight to your office and hang there until you're ready to go home." The UCLA campus, where I'm trying to finish my last year, is a sprawling complex, and during the day, full of students. The student body is *huge*.

"It'd take some mad skills and serious *cojones* to pull something off there. I'm more likely to get jumped in the parking garage again than on campus."

He threads his fingers through my hair, rubbing the muscles of my neck until I want to purr with contentment. "You're not helping, love."

My heart sputters at the endearment. I went a month without hearing him say it. A month where I hadn't heard *anything* from him, and as the days bled into weeks, the doubts started creeping in. He's ten years and a world of experience older. I wouldn't blame him for not wanting to be tied to someone as young as me.

Yet every day since he's been here, he's proving it's not just heat and blind lust between us. The things we went through together and the forced proximity have thrown us directly onto the *this is more than just sex* track, and I'd be foolish to think the connection we forged isn't strong enough to withstand a few weeks apart.

It's not love. But it's getting closer every day, and it's scaring the poo out of me.

"C'mon. You've seen the campus. You'll have a copy of my schedule. You can have someone pick me up instead of letting me drive myself." I tip my head back. I hate the glimmer of fear in his dark eyes, hate that it makes me question his motivations, because it's the one doubt he can't lay to rest. A part of me is convinced this protective bent he's got is because someone in his family tried to kill me.

Not because he cares about me.

Whenever I stumble down that rabbit hole, though, I claw my way back out, determined to give him the benefit of the doubt. *He came for me.* He could have ushered me onto a plane as soon as he arrived or moved us to a hotel where we could have separate rooms. Instead, he stayed. I lost a lot of strength and stamina confined to bed for two weeks in the hospital, then off and on over the past month recovering from plastic surgery. So all we've really done is wander at a snail's pace through Phuket, trying to get the other to eat the fried grasshoppers from the various food carts. And that's only when we're not staying out of the heat of the day in my hut.

Honestly, those are my favorite times. The times when we're just sitting here, talking. The times that mimic the evenings in his condo in Manhattan Beach, where he distracted me from my guilt enough to eat.

It might have come out eventually that Nick's favorite food is an In and Out burger, but because we're here, with little else to do, I learned it earlier. Like I learned his favorite color is green, his favorite movies are *Stand and Deliver* and *Billy Madison*, and that he and Constantine grew up like brothers, much like Marc and Isaiah.

He presses his thumb into my lower lip, then lets it slip down to my chin. "How many classes?"

I can't stop the giddy joy rising in my chest and smile. A normal life. I get to go back to a normal life. Or as normal as I get. "Four. If they have the last courses I need to graduate during the summer term, I'll be done by September." Then I have to worry about getting a job, what to do with the rest of my life, and my lack of work history. Somehow I don't think putting *assassin* on my resume will score me any interviews.

His hand drifts farther, brushing over my neck and along the faint scar left by Josef, a member of the family who tried to kill me on Isaiah's orders. The doubts stir from their slumber at Nick's constant touch tonight. His attention should make me happy. I *am* happy. I step back and tell those doubts to shut up.

He studies me a minute more, the light on the little porch buzzing when another fly gets trapped. It's so damn loud, that buzzing, filling the silence. "Fine," he says. "I get a copy of your schedule?"

The worry line between his brows makes my heart sputter just as badly as when he calls me "love," only in an entirely different way. "Yes. A copy of the schedule, and anything else you think I need to stay safe. *Except* a babysitter. I've still got Josef's knife." Somewhere. It's probably buried in a bag at Nick's.

"I'm getting you your own. Something that fits your hand better." He picks up my hand, holding it palm out, and uses his thumb to trace the creases.

My excitement dims a smidge. Carrying my own weapon is permanent, one that speaks of Nick's faith that I can handle myself and the scrapes I get into. It's also part of the life I'm trying to leave behind, if only Isaiah would pop up from whatever rock he's hiding under.

And I wonder, not for the first time, if staying with Nick means I can't shed that identity. If it'll dog my steps like an unfriendly ghost.

Nick's phone rattles angrily across the table. He kisses my palm, drops my hand, and reaches around me to pick it up. "Kosta."

Knowing the call could take anywhere from a couple of minutes to an hour or more, I grab another bottle of water and wander out onto the porch.

The sticky heat of the night drops over me like a wet blanket, smothering me in its weight. The humidity around here is insane, giving the air a tangible quality, like I can squeeze it between my fingers and watch it ooze out like syrup. The hut is at the end of a row of other huts just like it, some with their porch lights on, some dark. This close to the beach, there isn't much of a bug problem, and I lean on the railing, staring out over the black water.

Funny how oceans are the same no matter which one you're looking at. People earn their living on them. Swim in them, play in them. The color is different. So's the temperature, and the creatures swimming through them.

The ocean's always changing too. The way it breaks apart and reforms, holding on to most of the old stuff that keeps it recognizable as a salty body of water, letting in enough of the new that scientists either scream with delight over previously undiscovered species or moan about the fate of the planet as its levels rise.

It's also not mine.

My ocean is the one near the Santa Monica pier. The place I go after a job, a kind of meditation that allowed me to slip back and forth between Cass the College Student and Cass the Assassin. I miss my ocean. I miss Los Angeles, I miss my friends, and I miss my mother.

I miss Turner something fierce.

The door opens behind me, and Nick steps onto the porch. He props his elbows on the railing. Our bare shoulders touch, the only body parts that do, and out here in the messy heat it's almost too much. "Good news? Bad news? Indifferent news?"

"Har." He shifts to wrap his arm around my waist, pulling me to his chest, ignoring my half-hearted protests that it's too hot to cuddle. "That was Con. LAPD raided one of the escort agencies, and the manager's being brought up on charges. Con's concerned he'll talk."

"You let a man run that service?" In the movies, it's always women who run those businesses.

"He did a good job of it until he got greedy and started selling drugs out of the office. Been charged with possession with intent to distribute. Fucker had a couple kilos worth of cocaine waiting to be doled out. Tough as the drug laws are, he'll be going away for a long time."

Well, shit. "What are you going to do?"

His chest rumbles at my back as he growls in frustration. "Let him use our attorneys. Pretty much the only way we might have a chance of him keeping his mouth shut."

Which means if he doesn't, his fate will likely be very different. I turn around and place my hands on his chest, needing some space. I can't stumble around in the dark anymore. I've already done two jobs for his organization. With Isaiah in hiding, the chances of me taking another life are pretty high. I need to know what Nick does with the people who betray him. "What happens if he doesn't? What if they offer him a deal? If he was stupid enough or desperate enough to run drugs while engaging in other barely legal activities, his loyalty might snap."

He dips his head, his gaze locked on mine. "I think you can guess what happens." His voice is quiet, the words final and brutal, the last swing of the gavel. "The organization demands loyalty. Learning the scope of who we are and what we do is only given once trust is earned. You break that trust, you pay. Whatever that price might be. It's always high, and it's never what you expect. Right now, he's probably thinking if he talks, we'll come for him. We might. It might be his brother. It might be his wife."

My stomach clenches in a violent, shuddering knot, my mouth dry as I stare at him. No. No *way*. Innocent people. He uses them like…like… tools. "His *wife*? You go after women? Do you murder children too?" *Say no. Please say no.*

In the low light, the shadows on his face take his blank expression and twist it into something sinister. "We do what needs to be done, Cassidy. Sometimes that means using whatever leverage we've got. Sometimes that's women and children, though those are last resort measures."

I back away, out of his arms, skin prickling as the truth hits home. I knew Nick was as deadly as me. Without seeing it in action, I guess I didn't really believe it.

I sure as fuck do now.

About the Author

When she's not plotting ways to sneak her latest shoe purchase past her partner, **Amanda K. Byrne** writes sexy, snarky romance and urban fantasy. She likes her heroines smart and unafraid to make mistakes, and her heroes strong enough to take them on. Amanda lives in the beautiful Pacific Northwest, and no, it really doesn't rain that much.